changeling

prelude to
the chosen chronicles

karen dales

Dark Dragon Publishing
Toronto, Ontario, Canada

This book is a work of fiction. The characters, incidents, and dialogue are drawn from the author's imagination and are not to be construed as real. Any resemblance to actual events or persons, living or dead, is entirely coincidental.

Changeling

Cover Art, Design and Author Photo
© 2010 by Evan Dales
WAV Design Studios
www.wavstudios.ca

Dark Dragon Publishing
313 Mutual Street
Toronto, Ontario
M4Y 1X6
CANADA
www.darkdragonpublishing.com

For more information on the Author,
Karen Dales and The Chosen Chronicles
www.karendales.com
www.thechosenchronicles.com

For Calista...

prologue

 scream cut through the night, intruding upon the solemn celebration of the first of winter. Villagers, afraid of what the night would bring, huddled in groups in the larger lodge of their Chief, each trying unsuccessfully to ignore their own increasing terror as they attempted to reassure their crying children. It was not the first shriek to shatter the sacred night—a night when those of the Otherworld rode through the dark, taking poor lost souls to the Lord of the Underworld. Noslen was a very poor time to bring forth a child, especially the Chief's newest grandchild.

The Chief worried his long grey moustache and stared at the door. There was nothing he could do and trusted his wife to tend to his daughter. It was in the hands of Dôn, the Goddess of All, and if She decided to take his only remaining child it seemed the most appropriate time of the year. But tonight was not a night of the Mother, so he whispered a prayer to the Dark One, the Lord of Death, in hopes that He would ride on past, taking no notice of his daughters screams.

"Push! I can see the baby's head." The older woman instructed her daughter. "Don't just stand there with your jaw on the floor," she yelled at her daughter's husband. "Grab a blanket. Your third child will be born very soon."

She never understood what her daughter saw in Geraint. Then again her own mother had never understood her choice to Handfast to her husband. Esyllt shook her head and sighed.

Daughters.

The Mother had sent plenty of those to both she and Enid.

Let it be a son this time, someone to become Chief after my beloved.

She bent to see her daughter's progress.

Geraint left Esyllt's side and grabbed the soft birthing blanket his wife had woven. Turning back, he was stunned at the sight of his beautiful Enid. Supported by her dark haired cousins and sisters, her mother applied a soothing hand to help guide the crowning head of his child. He had refused to leave even though he knew it was not a man's place to be at the birth. He needed to see this for himself. The child was early. Too early for a child of the Mai, and he knew the risks this posed to his precious wife, who hung lank and exhausted between two other women. Her jet black hair plastered her face as she panted with the oncoming pain of a new contraction. Unsuccessfully hiding his worry, Geraint handed the woollen cloth to the old woman. "Will she be all right?" he asked.

Enid lifted her gaze and saw her husband without seeing him before the crest of the contraction pulled her back into herself. She let out another ear piercing cry.

"I don't know." Esyllt shook her head, concentrating on the weak young woman. "Her first two children were never this difficult."

Geraint took a deep breath and moved to take hold of his wife's limp hand, staring at her sweat-beaded face. He ignored the scowls of the other women. He would not leave.

"Cariad," he whispered. Enid's black eyes fluttered open to look at him. Her face grimaced in a pain he could never imagine. "Our child needs you to be strong." She tried to nod but another contraction wracked her body, forcing another scream to escape from her lips. The old woman yelled instructions for the writhing woman to push. With the help of the other women, Enid tucked and grunted. Before long the old woman leaned back with a smile, holding a purple-faced baby. A new cry cut through the night as small new lungs filled for the first time.

"You have a healthy son," Esyllt declared to her children as she tended to the little boy.

The new father should have been happy, but looking at the little boy, born three months early and properly grown, only told him the truth. Geraint closed his eyes and asked himself if he could accept this child. He honestly did not know until his wife's cousin gave him the snuffling, swaddled babe, and he realized he wept for joy.

"I don't know what to do." The father of three paced his mother's small hut. "She just lies there, ignoring the baby and when she looks at him she bursts into tears." He stopped to stare at his seated mother, realizing for the first time how old she appeared.

Time and hardships had withered the old woman to a frail and shallow husk, but she still had the heart of a dragon and was not afraid to let it show. Glad that her son had stopped his irritating pacing, she rose unsteadily to her feet.

"Has she paid any care to the other two?" she asked, bending to grab a dry log. She placed it carefully in the hearth so as not to send sparks into the dangerously dry thatch above. The flames enclosed the wood and new heat radiated into the room, warming her arthritic joints. She waived her son over to her.

He took her outstretched arm and guided her gently back to her seat near the fire. "She will only recognize the existence of the girls. When I remarked that we should name our son she flew into hysterics. The only time I managed to get her to discuss the child, she declared that our son wasn't human and tried to smother him. She will not nurse him. I have to feed him goat's milk by soaking it in a rag and letting him suckle off of that. No other women in the village will help. I don't know what to do! Even her parents have turned a blind eye to the situation. Maybe you should come with me to see her. Convince her she needs to care for our son. Please."

Geraint had a way with those puppy dog brown eyes of his and she sighed heavily. "All right, I will come, but I can't promise that I can change her mind if it is set in her thinking. Hand me my shawl."

Her son turned and took the woollen piece of clothing down from the peg beside the door, handing the ratty material to the older woman. Gathering her strength, she pushed herself to her feet yet again. She had hoped to have a quiet night by the fire and maybe, if she was lucky, fall asleep in her chair. Lately the pains in her joints kept her up at night and no mixture of herbs seemed to help. "Alright, let's go. And you had better make me some hot ale when we get there."

Taking his mother's arm to steady her, Geraint smiled at her usual request and opened the door to enter the snow-laden landscape. Snowflakes fell in wet clumps from the thick black sky as they trod through the deep snow to the farmer's hut. Their warmth stole into the night and allowed the bitter cold to enter; fingers and toes quickly grew numb in the short distance. The constant crunch of snow compressed upon snow under thickly wrapped feet and legs was the only sound accompanying the two. The falling snow seemed to deaden the night even further. Clouds of frozen breath followed closely behind, marking their trail in the air.

It did not take long to reach Geraint's small circular hut and with a frozen hand he pushed the thick leather door open. Guiding his wheezing mother into the embracing warmth of his home and closing the door behind him, he let the door flap hang loose before any more frozen night air could steal into his home. He offered to take the old woman's shawl but she waved him away, shuffling stiffly to the hearth for warmth. Shrugging, he took off his extra layers and placed them on the empty hook by the door.

The roundhouse was small, with the hearth in the centre to provide heat to the whole structure made from wattle and daub. The front of the hut included a table with two benches, one on either side, serving as the dining area and a place to mend broken tools. There was one chair by the fire so that his wife could tend to the cauldron hanging from the tripod over the blaze. On the ground, by the chair, a drop spindle sat untouched, its red wool linking itself to a basket beside the spindle.

The old woman sat herself down in the chair, arranging her position so that her feet would be the first to warm up, if not catch fire. The back of the house included two beds behind curtains of colourful fabric. In one, his two daughters slept, holding onto their dolls made out of cornhusks and cloth. In the other bed lay his wife curled up into a ball, her eyes tightly shut as if waiting for a sword to fall. Beside their shared bed was the cradle his wife's parents had given as a present to celebrate the birth of their first child. In it was his son of two months, sound asleep.

The farmer moved to sit beside his wife, gently touched her hand and leaned over to whisper that his mother was here. She opened her eyes in dumb recognition, got up and pulled a thin blanket around her slim shivering form as she walked over to the other bed. Oblivious to the sleeping babe in its cradle, she kissed her little daughters on their brows.

The elder girl woke. "Mama?"

"It's all right, Eira. Everything will be all right. Just shut your eyes and go back to sleep."

The six year old girl yawned and closed her eyes. Her mother walked to meet her husband's mother as her husband ladled steaming ale from the cauldron into a drinking horn before handing it to the old woman.

"I know why you have come," she said to the older woman. Enid's once glossy black hair was dull and streaked with grey, and her brown eyes were red and swollen from crying. "My husband went to you in hopes that you would be able to talk me out of—What did he call it? My craziness?—Regarding that thing lying in that cradle." Her husband visibly winced. The old woman listened unfazed. "I may have given birth to it, but I am not its mother. Its parents are not us. Not human."

"My son witnessed the birth from your loins, child." The old woman sat quietly. "What more proof do you need? Your husband was there, holding your hand."

Raising her voice, "It's not my child. It's not my son. You have only to look at it. It doesn't even look human." Glaring, she flung out her arm to point accusingly at the old woman sipping her ale. "It must have been you. You must have changed him!"

The little girls woke at the rise in volume but stayed under their covers, afraid that their mother's erratic behaviour might turn onto them, as it had wont to do since their brother was born. The baby began to wail and Geraint picked up his son. The baby instantly quieted, cradled in his father's arms.

The old woman looked over the rim of the drinking horn; blowing to cool it off. Steam rose to obscure her face. She chuckled and shook her head. "That is the most inane thing you have ever said to me, child. I did not change your child anymore than I changed my beautiful grand-daughters into boys." Smiling, she gave the little girls a wink, which sent them throwing the covers over their heads to hide further down in their bed. Silently chuckling, the old woman returned to her careful sipping of the liquid.

"Just look at it." The young mother turned to her husband. "Its eyes are as red as the demons the Christian priests always talk about. And look at its hair. It's white. Now look at your hair and eyes, and mine, and our daughters." She tugged at her hair making Geraint fear she would rip hers out. "We all have dark hair and eyes. This baby cannot be ours."

"Then what do you think my grandson is?" asked the old woman.

The younger blinked, caught off guard. She never thought about what it was. All she knew was what it was not. Then the answer came to her as she stammered, "I—it's a *crimbil*. Yes! That is what it must be. Our real child was taken by the Tylwyth Teg and replaced our son with this." She pointed to the bundle in her husband's arms, his mouth slack with shock at such an accusation.

"You must be crazy!" he declared, bringing both little girls again to peek carefully over their blankets at the spectacle.

"Have you no better explanation?"

Before he could find an appropriate retort his mother spoke up. "Enid!"

The younger woman snapped her head around to look at the hag in her chair.

"Enid, will you care for this child whether or not it is of your flesh and blood?"

The young woman drew herself up to her full height. "No. I will not care for any changeling child."

Geraint made a move towards his wife. With a gesture from his mother he halted, the fate of his son forever out of his hands. Since his wife would not care for the infant, and the rest of the village would not help, there was nothing more he could do. Going to his mother had been his last hope and now that seemed lost.

"Then what do you propose we do with this child?" asked his mother.

Enid thought for a moment, remembering the tales her own mother told to her about *crimbil* and the fairy folk. "We must leave this changeling where the Tylwyth Teg will find it and hopefully they will return our real son."

"This is ridiculous! This is my son!" Geraint shouted and tried to hush the crying infant in his arms.

"But it is not mine! It goes! Tonight!" Enid glared at the

child. A look of disgust twisted her once beautiful face.

"He will die if left out in this winter!"

His wife turned her back on him, refusing to listen. He looked pleadingly to his mother. She shook her head sadly. It was the decision of the child's mother whether it lived or died. "Take him," she said sadly. "Leave him where he will die quickly." Her son stared in shock at his mother.

"No!" He could not believe what he was hearing. His son, the Chieftain's only grandson, was to be left out in the freezing cold to die all because his wife would not care for it! It had taken little time for Geraint to accept that his wife had been with someone else to conceive this baby, but it also had not taken him long to accept him as his own.

His mother sighed. This time his sad brown eyes could not save him. She closed her eyes. "Geraint, take the boy away. At least let him have a fast and clean death rather than a slow and painful one because his mother refuses to feed him."

The cries of the baby grew, his face curled up in a furious fight to convince his father to let him live. Geraint's heart broke as tears flowed freely down his face as the futility of the situation encompassed him. His mother was right. No one would help this babe live.

Ignoring her husband, Enid turned and went back to bed, curling into the same foetal position he had found her in. This allowed his two daughters permission to run to him, crying. "Dada, where are you taking the baby?" cried his eldest.

Geraint wiped the tears escaping from his eyes. "I am taking your baby brother to a place where people can care for him until your mother is better," he lied.

"But you said he was going to die."

"No, the baby isn't going to die." He could not believe how hard this was, hating his wife for making him do this. "He's going to go to the land of everlasting life, to Tir na n-Og."

"Glenys not play with pink-eyes no more?" asked the youngest, her thumb in her mouth.

"No. Not for a while," said Geraint's mother, coming to his rescue. "Now off to bed, the both of you."

The girls hesitantly turned away, moving slowly back to their bed. Once under the covers, their eyes closed. Geraint handed his son to his mother to hold while he put his winter layers back on. "You might as well stay the night," he said, taking his son back in a shaky embrace. "You can sleep with my wife. When I come back I'll go with the girls." The old woman nodded. He turned to look at his wife and through gritted teeth he whispered, "I'll never forgive you for this."

Geraint opened the door, letting a blast of cold air in. The hearth fire flickered. He looked back at the deceptive warmth of his home and walked into the cold night, his son in his arms, allowing the door to close with a flutter.

The baby nestled against the warmth of his father's breast, quickly settled into a quiet slumber. The snow had stopped falling, allowing the thick clouds to move further east to reveal a star filled black curtain. Only the crescent light of the moon guided the farmer's journey as he headed towards the dark of the forest beyond.

The air had chilled with the clearing of the sky. Each exhalation clung to the farmer's moustache, turning the dark hairs as white as his sleeping son. His tears froze on his cheeks as they left his water filled eyes. He tried to think of who would take his son and ruled out any of the other villagers. They knew the reason why his wife did not want the child. Her own father had approved of the idea of letting his grandson drown, but Geraint had put his foot down. If there was no one to care for his child then letting the child die quickly was the most merciful thing to do.

The skeletal arms of the trees embraced him, blocking out the silver light. Geraint's path became unclear so he slowed his pace. The sound of crackling branches replaced the crunching of the snow. He walked faster, fear creeping up his spine, sending the short hairs on the back of his neck to rise. A thousand eyes peered at him through the dark blotches between tree and snow mound, or was it a trick of the moonlight? It was ludicrous coming out at such a late hour, an invitation for the whim of the Tylwyth Teg to make a plaything out of him. A little bit farther and he would place his son in the care of the elements and return, very quickly, back to his dishevelled home.

Closer to the heart of the forest Geraint stopped his travels, looking around for an appropriate place to put his doomed child. No sound, except his breathing and the gurgles from the child, could be heard. He noticed a dip in a snow mound and gently placed his son in it. As he turned to walk away, the babe woke and began to cry. Its piercing screams crying out to be held and loved cut the still silence. Geraint increased his pace out of the forest; fresh tears flowing freely down his cheeks.

The haggard old woman grumbled as she walked through the forest, quickly waddling with her heavy skirts lifted in her hands to allow easy passage over the tangled brush above the snow. "That is the last time I get dragged out in the middle of such a horridly cold night for a simple case of the sniffles," she muttered under her laboured breath. "Phagh! Maybe I'll give them a diuretic rather than an expectorant. Now wouldn't that be a sight." Laughter in the form of successive wheezes wracked her body. *Maybe I'll just give myself that expectorant.*

A sound from within the forest halted Llawela in her tracks. Frightened, she crouched down, cocking her head to the side searching the darkness for the source of the strange sound. *Can't be a cat.* She listened to the wailing. Curiosity piqued, Llawela stood, focused on the direction of the sound, and moved off into the forest, following the wails.

She may be old but her hearing was still as sharp as when she was a girl. The forest wrapped its dark wooden cloak around her. Fearless of the woods she knew so well the old woman moved quickly, yet cautiously, following the increasing sound. Before long she came upon the source of the cries. It was a baby! *Who in their right mind would put out a child on a night like tonight?* She thought for a moment. *A crimbil!*

Such children should not be touched but something about this one called out to her heart and after a bit of internal personal debate with the rights and wrongs of such an action she picked up the crying bundle, cradling it in her arms to pull back the cloth that covered its face. "Well, hello there. What are you doing out here all by your lonesome?" The baby ceased its crying and looked up at the shadowed face of the stranger.

Glancing around to see if the ones who left the child were near, Llawela turned her gaze back to the babe. A shiver ran up her spine, letting her know that creatures not of this world watched her. "Are you a child of the fairy folk, my *crimbil*?" She noticed wisps of white hair on the babe's head as broken moon-light shone down. Llawela clicked her tongue in her cheek. "I must assume that you are."

Contemplating her next decision, she asked the babe, "Are you for me to care for?" The baby gurgled with pleasure as she tickled his chin. Sighing, she silently cursed the Fay for knowing her soft heart. "I guess you are."

Llawela smiled and cuddled the infant closer, before turning to head back to her hut by the forest.

Í

he boy ran joyfully though the woods, keeping close to the trees and the deep shadows they created. It was wonderful to finally be free of the stuffy hut that he shared with his Auntie. He did not understand why he was supposed to stay indoors on bright sunny days. Even on grey dreary days he was only allowed to go out for a little while staying close to home, but today, like every ninth day, Auntie let him go out to play in the thick forest that backed onto their small piece of land, always with a warning to stay out of the sun and to keep the eyes of strangers from him. He could only go in specific directions that Auntie gave him, telling him to keep to himself.

The boy did not understand Auntie's fears, but she made them clear enough that if he was ever seen, or worse—caught, the repercussions on her and the boy would be severe. So he stuck to the trails left by the deer and other forest animals.

Auntie had given him a wedge of dark yellow cheese and a couple of slices of bread telling him not to come back until sundown. The boy knew that today would be the day that people from the nearby villages would come to buy Auntie's simples and cures, to hear about their futures and be given the spells necessary to bring their desires into their lives.

When he was younger and Auntie did not trust him as much as she did now, the boy would sit silently behind the drape that hid his pallet, for the whole day. There was only one day in which he peaked through the drape to see a woman with a babe to her breast. The boy was so fascinated, having never seen another person, let alone a baby, that he did not realize that the mother had felt his eyes upon her and turned to see a pair of blood red ones staring back at her. The woman had screamed and ran out of the hut. The whipping he received from Auntie that night was severe, leaving him weeping and heart sore. He knew he had jeopardized their life together though he did not know why.

Since then he followed Auntie's rules, but today, with the spring sun warm on his bare shoulders and the sounds of the forest as his friend, the boy was able to shake off the demands that Auntie made to keep him hidden from the world. Today he was part of the world and he revelled in it.

Not much farther along the path the boy came upon his favourite spot; a glade with a stream burbling through. He sighed and smiled at the sight of the sun dancing off the water as it gurgled over the pebbles and rocks. The stream was too wide to jump over and when he went fishing the stream would be as high as his thighs.

Today he would bring back the biggest fish he could catch and Auntie would be so proud that they would feast on the fish, leaving nothing but bones for soup. The boy smiled at the thought and checked to see the position of the sun through a lifted hand and watering eyes. It was still too early. He would have to wait until the sun was behind the trees to give him the shade he would need to take his time fishing.

Sitting down beneath the old oak tree that stood guardian over the glade, the boy closed his eyes and leaned his head back against the rough bark, enjoying the smells of the green growing things and the white petals of the hawthorn that the slight breeze brought to him. A sense of contentment washed over him. This was his sacred place where not even Auntie could find him. Her fears were not welcomed here.

He did not understand her fears and why she kept him away from others. Auntie was his only friend; the only person he knew and he loved her dearly. He gladly learned what he could of healing and the positive magics that she let him participate in. He loved to hear her tell stories about the Goddess Dôn and Her children. His favourite were the stories of Gwyn ap Nudd.

Every night, before they would go to sleep, he would implore

Auntie to tell another story. Now he could almost recite the stories by heart, but he still loved to hear her old, shaky voice become musical as she recalled the stories she was taught when she was his age.

On the nights of the full moon, if Auntie allowed, he would join her outside to dance and sing. They would pour milk onto the thirsty earth and would leave special cakes made of oats and honey by the trees nearest to the forest. Maybe tonight they would be able to celebrate together if Auntie did not have more serious work to do. They had not been able to do so for several moons because of the cold sapping Auntie's strength.

She had grown old of late, but then again she had always been old. The boy knew Auntie was not his mother. He knew the words; mother, father, brother and sister. The stories Auntie told made it clear that all the Gods and Goddesses were related, but the boy did not have any relations. He only had Auntie and though that should have been enough, it was not. He wanted more but it was denied to him for reasons Auntie would not explain. She would always tell him that he was too young yet to understand and that when he was older she would tell him. Until then the boy sat in the darkness of his origins and it did not comfort him.

He frowned and opened his eyes to the bright sunlight filtering through the heavy leaves and quickly closed them, letting the tears wash away the sting. It still was not time. Checking to see that he still sat in the shade of the oak, the boy took out the wedge of cheese and bread from his brown leather pouch that was coated with grease to protect it from water. It was still some time before midday but he was hungry so he portioned out a bit of the bread and ripped off a chunk before putting the rest away.

Auntie complained of late that he was eating her out of house and home. She expected it, she would say when she noticed that he could not fit into his clothes. Always clucking like a hen she tried in vain to make his kilt and shirt fit him properly. The kilt was easy to let out, even though it grew shorter and shorter until it hung above his knees. The shirt was beyond adjustment, and since it was now warm enough, it was in the rag bin to be used for other things.

The bread, being freshly baked, was soft and a perfect accompaniment for the sharp cheese that had been given to Auntie as a gift from a villager whom Auntie helped survive a nasty sickness. The boy had been left alone for a few days. He had to take care not to be seen when others came by on Auntie's regular ninth day and she was not home. That day he had to stay as quiet as a mouse as people from all over would knock on her door post expecting her to be home. Every time the sound of strangers came to the door the boy caught his breath and stopped what he was doing in fear of being found. Eventually the visitor would leave and he would breathe a sigh of relief until the next person came by.

Auntie's fears had become his own without knowing why.

Popping the last bit of crust into his mouth, the boy checked the position of the sun and the shadows once more and saw that he could start fishing. A smile lit up his face. Maybe a big salmon would jump into his hands. Now that would be wonderful!

The boy carefully unwrapped his footwear consisting of old rags and strips of leather tied to his feet and left them next to his little leather bag that held the cheese and bread. Feet were easier to dry than wool and leather. He wiggled his toes in the air and stood up, enjoying the cool green. Once more taking note of the sun's position and the shadows, he walked to the stream and tested the water.

He gasped at the cold shock. Maybe fishing was not the best idea but he did not want to disappoint Auntie. Swallowing his courage, he stepped into the freezing water and waited a bit before carefully walking in deeper. Each step brought a new wave of chills as the ice water met with pale flesh. By the time he reached the middle of the stream he could not feel his toes and his teeth began to chatter as he tried to catch his breath. The tug of the fast flowing water threatened to pull the boy off balance but he adjusted his stance. If only he could stop shivering he would be able to put his arms into the water to tickle the fish. Gooseflesh covered him and he knew had to master this. Taking a deep breath, he unwrapped his arms from his sides and stuck them into the water when he sighted a salmon meandering his way.

The shock of the water caught his breath once again and he gritted his teeth as he allowed his fingers to wiggle in the hopes of enticing the fish. His breath came in gasps. He was not adjusting to the near frozen water, and he desperately hoped that the fish would come closer. Staring hard at it, he tried to will the fish to him. It inched ever so slightly towards him as it fought the current. Maybe it would swim between his legs and then it would be easy. A tickle of a scaly body and a toss to land it on the green grass would end his frozen misery. The fish did not pay heed. It began to veer to the left, away from the tasty worms his fingers tried to be. The boy swore under his breath. He did not know how much longer he would be able to stay in the water. His legs had started to lose feeling.

Come here fish! He tried to block out the discomfort of his body and focus all his attention on getting that salmon closer to him. With a flip of its tail the fish changed direction towards his fingers and the boy was able to relax in hopeful anticipation of the feel of the salmon's scales on his fingers.

Time went by. His fingers lost their feeling and he did not know why the fish played with him. Salmon were known for their wisdom and if this was truly the case then what the boy had here was the smartest and wisest salmon in the entire world. The boy could only be patient as his body slowly lost feeling.

Warmth touched his shoulder and he looked up to see that the sun had moved, bringing him out of shadow. It felt good to have the heat of the sun on him, but he knew he had to move fast. The sky was clear of clouds and he could not stay exposed to the sun for long. The reflected light off the water created spots in his eyes, making it near impossible to see the fish. If the salmon did not come to him soon he would have to leave the stream and wait for the sun to go behind the trees again. The boy did not relish the thought of coming back into this frigid water.

Please, Dôn, he silently prayed.

He lost feeling in his arms and his back began to ache with having to bend over while the muscles fought to keep their heat. A feathery touch flicked across the fingers of his left hand. He could not see the fish, but was rewarded with the sensation letting him know that it was finally falling for his rouse. Slowly bringing his other hand closer to cup under the salmon, he allowed it to gain a sense of ease before he lifted and tossed the fish in one fluid motion, sending a spray of water across his face.

Spluttering at the shock, the boy hesitated a moment before seeing where the fish landed. It squirmed and wriggled on the mound next to his lunch and footwear. He let out a whoop of glee as he ran on unresponsive legs out of the stream and up on the grass, a large rock in his hand. It took a moment for him to tackle the fish and hammer the rock into its head.

Cold water dripping from his milk white hair, he smiled in

triumph. Making sure the fish was truly dead, he got onto his hands and knees. He could not believe his eyes. It must be the biggest salmon he had ever caught. It must have been as long as his torso. Auntie would be so proud! Not only would this fish be a feast, but also there was probably more they could eat in one setting. Fish soup would also be on the menu. It had been so long since they had salmon.

A snap of a branch drew his attention to the dark of the woods to his left. The smile left his face to be replaced with a worried frown. Was there someone out there? He did not know. Maybe it was a bear coming to sample from the stream.

Another sound of breaking was followed by voices.

Panic struck the boy and his breath came in sharp pants. His heart pounded in his ears for him to flee. People were coming to his glade!

He had to hide. He must be quiet. Maybe the people would pass by, leaving him unnoticed, but where to hide?

Bushes of hawthorn flowered next to the spring on his side. It would have to do.

The sounds came closer. Dashing away, the boy left his possessions and the fish. He crawled carefully through the mayflowers so as not to feel the bite of their thorns. He managed to hide just in time before four people noisily burst onto his sacred place.

His breath caught as he saw that the two young men carried long sticks, and the younger of the two women had a smaller version of the same. It was the older of the two women who came defenceless to the glade. Covering his mouth with his hands to stifle the sounds of his terrified breathing, the boy sat staring wide eyed though the flowering branches.

"This is ridiculous, Glenys!" stormed the older girl of fifteen years. Her raven black hair hung long and straight, and her dark eyes flashed angrily. "You know that father does not want you to learn to use the sword."

The two older boys looked at each other, wondering the same thing, stood waiting. When were these two sisters ever going to stop arguing?

"I don't care what father wants, Eira. I'm not going back home!" shouted the younger girl. "I'm going to be a Sword Maiden like the stories that Grandmother tells us!" Though she was several years younger than her sister, they were remarkably alike in their looks, and their temperament. "Okay Huw," she said, twirling around to face the younger of the two boys. She ignored her sibling and held up the wooden sword in hope of finally being taught. "You promised to teach me. Let's go."

"Finally!" said the boy with chestnut brown hair that curled playfully to his shoulders. He brought his own waster up to face hers. He looked forward to giving his foster sister a good lesson in why girls did not learn the sword. She was always a pain. She would not even wear a skirt and demanded to always dress as they did. He could not imagine why his foster father allowed it.

The older girl opened her mouth, closed it and chewed on her lip. No matter what she could say it seemed as though she was going to lose this battle. Glenys had been bothering their father for months now to teach her the sword and every time he forbade it to them both. The Priest made it clear that girls were meant to be in the home. Eira did not believe that, but she did not want to bring dishonour to their family. Ever since their mother passed away when she was a little girl, Eira's sole purpose was to try and make her father happy, most of the time it worked. She learned what her Grandmother would teach her. She took care of their home, and when their father was made Chief after her grandfather passed away, she tried to ease his burdens by learning what he knew of ruling his people.

Glenys was not interested. She was always focused upon what she wanted, damning the consequences of her actions. Arguments between father and younger daughter would always end up with Glenys stomping away muttering how their female ancestors would join their men in battle and that they were the true rulers. Their father would shake his head knowing that times had changed and with that they had to change. That meant his family had to grow into the present. It was his fore-thinking that convinced the Elders to make him Chief since the old Chief had left no heir. Eira wanted to follow in her father's footsteps. To make him proud even as Glenys confounded him. If she could not make her younger sister see reason then maybe Glenys would anger Huw enough to give her a good bruising.

Huw and Rhys had come to them two years ago from their cousin, as fosterlings to her father. Rhys was quiet and contemplative, but Huw was brash and unthinking, always looking for a way to prove himself a man. Having her sister ask him to teach her to use the forbidden weapon had stroked his ego, but today was the only day they could practice without the all-watching eye of her father. That meant the practice would cut into the time Rhys and Huw had hoped for themselves. Maybe they would teach Glenys something that would change her mind.

"If you get bruised, don't come crying to me or Grandmother for a salve," said Eira coldly as she went to sit by the stream in a billow of grey and brown woollen skirts.

Having enough of the pettiness, the older boy came up to Huw, put a tanned hand upon his friend's shoulder and mischievously smiled at Glenys. "Give her a quick lesson, smack her hard on the behind and then let's get to *real* practice."

"Aye, Rhys. I'm not here to play with little girls." Huw gave a knowing wink to the older boy.

"I'm not a little girl!" Glenys swung her wooden sword, making the two boys jump back, but the swing unbalanced her and she spun and fell.

Eira clapped her hands and howled with glee. This was perfect. Even the two boys laughed.

"Stop laughing!" shouted the girl. Tears threatened to spring from her eyes. The two boys managed to stifle their giggles.

"Thanks, Glenys. I needed a good laugh," said Huw, wiping tears from his eyes. "You weren't kidding that you needed lessons."

Glenys crossed her arms across her flat chest and pouted in hopes that maybe one of them would take pity upon her and finally show her something with the wooden stick. Unfortunately, her magic worked on the wrong boy. Rhys walked over to her, picked up her waster and held out his hand to her.

"If you truly are serious about learning the sword, you are going to have to first learn how to block."

Her small hand fit into his and she stood, wiping off the loose grass from her breeches. She was small next to him and her smile was radiant.

Huw rolled his eyes and coughed. It seemed he was off the hook to teach his foster father's daughter. If practice with Rhys was off then he was not unhappy with the prospects of sitting with Eira. She was beautiful. She had to be the most wondrous woman he had ever seen, and though he was only a year younger than her, he already had dreams of the two of them together as man and wife.

Watching Rhys show the proper stances with the waster to her sister, Eira plucked nervously at the grass when Huw came to sit beside her.

Huw sensed her agitated state and remained quiet for a few minutes while he watched Rhys try and teach Glenys how to stand and block with the sword. The sun lit up around them, and he could see the young girl's face aglow with hunger and excitement. Within a short time the sound of wood hitting wood rang throughout the grove, shortly followed by a smack of wood against skin.

"That's not fair!" Glenys howled and rubbed her backside while Rhys chuckled, keeping to his balanced stance with sword in hand.

"Life's not fair, little one," called Rhys. "Let's go at it again and I'll show you where you went wrong."

The slow dance of bodies and wood began again. This time Glenys thought about what she was doing and took her time.

Huw turned to look at the older of the sisters. The sun glittered blue highlights off her glossy mane and her high firm breasts made him stir. "She's not that bad at this, aye?"

Torn grass fell from her long, delicate fingers and she looked up with a sigh. Her sister seemed to be holding her own, but they still should not be here. She should be home preparing for when their father returned.

"I guess she's doing okay. But..."

"What?" Huw leaned closer, her brown eyes drawing him in. He enjoyed hearing her soft melodic voice and he could not believe his luck that she was actually spending time with him rather than getting up and leaving as she tended to do when he came around.

She pulled away when he tried to touch her hand and saw him look down, a frown on his face. Regardless of how she felt about the boy, Eira did not like to be the cause of anyone's unhappiness.

"I'm sorry, Huw. It's just that I'm worried."

The boy looked up, concern on his face. "What about?"

The cat was out of the bag. She had held in her worries for so long, only able to talk with the other women in the village and her Grandmother. It seemed no one else knew what was going on. Maybe her father did, but he did not say anything.

"I don't know if you've noticed, but the village has been going through some very bad luck." She looked into his hazel eyes, searching for any recognition that he knew what she was talking about.

"What do you mean 'bad luck'?" He frowned, wondering what this was all about.

She took a deep breath and decided to continue. "Haven't you noticed all the strange things happening since the Priest came back?"

"What are you talking about, Eira? You always talk in riddles."

She rolled her eyes. "Okay. You must have noticed the strange things like the milk turning sour as if it came from the cows that way. Things going missing and then turning up in the oddest places. Don't you remember when Father couldn't find his newly fletched arrows and the next day they turned up in the cauldron when we all awoke? People in the village are worried, Huw. Ever since Father agreed with the Priest that leaving offerings to the Fay had to stop things have gotten worse."

"But the Priest and your father are right." Huw could not understand the strange occurrences and chose to believe what the Priest said at his weekly sermons. "The Priest says the Fay are demons and we have to pray to the Christ to save us. Then the demons will go away."

She could not believe her ears. The Fay were not demons, as the Priest would like them all to believe. They were part of the land. They gave life to the land and were children of the Goddess just as they were. Eira could not believe such stories of demons, but the Fay were known to cause mischief at times.

"So you believe demons are causing the problems?"

"That's what the Priest says," replied the boy, fully believing what he said. "The Priest says that we have to drive the Devil out of our village lest the evil becomes worse."

"And how does the Priest think we can do this?" She was curious as to how much Huw was taken in by this wandering man.

"He says we should pray harder. I don't believe that." At last some sense seemed to come from him. "If I had my way it would be with this." He brandished his waster and then let it drop.

She laughed. "I don't think a Christian devil would be afraid of that."

"It would be if the sword was of steel," he said in all seriousness.

Her laughter was cut short by the coldness in his voice and

she was suddenly afraid, knowing that Huw could become a very dangerous man. Eira did not know if she was afraid of him or she was afraid for him, but the fear cut her deep to the bone.

A shout from Rhys turned their attention from the sudden gulf that had expanded between the boy and the girl.

Standing up, Huw called back, "What is it?" He was glad for the diversion as he helped Eira to her feet. They went to join Rhys and Glenys under the shade of an old oak tree.

The boy behind the hawthorn stared in horror and tried to get a better look through the leaves and flowers. He could not believe what he witnessed. They had found his belongings! He had sat quietly as he watched the four strangers take over his sacred place, and in fascination as the younger girl and the older boy started trying to hit each other with the sticks. The hammering of his heart in his ears made it difficult to hear their conversations while terror kept him rooted in place. Now that they had found the items and the fish he had left behind when he had hidden, the pounding upped its tempo. He tried to swallow but could not. His mouth went bone dry.

"Someone was here before we came," he heard the older boy say, looking around for him.

"No one would have just left this stuff," said the tall girl with the long black hair. "Whoever left it must still be around."

"I didn't see anyone when we came here, did any of you?" asked the younger girl.

The other three shook their heads.

The boy let out his breath in relief that he had not been seen, not realizing he had been holding it. He licked his lips nervously and tried to see what was happening.

"Well, no one can just up and disappear," said the younger boy, who held his stick in a fierce grip. A look fell across his freckled face that made the boy behind the bush shiver. "Eira, you said that someone was causing a lot of mischief in the village."

"I said the Fay, not someone."

"Fay, demon, whoever or whatever has been causing all the bad luck could easily disappear, couldn't they?" He started looking around.

The older girl nodded. "I guess it could, but maybe we should leave this place if it lives here. Maybe it doesn't like us being here and will cause us more problems."

"No. I like this place." A malicious tone crept into his voice. "Maybe if we can flush it out and teach it a lesson it won't come back to cause more problems for everyone else."

Hearing this, the boy knew he had to run, now, to get away from this place and never come back. He looked to see how he could get out of the tangle of hawthorn without drawing attention to himself and then glanced back to see what the four were doing. To his horror they had fanned out, looking for him. He had no choice. The younger girl came his way. Turning, he put his hand down to give him the push needed to get up from his sitting position and was met with a thorn in the fleshy part of his thumb. A cry came unbidden to his lips and he pulled the finger long thorn from his hand in time to have his eyes meet the brown ones of the smaller girl through the bush of flowers and leaves.

She screamed and jumped back, bringing the other three running to her. "It's in there! I saw it!" She pointed at the spot he hid in.

The older boy pointed his long stick at the bush and the boy behind it. "You'd better come out of there if you know what's good for you."

The boy sucked on his bleeding hand. He did not know what to do. Everything in him told him to flee, but if he ran they would most likely catch him. Where would he run? He could not go back to Auntie with them hot on his heels. He had waited too long, been too curious and now he had no choice. Swallowing the fear that turned his stomach sick, he carefully dislodged himself from the mess of thorny branches and foliage.

"By the Gods!" The older boy's face grew pale with shock, his sword suddenly hanging limp in his grip, as the sight of the pale creature with red eyes came fully into view.

The boy stared back at the four, easily recognizing fear in all their eyes and looked down at his bare feet. He found it hard to catch his breath, his own fear stealing the air.

The older girl, curiosity in her eyes, took a step towards him, hand outstretched as though to touch him. He backed away before she could come any closer, fearful ruby eyes met brown. Before she could touch him the younger boy named Huw pulled her away.

"Don't touch it! My God! The Priest was right! It is a demon!"

The venom in his voice struck the boy as if he had been slapped, and his gaze landed upon Huw who was of a height with him.

"Just look at its eyes! No natural eyes are red, and look at its skin and hair. This… this creature is not natural!"

They had not done anything to him — yet, but the boy did not want to wait around to find out what was next. Not with the blatant hostility that the other boy showed him. It was exactly what Auntie told him to expect and to make sure never happened. Fear and drilled in instinct snapped into him and he bolted for the cover of the forest. He did not get far before a hand grabbed his arm and violently swung him around and back into the glade and the sun. Catching his balance in a crouch, he slowly got back to his feet as the other boy back fisted him across the jaw.

The blow sent him reeling and the taste of blood exploded in his mouth before he landed hard on his backside. Auntie had warned something bad would happen if anyone caught him. He had grown up with those same fears, but never, until now, had they become a reality. Her constant predictions were right, no matter how much he had hoped and even dreamed that they were wrong—Auntie was right! In shock, he stared as the boy named Huw came at him, stick raised, as the other three yelled after their friend.

"I'll teach you to cause us problems!" shouted the other boy. "Be gone, demon!"

A flash of brilliant light and pain cracked across his skull before sweet oblivion enfolded him into its embrace.

She stood in horror as the white creature extracted itself from the hawthorn. When she saw his red eyes, her breath caught in her throat.

Was this the creature terrorizing her village?

It must be Fay to have hidden in the mayflowers, she thought.

It shivered in fear. She could not believe her eyes; could not believe he was real.

Did this mean that all the stories that Grandmother told about the Tylwyth Teg were true? It must.

They had found one of the Fay!

Wanting, no needing, to see if he was real, Eira stepped closer, her hand outstretched, but he had stepped back. She could not mistake the terror in his eyes—his beautiful eyes, bright as spilled blood, locked with hers, stirring a deep memory. Did someone say something? She did not know and was suddenly pulled away from the Fay, breaking the spell for both of them.

Unexpectedly, the Fay made its escape towards the forest, but was caught and flung back into the glade. Bright sunlight shone off of his moon pale skin, red blood dripping from its split lip. The violence of the action snapped Eria back to the present. She shouted for Huw to stop. Rhys held her back, shouting words she could not understand. All she knew was that she wanted to protect this creature from Huw's temper, but it was too late. The waster made from ash connected with the Fay, spilling it onto the ground until it came to rest face down on the green earth.

"Let go of me!" she shouted, shaking off Rhys' tight grip. Ignoring them all, Eira picked up her skirts and ran to the Fay lying prone in the grass, a red puddle starting to form beside its head. "Dear Goddess, what have we done?" she whispered behind her hand.

"Eira, get away from it," ordered Huw, wiping his waster on the grass. "It won't be bothering us anymore."

How could he be so cold? Eira could not believe him. She knew, had always known, Huw had a temper, but she could never imagine such unrestrained violence. She knelt beside the unconscious creature and put her hand to its warm neck as her grandmother had taught her to do and found a faint pulse.

It's alive! Thank Dôn! She sighed in relief and caught herself. She had touched a Fay! She wanted desperately to heal it, to care for it—something within her somehow knew this creature. Dare she touch his long white hair? Her hand traveled up its neck and to her amazement found its hair downy soft.

Her reverence was broken as Rhys snatched her to her feet to face him. "What do you think you're doing?" he hissed, taking her by both forearms and shaking her until seemed to come out of a deep sleep. "We have to go—NOW!"

He looked to where Glenys stood with tears in her eyes and then to Huw who looked away in disgust, as if the others should really care about what he did to the demon. "No one, and I mean no one will ever tell anyone what happened today," ordered Rhys and to Huw, "If I ever hear one word out of your mouth to anyone about this, cousin, I will make you eat a real sword."

Huw's eyes lowered and Rhys could see the hostility in his

cousin's stance, knuckles white as it gripped the waster. "I won't say anything."

"Your word, cousin."

"My word." Cold fury had encompassed the boy, and without another word he walked out of the glen, leaving the three with the body.

Rhys turned to the two girls. He did not trust his cousin at this moment, but never before had Huw given him reason. "Let's go."

Glenys nodded her tear-streaked face as she hugged herself. She had wanted to learn the sword, but if a wooden one could do so much damage, she decided that maybe learning to use a real one would not be the best thing. She followed her cousin out of the glen, treading the path back to her village.

Left together in the glen, Rhys glanced sideways at Eria. "Come on."

"We can't leave him here, Rhys," she implored. "He'll die if he does not get help."

"He's dead already, Eira." Fatigue filled his voice. They had come to the glen to have fun. Today they would go back to the village forever changed. Taking Eira's arm, he guided her out of the sun and into the darkness of the forest.

II

ark tendrils encompassed him as he floated downwards, buffeting him against the gentle winds that slowed his fall, cradling him against forces he sensed about him but could not see.

Was he dead?

He did not know, and nor did he care. He was away from the pain, away from the fear. Here he could float on the winds of un-consciousness. The comfort astounded him and he nestled deeper into the darkness, breathing in its sweet essence.

A shift in current.

A minute change of direction.

An unwelcome force applied to his flight bringing a twinkling of fear and a whimper.

Far off a brilliant white light tugged at him, pulling him closer. Is this where he wanted to go? He did not know, but the light frightened and enthralled him, forcing him to gaze into its blazing radiance.

The supporting blackness dissolved, burning away in the flames of its heat.

The pull downwards to the growing light became stronger until he saw within its glowing surface a green garden full of flowers. Its bountiful beauty more ecstatic to his senses than anything else he had ever seen. Flowers of gold, silver and every *colour of the rainbow grew. Trees so tall that their tops could not be seen yet did not diminish the light at their bases, allowing smaller plants to flourish.*

In awe, he allowed the tidal forces that pulled him to draw him closer.

The light flared encompassing him, and he gasped at the pleasure as it flickered gently across his skin. His body shivered at the sensations.

Slowly, the light moved along his body, caressing him. He closed his eyes and swallowed in anticipation as the brilliance brushed up his chest, his neck, and his face. Feelings of love and compassion reverberated through his whole being until the light reached his head.

Pain!

Blinding pain forced his eyes open and as suddenly it had come upon him it dissipated.

The ball of light with its garden was so close now that he could see three female figures. All with outstretched arms imploring him to their company. One as white as he with eyes the colour of snow, the other with flaming red hair and eyes to match, and the last, which looked so much like the girl at grove.

The grove!

Memory crashed into his consciousness and he cried out. The pain, the humiliation, the fear, all encompassed him and cried out. His body convulsed.

The light withdrew, leaving him cold, vulnerable to the darkness that claimed him once again. His cries echoed in the wails of the three women as he twisted and turned, cast adrift, pulled away from the light and its garden.

Darkness filled him, yanked him away until not even a pinpoint of light remained.

Utterly devoid of any light, he let the blackness comfort him, drawing the memories away leaving only numbness.

No thought.

No feeling.

No emotion was contained within him.

He relaxed in its embrace, revelling in its ebon caress sweeter than the light.

"Yesssss." The darkness hissed.

Unseen fingers flickered across his body draining him of all pain, numbing his mind of fear.

"Sooooo delicious."

In the void, he could not see the fingers as they made their way to his face, tracing his features, drinking in his memories. He closed his eyes to allow easy passage across his face.

The fingers from his body evaporated.

"What isssss thisssss?"

The apparent shock of the veiled voice drew the boy back to the awareness of the deep chill of the dark and he hugged himself in an attempt to keep warm.

Where was he?

What was going on?

He did not know and this time he cared as fear darker than the void washed through his body.

"No. Not yet. Too sssssoon," said the voice from everywhere and nowhere.

"W-who are y-you?" called the boy, shuddering from fear or cold, he did not know.

"You have made your Choice too sssssoon, but Choice has been made. Take back your memories, your fearsssss and your pain. We will come when the time isssss right."

A silvery white mist began to develop and swirl before him. Wisps being drawn into a core that became more and more solid, taking form. With a slack jaw, he stared as this thing of mist coalesced until it had a partial form of something not quite human. The wisps of silver fluttered like a ragged cloak that was the creature. Then he saw its face, or what was possibly left as a face.

Red glowing eyes stared back in a skull ravished by decay. Its black maw open with pointed teeth. It had no nose and then it did something that horrified him even more... it smiled.

Laughter echoed through the void.

He desperately needed to get away, but he could not move.

The creature floated towards him, its white tendrils caressed him, and this time he shuddered in revulsion.

"Sssssweet, sssssso sssssweet." It was face to face with him.

If it had breath it would have smelled fetid. The figure before him conjured images of putrescence, death and decay.

If he could have run, he would have, but there was nothing in this void save for this creature before him.

He turned his head away and closed his eyes.

A greater pressure on his face made him open his eyes and

face front, gazing into its eyes—were those red orbs eyes?

"Sssssstrong," it hissed, a slight smile on its ruined face. "A gift assss well, then."

It drew back and swirled around him, gaining speed. He could only stare at the vortex of silver mist surrounding him. As it reached its peak above him, it crashed downwards, into him, showering him in its frozen being, entering every part of him.

The pain of the bitter blast forced a scream from his tortured lungs.

A scream that could not stop.

ÍÍÍ

Awareness slammed into the boy, pulling him from the dark void and its ghoulish creature. Gasping, trying in vain to catch his breath while his heart hammered through his battered skull, the boy lay on the grass in shock. Mastering his breath, he managed to become aware of his surroundings and opened his eyes to the darkness. What time it was he did not know, but he could not remain where he was and he lifted his head.

Nauseating pain flashed in his eyes and he was able, just in time, to get to all fours before retching out an empty stomach. The pounding renewed its vigour and he felt the world spin. He clutched onto consciousness as hard as his hands held onto the grass and earth, waiting long minutes before the sick feeling decreased enough to move again, but slowly this time.

He was still in the grove, but the sky was indigo, quickly surrendering its fading light to the night. The boy moaned, fighting back another wave of queasiness and the flickers of light it brought. Still on all fours, he lowered his head to the soothing cool earth, gasping in its clean green scent and tried to remember what happened. He found his memory ended after the first blow from the boy with hazel eyes and a freckled face.

Dear Dôn, what did they do to me?

The answer was evident in his being.

Ever so carefully, the boy tried to shift into a kneeling

position but a new pain wracked his body. Intense fire flowed along his legs, back and arms, causing him to cry out. Bringing fingers to touch his forearm, he found his skin ablaze in heat and pain. Again he had to fight off another swoon, his breath coming in short gasps. Closing his eyes, he could feel the cool breeze eat at the heat and the violent shuddering began. He knew he was sick. Something was terribly wrong. He could not even hug himself to try and keep warm for the pain his own touch caused his body. Tears seeped out of the corners of his eyes as the suffering rocked him, its salt stinging his swollen and broken lip.

He needed Auntie, needed her badly, but the boy knew that she would never find him. Somehow he had to get home where the only person in the world who cared about him could comfort and heal him. All he wanted to do was fall into her embrace and let her dry old fingers wash away his tears. How would he explain what happened? He did not know for certain either except that she had been right. He had to remain hidden. The pain of the attack was inconsequential compared to the lack of reason as to why it occurred. Auntie had always said he was different and that such difference would always be a threat to others, but she would never explain. Now he knew. He was perceived as something not human—even to Auntie!

That realization hit him harder than the blows he suffered, making the tears flow faster. That was why she would say it was his Fay nature to act in ways she could not comprehend. Why he always seemed a mystery to the woman who raised him. Could that be why she never gave him a name and only called him boy? That thought horrified him even more and a sense of betrayal began to wrap around his heart, but he still had to go home, to face her and hopefully to heal.

Climbing to his feet nearly caused him to pass out. It was his strength and determination that steadied him. His head throbbed in time with his pounding heartbeat. His skin ablaze in unseen fire, the boy took a first unsteady step. The nausea became less fierce and he sighed looking into the dark forest he had to pass through. The thought of branches and leaves touching his burnt skin scared him, but he had no choice but to enter.

A few steadier steps brought him to the tree line. Closing his tearing eyes, the boy took a deep even breath, gaining the courage to make the assay. One more step took him out of the glade with the firm knowledge that he would never return to this place.

*   *   *

He sat at the small board and accepted the second bowl of stew from the small old lady; too courteous not to say that he was already full from the first generous helping. The black hard bread came next and he did not believe he had room enough within him to manage the bounty she honoured him with. For her he broke off a piece of bread, dipped it gingerly into the bowl, letting it soak the beef juice as he rolled some meat and vegetables onto it with a practiced knife. Carefully, he brought the steaming bread to his lips and popped the whole thing into his mouth. Chewing noisily and sucking the juice off his thumb, he watched the sister of his wife's father settle herself across from him.

She was a strange sort. Having never married and choosing to live a life of solitude, Llawela's reputation was replete with stories ranging from the most innocuous, to some that, if heard by the wrong kind of folk, could cause her a lot of problems.

It was common knowledge that the Old Woman was a witch—one of the Gwyddon—and where she learned her lore and magic was part of her mystery. Those who knew her knew that her heart was dedicated to the service of the Old Ones. It was a matter of perspective that dictated whether this so called service was benign or malicious. He liked to think that she was a crazy old bitty who, on the rare occasion, would be able to make others believe in better things, in a better world. It was a damned hard world to live in.

Ever since he had the mantle of Chief thrust upon him by the Elders, Geraint had seen more than enough of his share of skirmishes, battles and war. It was not a good time to be alive, and even worse to be a Chief of a people who were as stubborn as he. He managed the best he could and worried who would become Chief after him since he had no living son. It was one of the many reasons why he took on his cousins' sons to foster. Rhys was a good boy, but Huw—he grimaced at the thought of the younger boy—he would leave that line of thought for another time when he could devote more time to what to do with that impertinent pup.

He brought his gaze back to the bowl and realized he could not force another bite down. She had asked him to come today and when he arrived she had him tether his horse behind the house—which was strange—and then she proceeded to have him wait, filling the silences with trivial talk. Okay, his girls were not trivial. Eira was every bit of a woman his wife had been before… No! He would not go there with this either.

Damn you old woman. Just tell me why I'm here. He realized then that Llawela fidgeted nervously and kept glancing at the door. She had not said anything since offering him another bowl of stew.

Geraint huffed in annoyance. It was already dark and traveling at night was not something he relished. He needed to get back home before his family started worrying for his safety, if they had not already.

"Okay, Old Woman, enough," he broke the silence with his gruff voice and was surprised to see her startle as though she had forgotten that he was there. He started in with a gentler tone. "You asked me to come here today and then you have me sit and wait."

She turned to face him, her eyes grey and rheumy, appeared very worried. This in turn made his stomach tighten. Llawela was not the sort of woman to worry or be concerned about anything. Whatever bothered her must be damned well important.

"I'm sorry, boy," she said, her voice warbling with age. He liked that she called him boy; then again to her ancientness any man would be a boy to her. "I don't mean to keep you, but…" She let her words fall away as grey brows furrowed in worry and eyes turned back to the door.

They must be waiting for someone, Geraint surmised, but who would come now that it was dark? Whoever was supposed to come was obviously delayed, judging by the Old Woman's distraction. Late or not, it was late for him and regardless of what she wanted he had to get home. Standing up, he lifted the sword from where it leaned against the board and strapped it onto his belt.

The sound drew her attention back to her guest and she rose to her feet. "Please, Geraint. Don't go," she implored.

Geraint closed his eyes and sighed. Shaking his head, he said, "I'm sorry Llawela, but I've waited too long as it is. I must get home."

Frantically staring about, her eyes fell upon the slightly indented stew and bread. "You can't go until you finish the stew. It would be a waste."

He could tell she was grasping at anything that would hold

him to this place and smiled sadly. "I appreciate the food. I really do. But if I eat any more I swear I will burst." It broke his heart to see the Old Woman's shoulders slump in defeat, and he walked around the small table and kissed the top of her head as he would have done with one of his daughters. "I really must go now."

She nodded, not daring to look up at him. "Will you come back soon?"

"I'll try." He could not make any promises. He did not usually come out this way since the hovel bordered on the lands he governed. Having taken his leave, he made way to the door only to stop short at the lithe figure that suddenly stood in his way.

Eyes wide in shock, he took a step back. The creature before him was a ghastly sight. Slightly shorter than he, thin without looking scrawny, it stood in the doorway, arms red and torso white as snow, clad in a rough woollen kilt. Bringing his gaze to the creature's face, he could see the large blackened bruise on the right side of the jaw and the dried blood where a split lip began to swell.

It was the eyes of the creature that took Geraint's breath from him. In the orange firelight from the hearth, the eyes glittered red, and were puffy from...crying? He noticed that there was more dried blood on the side of its face, and saw rust coloured blood staining its milk white hair from a bad wound that still leaked red on the left side of its head.

Geraint stood numbly, staring back at the red eyes that glared at him. Pain, hatred and above all, fear reflected back at him as the old woman rushed past.

"Oh dear Dôn," she prayed. "What happened?" Lifting her hand to touch the creature's battered jaw, her face ashen as it took an unbalanced step back and brought the full brunt of its gaze onto her.

Tears threatened to break, making its eyes glitter like rubies. There was so much pain there that Geraint could only stand and stare. The red eyes, hair the colour of the moon and skin so pale brought a hidden memory to the surface forcing Geraint to take a step towards the boy.

Noticing the movement from the stranger in his home, the boy turned back to face the man. Finding him there, sitting across from Auntie, was a shock that sent his mind reeling into believing that what was done to him in the grove was just the beginning of worse. The man wore leathers as a warrior would, that accentuated his barrel build and strength. His dark hair streaked with silver and his moustache hung long. It was the silver dragons that made up the guard of the man's sword glittering in the firelight that caught his attention.

The boy began to visibly shake and Geraint did not know whether it was from fear or from the injuries. Following the gaze, he noticed that the boy's eyes were glued to his sword and blinking very rapidly. It was then he noticed that the boy did not seem able to catch his breath.

"Geraint!" cried Llawela, as the boy's eyes rolled back and he collapsed.

He managed to catch the boy before he hit the ground, and scooped him into his arms.

So light, he thought.

Thrust into action, Llawela forced back the curtains that divided the pallets that served as beds and the rest of the home. It was the first time in which he noticed that there was a smaller bed set next to Llawela's.

"Here. Put him down here," she ordered. "On his stomach."

Geraint did what he was bidden and only when the unconscious boy was on his bed did he realize the extent of the damage. Not only were the boy's arms red, his back, shoulders and calves were on fire. Blisters formed and some had broken when he had lifted him into his arms. Geraint had seen many wounds but this one baffled him and he took a step back, giving the old woman enough room to manoeuvre to get her healing herbs.

"Wh-what did you say?" Geraint came out of his shock, realizing that the old woman had asked him something.

"Wake up, man!" Clearly she was angry. "There's a bucket over there. Go get some fresh water from the stream."

Geraint saw where she pointed, picked up the bucket and left the small home for the little river that flowed to the west. Shaking, and not from the cold, his mind staggered through the events of the last few moments and knew, without a doubt, his life was forever changed.

Llawela watched as her guest, and she figured—her Chief—leave her home with the bucket in hand. She had expected a reaction from the man once he saw the boy, but circumstances had changed everything. Bringing her attention to the boy on the bed, her eyes brimmed with tears. Something terrible had happened and somewhere deep inside she knew that her long held fears for the child had finally come true. The question she had to concern herself with now is whether this signified the end of their lives together?

Then another thought came to her that shook her to the core. Would Geraint go off and tell of what he has witnessed or come back? Regardless, she knew that the choice was in his hands and she had no right to try and change it. Dôn would hopefully protect them and hide them as She always had. It was so hard to keep faith with the boy lying there, skin burnt and bleeding.

Pulling down some of her dried herbs from last year's harvest, she plucked off the amounts she needed and dropped them into a carved wooden bowl often used in her blends. She had to work fast; the boy shivered from the wounds and the illness they created.

What worried her most was the head wound. The cut lip was the least of her concerns. What confounded her was that the boy's skin was burnt as though someone had taken a torch to him. She prayed to Dôn that had not been the case. She put her healing powers into pounding the herbs together, blending them and letting their magics interlink and then put them aside for when, or if, Geraint returned with fresh water.

There was something else she needed, but could not put a name to it. Letting the Goddess guide her, she searched the shelves until the knot in her stomach loosed enough to tell her that she had found what She wanted her to find.

The old bottle of wine that sat on one of her dusty shelves seemed to pop into her diminished sight. She could not imagine what wine could do in this situation. Maybe Geraint would need it; at least she could finally get rid of it. Grabbing it, she used the knife she kept on her belt to get the stopper out and took a whiff. She wrinkled her nose and held it at arm's length. Whatever it was supposed to be, it was not wine—at least not any more.

Another intuitive flash came to her and Llawela knew that the Goddess worked through her to heal as She had done throughout her life. Letting instinct and the Goddess guide her, she took a rag that was once the boy's old shirt and she soaked the cloth with the vinegar. Carefully, so as not to hurt the child, she laid the sodden rag on the boy's back. A sigh escaped from his unconscious lips and lifting a corner she tested the reddened skin. Heat radiated off, but it seemed a bit cooler. Unfortunately, the child's shivering did not cease. Only time would heal those burns. In the meantime, she could help by keeping them clean.

Lowering herself onto the floor next to the boy, old joints cracking, she groaned at the effort to put a hand to his forehead, feeling the fever that racked his lean and graceful figure. It was so hard to see him like this; so helpless and in such pain. She shook her head. She had dealt with so many wounded and sick people in her very long life, but to see the boy she raised from a foundling lying helpless on his pallet gripped her heart. She finally understood the fears mothers had when their babes fell ill. Silently, she asked him to forgive her, that she was too late—oh so late.

Hands thin and spotted with age searched through the white hair crusted with blood to find the swollen gash that ran from behind the boy's left temple to behind his ear. Dried blood flaked off of the wound allowing fresh to flow free but only for a moment. It looked as though it was healing well, but the swelling was what really concerned her. She wished that Geraint would come back so she could wash the boy's wounds and truly see the extent of the damage.

The door banged open and Geraint entered, pail in hand. He looked a wreck. She had not expected the boy's presence to take such a toll on the man.

"Where do you want this?" he asked. A twinge of sadness and shock simmered in his voice.

"Can you please pour as much as possible into the kettle and hang it over the fire," she asked gently. He did as he was bidden.

The bench was painfully hard under Geraint as he sat and watched the old woman work her healing magic, taking the heated water and gently cleaning the boy's head and face. He was astounded at the amount of dried blood that she washed off, but head wounds were notorious for the gruesomeness. He tried to tell himself that it would be okay, that boy would be all right. Shoulders tense and back straight as a rod, he found he could not relax, expectant for some word from Llawela, any word.

She focused all her attention on the boy, and when she had done all she could she looked up at Geraint and nodded, face drawn tight and fear in her eyes. "It's up to the Goddess now," she declared, washing off the stains from her fingers.

Her movements were stiff as the effects of her age and her craft took its toll and she sat down opposite Geraint, eyes lowered with anguish and fatigue. The silence in the hut was only cut by the crackle of the fire in the hearth. Geraint put his hand on top of hers, feeling their thin dryness that age and fate brought to her. How small her hands were and remarkably strong, just like her, admiring her even more.

"I've done what I could," she sighed. It seemed that she said this more to comfort him than anything else and the silence lengthened between them yet again. Geraint left his hand on hers since she seemed to take some comfort from his touch. Fighting his impatience to find out more about the child was hard, but he waited, eyes shifting to view the lithe figure trembling in the bed and back to the old woman before him.

"I was too late," whispered Llawela. "Dôn forgive me."

Her petition to the Goddess surprised Geraint and he drew his hand away, apprehension filling him. "Too late for what?"

Steel grey eyes met his. "Too late for him to meet you."

Shaking his head, Geraint's heart beat faster. Did her Goddess tell her something that only he now knew? Tentatively, he ventured, "What are you talking about, woman?" It then dawned on him. "Is that who you wanted me to meet?" Surprise filled his voice, making him louder than he intended. Normally, he would have been more courteous and not allowed his voice to rise, but the circumstances were too full of unanswered questions— something he did *not* like. It was time to find out what was going on.

Llawela nodded, a frown creased her already heavily wrinkled face. "I wanted the two of you to meet."

"Why, Llawela?"

She gazed sideways at him. Was there a hint of a smile lifting the corners of her mouth despite the sadness in her eyes? "Because I can teach him only so much, because I am very old, and because one day I will be gone and he will have no one to protect him. He'll have to do that for himself and I can't teach him that. Out of all the men I know, only you have the honour and the knowledge to teach him what a man needs to know."

"Blessed God," sighed the Chieftain. "Are you asking me to take him as a fosterling?" Despite his desire to know this boy, he could not bring him home.

Grey hair fluttered as she shook her head. "No. Not that."

"Then what? Speak plainly, woman." Confusion tinged with fear accentuated Geraint's words.

The old woman closed her eyes and took a couple of deep calming breaths. When she opened them again she stared into his deep brown eyes, making it impossible for him to turn away and impacting the seriousness of the words that followed. "I want—or rather *he needs*—you to come here when you can and train him how to defend himself. To use the sword, the bow, the knife, whatever the weapons of war are now. He needs to learn to be self-sufficient. He needs to learn, and only you can teach him that, Geraint. Only you. I've thought about other men in the area, but for the same reasons the Elders made you Chief I am imploring you to take time out of your life to teach him. I know you lost a son a long time ago..." Geraint gasped in shock. Did she know? "But this boy has never had a father, or a mother for that fact. He needs you even though he does not know it right now. Will you help him?"

It was hard to take his gaze away from her, but he managed to look away and found that his eyes naturally fell upon the unconscious boy. Clearly, Llawela did not know, but then again how could she. Pursing his lips together, he blew out in a huff. There was so much to consider. It sent his mind reeling, but the boy on the bed, so vulnerable, obviously needed help. Could he be the one? Could he open his heart up again after years of dust and neglect had rusted it shut? Could he have hope again for a true son? What about his daughters? He groaned. There was so much to take into account.

Brushing his hand across his weary and stubbled face, he regarded the old woman, trying to think things though and found he could not. "I'm sorry, Llawela—"

"Please?" she implored.

He closed his eyes and sighed, recognizing the emotional attack and knowing how effective it was on him. Living with three women taught him that.

"At least let me think about it."

Realizing she had gained a foothold, the old woman smiled and nodded, eyes lighting up. "That's fine. Very fine." She got up, agitated by the excessive energy that newfound hope had brought. "Since it is so late, you are more than welcome to stay the night."

Geraint accepted her offer. A warm hearth was better than getting lost in the cold dark. He made his way to the door to care for his horse before he could rest. Before exiting he realized something, turning back he asked, "What's the boy's name?"

The question startled her and she replied, "He doesn't have a name."

He took a step back into the building. "What?" This was strange. Everyone had a name.

"The boy is Fay, Geraint. One of the Tylwyth Teg. He will be given his name by his own people when they finally come for him."

The matter of fact tone surprised him. She really believed this, but what could he say? To tell her that he had witnessed the boy's birth from his own wife's loins would reveal the truth; a truth that *must* remain hidden for all concerned. "What do you call him, then?"

She seemed genuinely surprised by the question. "I call him what he is: a boy."

Shaking his head, Geraint went outside to unsaddle and care for his horse. At least with Cadfarch, his gelding, the world was much simpler.

It did not take long to brush down Cadfarch and see that the chestnut gelding had enough feed and water for the night. The sky had been a black veil littered with stars for quite some time and Geraint figured that it was well into midnight when he opened the door to the hut. Ducking under the lintel, he found himself in a home where the only sounds were of a snapping fire, banked for the night, singing with the soft breathing of the two residents who slept in their respective beds. It would be uncomfortable to sleep beside the fire with the ground so hard, but he had suffered worse in his days.

Geraint spread out his horse's blanket as padding and left his cloak as a blanket. He knew he could not sleep just yet. So much had happened in such a short time that he doubted that any sleep would ease his troubled mind, because it seemed to think in opposites to what his heart screamed at him. Was it a curse or a blessing to see that the boy was still alive? He did not even know whether to be happy as he stared at the boy sleeping on his small bed made of blankets covering straw.

Knowing he would not be getting any sleep yet, despite the weariness that weighed him down, Geraint stepped quietly, so as not to wake the two, and sat down on the hard packed floor next to the sleeping boy. The dim firelight glittered orange, and the deep shadows played with the boy's battered features, but Geraint could plainly see that the boy was in the grips of a nightmare.

He wanted to wake the boy, to make him realize that he was finally safe, to take him in his arms and hold him there, never letting him go. His arms ached for his lost son, and despite finding him after so many years of believing him dead, Geraint knew he could not. He was a stranger to this boy.

Oh God, what would the boy think if he knew that here was the man that was forced to expose him to a cold winter night as a way to kill him when he was but a babe? Guilt, anger and above all, self loathing filled Geraint. All the old emotions from nine years ago flooded back, but this time they came colliding with the joy, trepidation and the anxiety he felt at seeing his son.

The boy moaned and Geraint could not tell whether it was for the pain or the dreams the child suffered, but when the boy started to squirm and cried out, old paternal instincts kicked in and Geraint touched the boy's searing shoulder in an attempt to give comfort and hushed him, whispering to the boy that he was safe. He was rewarded with a whimper and then the dream was past.

The heat radiating off the boy was tremendous and Geraint could not imagine the pain the child was in, but he could see it clearly in the shadowed visage of the boy's face. He realized then, that even if he could not be the boy's father in truth, then he would try to be there as the old woman wished.

If God was truly giving him a second chance, then he damned well was going to take it. He would do as Llawela asked. Now it was a matter of how he was going to be able to take the time away from his village to come here and teach the boy without letting anyone know.

That could wait until tomorrow.

A yawn escaped him and Geraint knew that the tensions of the day were finally gone with the acceptance of this new and added complication in his life. He smiled. Tonight he would sleep next to his son; something he had not done in a very long time, and silently moved his blanket and cloak next to the boy.

Before the sun could break over the horizon, Geraint left his son, riding his horse home to his daughters. For the first time in a very long time Geraint was truly joyous.

ÍƱ

The mud and straw wall cracked and flaked off with the poking and prodding of the stick in the boy's hand. Lying on his stomach, he scratched out of boredom. It was better than picking at his flaking skin that itched him so badly. The worst was when the small of his back and the spot between his shoulder blades began to heal and peel after several days of feeling that if he moved his skin would crack apart.

Auntie tried everything she could, but what finally gave some relief was some foul smelling partially rendered tallow. Unfortunately, it did not stop his skin from peeling. At least it was better than lying in his bed for four days after he had regained consciousness.

Auntie told him she had been very worried for his life when he did not wake for three days, but even after three days the pain was enough to keep him abed. The fire on his skin had reduced, but coupled with the nauseating pain whenever he tried to lift his head kept him in place until he could rise without vomiting. Auntie could not believe that he had managed to stay alive, let alone come home on his own, and left offerings to the Goddess by the sacred elder tree in thanks that her prayers had been answered. The boy did not know whether to be happy that Auntie had been heard.

A larger chip of dried mud popped off and landed on his bed, leaving a large enough indenture that Auntie would notice. Abashed at his own carelessness, he tossed the stick behind him to hit one of the legs of the table with a thunk. Rolling over onto his back—a luxury after seven days of being on his front—he stared up at the thatched roof sitting on beams made of small trees. He let the world spin and come to a slow stop.

He still had bouts of dizziness, but they seemed to come less frequently now, only becoming a problem if he was careless. It was the blinding headaches that not even Auntie's herbals could fix he could do without. They came less often now that a fortnight had passed, but the damage from one single blow to his head was done. It was why he lay on his bed. Boredom mixed with the truth of who and what he was, and thus the reason for his suffering, created a despondency within him that not even the old woman who raised him could cure.

Unshed tears glittered in his eyes and a blink sent them flooding out. Biting down on his healed lip, he ran the events of his attack over in his mind again. It was not the first time, nor the one-hundredth time. He did so in hopes to find an understanding to the assault that would not lead back to what it always led back to, that he was considered something not human, even to Auntie. Because of this, part of him blamed her for what had happened. She had always known it would happen and why, and she could not stop it, did not stop it. He hated himself for what he felt and that only made it worse, because if it was not Auntie's fault then it was his for being different.

It was this difference that made Auntie hide him. Now he was found. A shiver of fear ran through him with the thought of a new attack coming because of him. Would Auntie be hurt for hiding him? She feared so. Was that why that big man had been in his home that night? Had the four in the grove told the man and he was there to punish them both?

The boy remembered the fear on Auntie's face. He remembered the man and the expression of horror he had exhibited at the boy's sudden presence. He could not remember what happened next. He was afraid that now these others knew of his existence, they would tell others or come to finish the job the four had started. The boy rubbed at his eyes in an attempt to force away that line of thinking and waited for the hut to darken with the sunset.

A faint sound of metal clinking against metal and the clopping of hooves upon earth clutched his innards. He sat up. It was unmistakable. There was a horse outside and that meant that someone was here! He was found! Panic took root. He had to get away. He had to hide. But where? The idea of hiding under his covers was ludicrous, something born out of childishness. If someone truly looked for him they would find him here, in his home. He could not hide here. He had to get out.

Climbing to his bare feet, ready to make his escape, his heart skipped a beat when Auntie appeared in the doorway, a smile on her face. Oh Goddess, was she happy to finally be rid of him? The thought shook him to the core, too afraid to say anything.

"I have some good news, boy." Not taking any notice of the boy's trembling, she continued, "Geraint has come back and he's agreed to—"

The boy bolted for the door and the freedom of the twilight, nearly knocking the old woman to the ground in his desperation for escape.

"What?" She twirled around, catching her balance. Realizing the boy had fled out the door, Llawela called, "Boy, come back!"

It had taken Geraint longer than he had anticipated in arranging things back home so that he could return to Llawela and his son. His son! It still mystified him, and though he hated lying to his mother and his daughters – not to mention the rest of the village and his advisors – he had managed something convincing enough to allow him to come to the Old Woman's every fortnight. Let them think what they may. He had lied close enough to the truth that his story and whatever news he reported back to the village from his visits would seem perfectly normal. He just had to make sure that he did not mention the boy.

Going to a lonely old woman to help her make sure she was well cared for and had what she needed was something a Chief of his people should do. Especially, since she was the sister of the old Chief. It was harder to convince his men that because she was kin he was safe to go alone. Begrudgingly, they had accepted. It was his mother that had voiced the greatest protests, but she did not have a choice in the matter. Leaving the running of the house for a couple of days every fortnight in her more than capable hands would give the women in his life a break from him and he from them.

It was hard living with three very strong willed women, he smiled. Sometimes he felt as though he was Chief in name only and his mother and daughters ran the show. It did not matter now. He was here again and he was anxious to see the boy.

Pulling on the reigns, Cadfarch came to a slow cantering stop beside the coop. The old woman stopped feeding the chickens some grain from a small wooden bowl and stretched her back, her face breaking into a smile at the sight of his figure atop the horse.

"I knew you couldn't stay away," she said, forcing the angrily clucking chickens out of her path so she could leave the pen.

Swinging his leg over the chestnut's back, Geraint dismounted and waited for Llawela to come to him, a smile on his face. "You didn't give me much of a choice."

He held out his hand to help her step over the old wooden fence. "Sure I did," she replied once both her feet were well balanced outside of the coop. "You could have chosen to stay away."

"After that surprise you dropped on me, not likely," he chuckled.

His laughter was contagious and she cackled, her face beaming. "So how long do we have the honour of having the Chief stay with us?"

"A couple of days," said Geraint, starting to strip down his horse from its bundles before he could take off the saddle. "I've made arrangements that I can come about every fortnight."

"Wonderful!" Llawela clapped, clearly pleased with how everything was going. "I'll go tell the boy."

Geraint watched the old woman waddle back to her small home as he undid one of the straps that held his kit. A sense of nervousness overtook him as he realized that this time he would be meeting the boy properly. What would he say when he saw the boy? Would he remember him? Suddenly, a streak of white caught his attention and he turned to see the boy running from the house. For a brief moment his eyes caught his son's before the boy disappeared into the woods.

"Boy, come back!" he heard Llawela cry out.

Ignoring his horse for the moment, he covered the ground between them with long powerful strides. "What happened?"

Llawela stood in the doorway; a hand on the wall for support. "I told him you were here and he ran." A sigh escaped her and she shook her head as if what had happened could be taken back and then looked up at the younger man. "You have to go after him."

Dumbfounded, Geraint was not prepared for this, but then again what had he expected? Open arms? To be enthusiastic about a stranger's visit? The boy's escape had surprised both he and Llawela, but more so for Geraint as he had never seen anyone run so fast or so gracefully. It was like watching the flight of a deer, or – Geraint shuddered – a ghost whisking off from being seen.

"I can't go into the woods, Geraint," she explained. "My eyes are not as they were when I was younger and it's already getting dark."

The sky was a deep blue with shades of pink and orange, the sun having set a short time ago. Looking into the darkening woods, Geraint grimaced. How he hated the woods, especially at night. It was a place that sane men were taught to fear. There were spirits in the forest. He had learned that the night he left his son as a babe. It had taken him until sunrise to find his home, his hands and feet and nose nearly frozen. He shuddered at the memory of the sounds of disembodied voices leading him in circles. Luckier than most, he had gotten out alive rather than falling into a bog, never to be seen again.

Going into the woods now, so close to the Beldân festival was an invitation for trouble, but he had no choice. Someone had to go and get the boy and it seemed that person was he.

Resolved, Geraint turned to face the dark forbidding forest. "Okay, I'll get him."

A hand stopped him before he could proceed forward. Looking back at the concerned old woman she said, "Thank you. I wouldn't ask this of you, but be gentle with the boy. Whatever happened to him still is an open wound."

"You mean he hasn't said anything to you?"

She mournfully shook her grey head. "He hasn't said anything. Nothing. Not a word about anything." Recognizing the inquisitiveness on the man's face, she stared into Geraint's soul. "He hasn't said a word since he came home that night."

The magnitude of what she said alarmed him. Had the blow caused some damage that made speech impossible for the boy? God, he hoped not. "He can hear, can't he?"

"Yes," she said miserably.

"Well, then, don't worry. I'll find the boy and bring him back. And I'll be careful with him."

Rewarded by a glimmer of a smile, Geraint nodded and walked to the woods.

It only took a couple of steps from the tree line to find that he was in a different world where night had fallen long before the sun had set. Swallowing his fear he put into mind his purpose in being here — to find his son, but where to start looking?

The trees stood as solid shadows that climbed to make up a canopy of darkness far above his head, cutting off the view of the clear night and the attempts of stars to permeate the new night. The trees were easy to manoeuvre around. It was the bushes and brambles that seemed to catch on his clothing, grasping at him as though they tried to stop him from finding the boy. Carefully he would have to stop and disentangle himself when his clothes caught in smaller branches and thorns.

The boy had to be Fay to be in here! he thought.

It would be nice to find a path, or find any sign of the boy, but in the darkness, not knowing the woods in these parts; it made it damned near impossible. Already he had to suck on his hand from the small scrapes and cuts that the brambles created. If the Fay wanted a blood sacrifice to give up the boy, Geraint was already the unwilling supplier.

Frustrated and fearful that he would get lost he let his hunting skills take over. Coming to a standstill, Geraint closed his eyes to listen. First it was hard to hear past his beating heart, but quickly reminding himself that doing this at night was the same as doing it in the day. He let the pounding fall into the background. Whispers of wind fluttered in the trees and bushes about him. A crack of deadfall and a screech of two fighting animals told him that a badger's nest was nearby. He let the sounds envelop him and found he heard something unusual. Placing his soul in the care of God Geraint carefully, quietly, followed the sound and prayed it was not the Tylwyth Teg playing games with him again.

It did not take him long to find himself in a small clearing, the indigo sky above with stars starting to become visible with the oncoming night. No moon would rise this night. Only the stars would be there to guide him back if — no, when, he corrected himself — he found the boy. The sound continued but louder this time. Turning to face the cause, he found beneath a tree off to his right a figure of white sitting with knees hugged to its chest. He had found the boy and the source of the sound.

The boy was crying. Then he stopped and stared at the man

who intruded upon his solitude.

Geraint did not require much light to see the boy's expression turn from surprise to terror. The boy's pale skin seemed to glow in the fading light. Geraint took a step towards the child and damned himself for a fool as soon as he did. The boy rose unsteadily to his feet and backed away, searching for a way to freedom, and bolted across the grove to a path hidden between two trees.

Cursing, Geraint, who was closer to the escape route, ran to catch the boy before he disappeared and barely managed to grab onto the slight white arm, whirling the boy to face him. A sharp pain shattered across Geraint's jaw, sending stars swirling. He almost let go of the boy, but gripped harder so as not to lose him and to steady himself. Gradually, the blinking lights popped out of existence, revealing the shocked and frightened boy in his bruising grip.

Following the boy's gaze he realized that his other hand was poised to strike back. Shame overwhelmed Geraint and he lowered his hand to test his jaw. *Damn, that boy can hit hard.* Testing his teeth with his tongue he found one loosened from the blow. Hopefully, he would not lose it.

"I'm not going to hurt you," Geraint explained, taking the trembling boy by both shoulders. He winced at the thought of the bruise that the boy would certainly have. "Llawela asked me to come."

A flash of a question crossed the boy's eyes, but he was too afraid to voice it. Geraint sighed and continued. "She asked me to come and train you in the warrior's way."

The boy shifted his stance, his body speaking the words. Geraint could see that the child was wary but curious. Not blaming the boy for not trusting him he released the boy and was relieved that he did not run again. More explanation was needed. Obviously, Llawela had not said anything to the boy about him.

"She wanted me to teach you so that you could defend for yourself when the time came."

The silence in the grove broke to the hooting of an owl in a nearby tree and the hairs on Geraint's neck rose, catching his breath in surprise. The boy seemed nonplussed with the sound.

"Do you mind if we talk about this on the way back?" asked the man. It was completely dark out and he did not want to spend a night in the woods.

Taking a step back, the boy turned and without so much as a word, found the path to lead them out. Geraint followed as best he could. The trail was obviously meant for someone shorter than he, but it was much better than floundering in the woods. Having no other recourse, he trusted the boy, but when the slight pale figure ahead of him suddenly disappeared, Geraint called out for him to slow down. He could not even hear the boy's footfalls on the hard packed earth. In comparison, he felt the clumsy oaf. He was better at this during the day when he could see what he was doing and where he was going.

The white figure reappeared before him, standing very still with his back to Geraint, allowing the man to come up to stand beside him. The forest parted to reveal the old woman's hut. Guardedly, the boy glanced up at Geraint almost as if daring the man to take the next step. Light from the bonfire Llawela must have built in their absence, reflected in the boy's large expressive eyes rimmed with lashes so thick as to give the illusion of darkness. Mistrust overshadowed fear and Geraint saw a new expression. In eyes red as blood blazed cold anger. Geraint had seen such expressions in others, usually in older men, but in this boy the look filled him with dread.

This was not how he had wanted to start off. He needed a new approach. "I'm Geraint." He stuck out his hand. The boy stared at the outstretched hand as if it were a snake coiled to strike. "This wasn't how I expected things to go, but I'm willing to give it another try, if you'll allow it."

Silence filled the space between them as the boy studied the man. Brown eyes connected with red before the boy reluctantly slipped his slender hand into a rough and meaty one well accustomed to hard work. Geraint was surprised at the cool softness of the boy's skin, but ignored it, happy that some positive headway had been made.

"If you want, we can start your training tomorrow at first light," Geraint offered with a smile.

If it was possible for the boy to become paler Geraint could not imagine until that moment when the boy blanched. "What is it?" Concern fought with worry filled Geraint's voice. Was the boy going to bolt off again?

Eyes of liquid fire glimmered with unshed tears. "I can't," whispered the boy, his voice soft, barely audible through the anguish. "They took away the day." A tear escaped.

Geraint stared in shock as the boy relinquished the grip and strode away. *What the—?* He needed to find the old woman for her to explain what was going on here. He headed back to the hut as the boy made his own way to the enclosure that held their chickens, obviously wanting to be alone.

Llawela tended to the fire and was attempting to fix a large enough tripod to stand above the blaze when Geraint found her. At his approach, she looked up. "Did you find him?"

"Yes." Geraint could feel his own anger starting to boil.

Looking into the dark, she turned to him, "Where is he?"

"He's over by the coop." Geraint moved to stand in front of her. "Why didn't you tell me?" He strained to keep the anger from his voice.

Blinking in confusion, she stared up at him. "About what?"

Exasperation took over. "What is this about the boy having the day taken away from him?"

Understanding dawned over the old woman's expression, her mouth forming a silent oh. She turned back to her chore.

"He can't go out during the day anymore, Geraint."

"What are you talking about? Speak plainly. I get enough of this run around at home. I don't need it here where I've been asked to come," he fumed.

Llawela struggled with a cauldron she meant to hang over the fire. It was obviously too heavy for her and out of exasperation, Geraint grabbed it out of her hands, lifted the heavy iron pot and hung it on the chain that dangled from the centre of the tripod.

"Okay, it's very simple." She wiped her hands on her grey ragged skirt. "Whatever happened to the boy changed him, Geraint."

"That's to be expected. But—"

"But nothing." Irritation filled her. "He can't go out in the day anymore because if he does he can't see. The light blinds him with headaches I can't treat. That's not the worst of it, though." She paused waiting for understanding to spark in Geraint's head. A jaw dropped and she knew she got through. "When the light hits his skin, he burns. Just like when he came home that night." She had tried to explain things matter-of-factly, hoping to hide her own despair at the changes the Goddess had seen fit to bestow upon the boy.

She let the space between them fill with silence until Geraint exhaled noisily. "Dear God."

The full impact stunned him. Not being able to go out during the day? He could not even begin to imagine what that would do to a person. Life revolved around the day. Chores were done. Lives were lived.

From sunrise to sunset life flourished and now to be banished from that world into one of darkness, he shook his head. How could he teach this boy now? So much of it was dependent upon clear sight. He glanced back to where the boy stood at the chicken coop petting his horse. A pale figure stood out against the chestnut. Geraint knew he had to find a way, if not for himself then for the boy. Not wanting to disrupt the child, but having to care for his horse for the night, he told himself, Geraint left the old woman and quietly walked over to the boy.

Furiously wiping away the tears that slid down his cheeks, the boy walked to the coop and saw the horse. In the reflected firelight, the horse's coat glimmered like autumn leaves. It was the most beautiful creature the boy had ever seen. He had heard Auntie talk about horses. They were very important to the stories she told him about the Children of Dôn, but to finally see one in the flesh lifted his battered soul a bit.

The chickens clucked in annoyance and the horse nickered softly at his approach. Ignoring the birds, focused only on the horse, he held out his hand so that it could taste his sent. He did not want it to be afraid of him. It was already too much that he was so different. Could the horse sense that? If it did it refused to give any notice. Its hot breath puffed gently into the boy's hand, as if looking for a treat. A trace of a smile lifted the corner of the boy's mouth, but it did not reach his eyes.

Sensing it was safe, the boy put his hand on its nose, feeling the soft hairs under his hand, and began to pet it. It pressed into his hand, wanting more pressure, and the boy obliged. Finally, here was a creature that was not afraid of him.

The man had been afraid, the boy recalled, when he had entered into the little glade. Yet when the man, who called himself Geraint, grabbed him and swung him about as he tried to escape, the boy had flashed back to the similar situation a fortnight ago. He had not meant to hit the man, and a part of him was sorry, but all he wanted to do was to get away so that it could not happen again. Never again would he allow himself to be placed in such a position, but the man's tight grip on his arm did not release. It was the sight of that raised hand so ready to land a blow that proved to the boy that everything was repeating itself. The man would strike him, and then he did something that amazed the boy. He lowered his arm. The explanation that the man was there to teach him was dubious. Why now? Why could it not have been before?

The horse nuzzled the boy's chest, causing him to take a step back and he scratched it behind the ears. The horse whuffled in pleasure. It seemed that the horse liked him. To have a friend like this would be wonderful. There would be no judgments, no fear, but that was unlikely for a boy who did not have any friends and his prospects were none. Surmising that it was Geraint's, the boy refused to care. He was content to stand here enjoying the horse.

Would the man—his name is Geraint, the boy reminded himself, remembering the man's calloused hand gripping his at the edge of the forest—teach him to ride? The thought of being up on this beasts back, flying over the land with the sun on his face was intoxicating until he remembered. He would never be able to be out in the sun again. New tears formed and he moved to the side so he could bury his face into the horse's long mane, breathing in the musky horse scent. The man would not teach him now. There was no way anymore. The day was taken away.

"Cadfarch needs to be brushed down."

The nearness of the man's voice surprised the boy and he stiffened, afraid what his trespass on this man's horse would bring. Did the man think that his touching of the horse somehow contaminated it?

"I'm sorry," the boy apologized, and backed away from both horse and its owner.

The man ignored him and went into a saddlebag's side pouch, pulling out a hard bristled brush and tossed it to him. The boy managed to barely catch it in both hands and stared at the device.

"You can brush him down while I take off his saddle and bridle," directed Geraint. The boy stood and stared, confused at what he was being asked to do. Brush down a horse? He nearly dropped the brush when he noticed the man's eyes had lowered as if studying him. "You do know how to brush a horse, don't you, boy?"

He shook his head.

The man sighed and motioned him over. "Come on, I'm not

going to hurt you." Reluctantly, the boy took a step closer and watched the man back away, giving him space to reach the horse. "Now brush him, starting from the top, working down. Go with the way the hair grows."

Chestnut skin twitched as he put the bristles against the horse and tried to drag it downwards, but his own nervousness made the brush slip out of his hands. He managed to catch it before it hit the ground, but before he could apply it again to the horse, a rough hand enclosed over his and his breath caught as his body tensed. The man stood behind him. He could feel the man's warm breath on his bare shoulders and the rough woollen tunic against his back. Trapped between horse and man, the boy could not move.

"Left handed, eh?" harrumphed the man. "That will make training tricky, but I've always been up for a challenge. Now, Cadfarch likes firm strong strokes."

He let the man guide his hand up and down, up and down. Did he hear the man right? But how can that be? His arm went up and down on its own and Geraint had moved to remove the saddle.

"Keep that up, and don't forget his legs. He gets brushed down before he gets fed and watered," explained the man, his voice soft and encouraging. The boy dared a glance at the man and watched the mechanics of the removal of the harness and saddle. "I brought some feed with me. You can give it to him when you're done."

The boy looked up at the man, his task forgotten with his hand halted in mid-brush. Was he hearing right? Geraint was entrusting the care of his horse to him?

The man looked back at him. "Cadfarch likes a bit more strength and movement when he's brushed. I know you've got both, boy."

Brown eyes blazed into him and he saw the man test his jaw. Realization swept over the boy and he stammered another apology. He had never hit another person before. He had not meant to. Instinct and a desire for survival had won out.

The man waved the apology away. "More my fault than yours. What I'm wondering is, who taught you to punch like that?"

Embarrassed, the boy turned back to the horse and returned to his task. The horse snorted as if wondering what took him so long to get back to the job. The long careful strokes were unsuccessful in alleviating his mind of his turbulent emotions. A grumble sounded, and the man was beside him once again. Was he doing this wrong? The warm hand stopped his. The boy did not dare to look up, but stared at the ground between the horse's hooves.

"We're not going to get very far if you won't talk." Geraint's voice was gentle, but firm. "A few words here and there are not conversation, and I don't like talking to myself. If you want to learn, you're going to have to speak. You do want to learn, don't you, boy?"

The idea of learning what this man could teach him swam in his head. It seemed so impossible, but he so wanted to try. He nodded, eyes downcast so as not to look up at the man.

"Try putting words to that," offered Geraint.

"Yes," he whispered. "I want to learn."

"Why?"

The question surprised him. A quick glance told him the man waited for an answer, his muscular arm resting on the horse's shoulder. He could not even form the words in his own mind without opening up a floodgate he was afraid would never be able to close once a foothold was taken. Even though he wanted to learn, it was not possible.

Then a new thought formed and he spoke, his voice barely audible. "Why do you want to teach *me*?"

He felt, more than he saw, the man straighten obviously not expecting such a response. Turning to look up at the man, the boy felt something nudge his heart into a faster rhythm and the words poured out faster than he could think. "All my life I have been hidden away by Auntie. Told over and over that if *anyone* found out about me something bad would happen. She never told me exactly what, but I found out." He could not believe what he was doing. All those years of loneliness and fear falling out of his mouth to a stranger who could easily finish what was started in that grove.

His voice broke with emotion, tears welling in his eyes. Goddess, he wanted the tears to stop. "And now, you come and offer to teach me too late. Why? Because Auntie asks?" The boy looked back at the horse. "I now know why she has hidden me. Why she has feared me to ever be seen by anyone. I found out that day in the grove and now she brings you into the secret." His tears flowed faster, his breath catching as he whispered, "You can't teach me because... because..."

The man caught him as he crumbled to the ground, sobbing. He felt the man's strong arms hold him against his broad chest and through his cries he heard, "Because you are Fay, making you alone, but you're not alone anymore, boy, and no one will ever hurt you again. I promise."

Llawela stood by the crackling fire, a large stick in the cauldron to stir the fat and ash bubbling down to become course soap.

Finally, she thought to herself as she watched Geraint console the boy, pleased that the healing of both father and son could begin.

ome on, boy. Get that sword higher. You know better than that," Geraint chastised his student as he held his own practice sword ready.

He could hardly believe that seven years had passed, but the grey in his once dark brown hair and moustache bore the witness of those years. In that time he had grown to love the boy who now stood a head taller than he. From a thin, almost delicate boned child to a tall, slender, yet muscular, young man, the boy had a natural grace that reminded Geraint of a large predator, and he had the heart of one as well.

Through the years of training, the boy had shown proficiencies in hunting and fighting with sword and knife. What astonished Geraint the most was the boy's incredible accuracy with the bow.

Today, though, they were out in the early morning fog with only a fire beside them for light for one last lesson in the sword. Well, he hoped it would not be the last, but circumstances as they were, made Geraint believe it to be the case. When the sun came up he would leave to meet up with his men before joining the others in a battle to protect their land and their king. He had not told the boy. Yet.

A yawn escaped from the boy. How many times had Geraint told him to keep focused and used this as a perfect opportunity to teach the boy that one final lesson. Bringing his own sword up, he brought it down in a swing that would, if the sword had been real, cleave the boy through the shoulder and down.

The boy no longer stood before him. The sound of wood smacking wood resounded in his ears, and then he spat dew soaked grass out of his mouth. He could not remember how he managed to lie sprawled on the lawn. Trying to turn over, he felt at the back of his neck the point of the wooden practice sword. He did not know whether to be furious or to be proud but accepted both feelings as he rolled onto his back to stare up at the young man who had felled him so easily.

The point lingered above his face for a moment longer before the boy lowered it and offered a hand up for the older man. Geraint begrudgingly accepted the cool white hand and let himself be lifted up. Was that a smile on the boy's face? It was not often that the boy smiled, always serious. He had tried to bring some laughter to the boy, but it was rare to even get the boy to truly grin. Thinking back, Geraint could only remember one time when he had seen the boy's face light up with happiness.

It was the first time he had taken the boy out to hunt. That was what? Five years ago? Geraint had wanted to make sure the boy had skills with the bow and tracking before going out into the forest at night. It had been a strain on Geraint. To teach at night things better taught during the day had at first been difficult, as he had to teach himself as he instructed the boy, but they had managed together. Geraint could not believe how well the boy had absorbed the lessons and the night they went out in search of a deer it was the boy who led the way through the dense woods.

The moonlight made it easier, dappling the trees, bushes and ground in silver ribbons. Geraint had spotted the red tailed doe first. Silently, he indicated to the boy the target and that they needed to stay down wind of the beast lest it catch their scent and bolt away. The boy nodded and followed Geraint, making no sound among the dead fall. When they were close enough, Geraint allowed the boy to take his long bow and an arrow.

Expecting that the first shot would go wide and possibly frighten the deer, Geraint had another arrow ready. What he saw astounded him. The boy, straining at the pull of the long bow, fired cleanly into the beasts shoulder. Frightened at the sudden pain, the doe tried to flee, but its front leg would not co-operate. The boy took the second arrow and shot it in the neck. Dark blood spurted out and Geraint knew the boy had gotten the artery. Down went the deer. Not knowing who was more in shock at the sudden luck Geraint turned to see eyes sparkling in the moonlight and a true grin broke on the boy's face. It was a radiant smile of pure joy and thrill of a successful hunt.

"You tricked me," stated Geraint, looking up into boy's pale face. Sweat mingled with the moist air, plastering long white hair to the boy's face. The half smile turned into a full one exposing perfectly straight teeth, second incisors and canines longer and pointed. Maybe that was why the boy did not truly smile often?

"You underestimated me," corrected the boy, his voice soft and melodic.

Releasing their grip, Geraint smiled and nodded. "Aye, I did. I won't be making that mistake again."

The boy nodded once, the smile gone as he looked into the increasing light of dawn. Through the dense mist of the summer morning they both knew that once the sun rose and burned off the fog it was going to be a sweltering day. One in which the boy had to be indoors before the first rays could do harm. Even in this increasing light the boy had to squint.

They had tried through the years to see if the boy's incredible sensitivity to the day had waned. It had not. After the third try nearly a year after coming into the boy's life, it was decided that this change was permanent. The boy had delved into another depression, but Geraint refused to let it last. He made the boy train doubly hard even though he could only come every fortnight. The boy trained in earnest and absorbed whatever Geraint could teach as though he were a sea sponge.

"Come on. Let's see what Llawela left in the pot." With a hand on the boy's shoulder they headed inside. Both had to duck under the lintel, but it was the boy who had to watch his head indoors lest one of the beams clip his head. The soft sea-saw snore of the old woman greeted them, and they quickly and quietly picked a couple of wooden bowls from the floor beside the hearth and dished out healthy servings of porridge before they left as quietly as they entered.

It was a ritual whenever Geraint came. One which both of them enjoyed, a time for the two to sit and talk, or even to listen to the music of nature as the day woke. They never watched the sun rise; the boy would leave to go inside before that point. They sat facing east, leaning against the wall of the hut and watched.

Taking a spoonful of the porridge, Geraint wished he had some precious salt to make it taste better. As if hearing his unvoiced complaint the boy passed him a small jar of honey harvested from Llawela's bees. Spooning some into the thick mixture of boiled oats and dried fruits, he placed the jar on the grass before him in case either of them wanted more. Honey was much nicer with porridge than salt, if one could get either. Geraint was grateful that Llawela was brave enough to care for the bees.

The two sat quietly in the mist and the growing light, enjoying a meal together. Geraint wanted to do much more for the boy, but could not without raising suspicion and felt a little self conscious at his elaborate and expensive clothing. It was important for a Chief to be well dressed, or so his mother explained before she passed two years ago to a wasting disease. He wished he could have brought some proper clothing for the boy who only owned one rough woollen shirt and kilt made from a blanket he had brought last year.

Both ill fitted the growing boy. The old clothing became rags that bound the boy's feet. At least Geraint was able to bring a gift this time. It was hidden in the house so that Llawela could give them to the boy once he was gone.

Concern washed over Geraint as he picked out a piece of apple and popped it into his mouth. Llawela was a very old woman. Not many people lived to see nearly four score of years, and her health was starting to fail her. What was the boy to do when the old woman was finally gone? His brow wrinkled in worry and he could see the boy giving him a sideways glance as if picking up on his thoughts.

It was time to talk to the boy. He may not get another chance.

Clearing his throat, Geraint broke the fragile silence. "Have you thought about what you're going to do when Llawela finally…um…passes?" He turned to look at the boy who stopped his spoon in midair.

Shoulders slumped as the boy dropped his spoon into the bowl and put both on the ground beside him. He shook his head, sending his straight waist length white hair shimmering.

Geraint knew he had hit a nerve, but he had to press. He wanted his son safe when both he and the old woman were gone, and he feared that it would be sooner rather than later. "She's not a well woman, boy. Llawela's seen more years than ours put together."

"I know," the boy whispered, staring at a spot on the grass ahead of them.

"Has she, I mean, has Llawela said anything about what you are to do when she's gone?" Geraint placed his empty bowl down, watching the boy's face. How like his mother the boy's soft features were. The boy was not handsome in the traditional sense, his features too much like his mother's, lending to another and more effective description—beautiful.

"No," replied the boy, his voice quiet. "I guess I would just continue to live here."

Geraint nodded. It was not a good plan, but it was better than nothing. "If you ever need of anything, you come to me. If you can."

The boy lifted his head and turned to face Geraint. It always made the older man a little uncomfortable to have those large expressive eyes, the colour of blood, stare into his. Eyes were never meant to be that colour, but he did not show it.

"You're not coming back, are you?" challenged the boy.

It was Geraint's turn to feel uncomfortable. The time had come. "No, boy, I'm not coming back." Surprised shock filled the boy's face and Geraint stopped the boy from saying anything with his own words. "Tomorrow I'll be leading a group of trained warriors to the king. Raiders have been attacking all along the coast line and the king has a plan to route them all out and send them back across the waters with their tails between their legs. If we win, and that's a big if, boy, then I may be able to come back, but I, like so many other Chiefs, think this is foolhardy."

"Then don't go and fight. Stay here." The boy's voice rose in alarm. "Or take me with you so I can help."

"I can't." Geraint shook his head sadly. "To either. We have to go and fight with our king or be charged with treason and have our lives, family and property forfeited. I can't take you with me not because of your inability at arms. God knows you are a natural and you are old enough, but because—" He hated to say this after so long. "—you're too different. The battle would be fought during the day."

The boy stiffened at the bluntness of his mentor's words, and then slumped in recognition of the truth. "You will try to come back, won't you?"

"I will." Geraint gave the boy's shoulder an affectionate squeeze. "I do want you to do something for me, boy."

"Anything." The boy looked up earnestly.

"Be careful when you're out in the woods," explained Geraint. "People have seen you." Ignoring the horrified expression on the boy's face, he continued. "Word is out in the surrounding villages of a spectre that haunts these woods. I can only assume they are talking about you based on their descriptions. Some are even saying that Gwyn ap Nudd has returned. That may work in your favour, as they won't want to come upon the God who takes people to the Underworld. Some may want to seek out the truth. Just be careful."

Surprise and shock flitted across the boy's face before he nodded. "I will."

"Good lad." Geraint smiled half heartedly, trying to be more optimistic than he felt. Worry did not convey the full extent of his feeling toward leaving the boy. "Now finish your food and get to bed."

The boy tilted the bowl of cold porridge with a long, delicate, white finger, his appetite gone. "I won't see you when I wake, will I?"

"No, boy, you won't. I'll be gone then." The sadness in the boy's countenance brought tears to Geraint's eyes.

The boy turned to face him, his own eyes wet. "Geraint," the boy's voice thick with emotion, "thank you."

That did it. Geraint grabbed the boy in a bear hug. He could feel the boy's slender yet strong arms wrap around him, returning the fierce embrace. "No, thank you," Geraint whispered, white hair soft against his weather worn face. Pulling back, he put his hand to either side of the boy's face, feeling the wetness of tears. "You take care. Now get to bed."

The boy nodded and Geraint let go of him. Standing with a fluid grace unmatched by anyone Geraint had ever known, the boy offered another rare smile before entering the cottage. Sunlight hit the home, illuminating the mist as it broke it up into millions of dazzling crystals before it was gone. Geraint could not see the beauty for the tears in his eyes as he burned the memory of their only embrace into his mind.

Carefully, the boy placed one booted foot down after another. Fallen twigs gave way to his weight but did not break as he looked through the leafy bush to his prey munching delicately on the foliage between its hooves. The boots were one of the gifts Geraint had left for him that morning four months ago.

The second of the gifts he swung off his shoulder and fitted with a black fletched arrow from the quiver strapped to his back. It was rare for one man to own one bow, Geraint had taught him. Most often it would be shared between two or three men because the yew tree they were made from was rare and it took a lot of effort and knowledge to make a bow. Geraint had one all to himself, but that was due to his rank of Chief.

Letting the bowstring relax, the deer forgotten, the boy closed his eyes. Goddess, he missed his mentor. That last day in the morning mist seemed so long ago that the boy still could not believe that such a short time had passed. Geraint had been right. He had not returned.

Word came from Geraint's daughter a month ago. The boy had slept through the visit of the now orphaned woman coming to visit her great aunt for the first time. It was when he woke to find Auntie sitting by the hearth, its fire almost out and tears on her face that he knew something was horribly wrong. Auntie never let the fire go out. It was something only a fool would do. Without fire there was no life. Through a quiet voice, broken with emotion, she told him that Geraint had been mortally wounded in the battle that felled the king. He had been brought back by litter to his home and within a matter of days lay dead. The boy had stood in shock before the realization hit him and he had to sit lest he fall down.

Without Geraint's visits it was back to just he and Auntie, but even she seemed to have grown old overnight. She stayed indoors more than before and stopped the visits from those who would need her help every ninth day. The silence between them grew. Partially due to the fact that she was firmly ensconced in living her life during the day and he had to live his at night. The love was still there, there was no doubt about it, but the distance was as far apart as night and day.

He missed her, and he worried about her. Geraint had been right about another thing. Auntie was not doing well. It pained her to walk, causing her to hobble since she refused a walking stick. She coughed, even in her sleep, and she could barely see. Most of the work done to maintain their home now fell upon the boy and every day he worried more about what he would do when she finally was called back to the Goddess. He was terrified of this obvious eventuality.

Until then he had to take care of them both and tonight he had to bring in the meat. There was precious little else and the on-coming winter was proving to be one filled with starvation. The loss of the king and the breakup of the nation under lesser rulers invited the raiders and thieves to make what they had done before seem like nothing. This year there would be famine.

Bringing his bow back up, he lined his sight to the unaware doe, notched the arrow and drew it back to his ear. A twang of the bowstring suddenly releasing and the startled expression of the dear as the impact of the iron tip drove deep under the ear, behind its eye, told of the arrow's fast flight through the air. A lucky shot, Geraint would say, and the doe collapsed to the underbrush.

The boy let out a breath he did not realize he held, stood and swung the bow over his shoulder before stepping silently to the deer. Kneeling before the dead animal, the boy took out his knife, a finely wrought piece of work that Geraint had also left him. With eyes closed, the boy muttered a prayer for the animal, thank-ing it for its sacrifice so that he and Auntie could live. This was not something that Geraint had taught him. It was something that felt right and proper to do. With a quick flick of the knife, he dug out the arrow and cleaned it off on the grass before putting it away in his quiver. Tomorrow night he would have to clean it properly lest it begin to rust.

Removing the bow from his shoulder, the boy unstrung it and placed the bowstring beside the quiver with the arrows. No longer under the stress from the sinew, the yew relaxed into a natural position that would allow the boy to use it as a staff. With natural ease, the boy hefted the carcass up and over his head to land on his shoulders. A bit of adjustment and the deer was balanced, albeit uncomfortably so, but there was no other way to get it back on his own. If Geraint had been there, they would have both carried it on a cross brace, but Geraint was not there and he would not be coming back. Bow in hand as well as the forelegs and back legs, the boy headed home.

The old woman woke with a start. She did not know what woke her, but something did not feel quite right. The fire from the hearth was blurred orange and yellow, lending light to objects she could hardly see. Sitting up in her bed made from straw covered with hides and blankets, she looked around in hope that whatever woke her would make its presence known.

Then she realized what had woken her. There was no sound, except the sounds of the crackling fire. Not even the crickets and the night birds sang their songs. That was what woke her, the silence. A sense of dread filled her belly. Looking down to the bed next to hers, she was relieved not to see the boy there. Unable to see into the darkness to see if he was there in the hut she whispered to him. Receiving no answer, she painfully stood up, grateful that she slept with her robe on.

Her hips hurt and every other joint in her body raged with a fire that made movement painful. Poultices only helped for a short time and willow bark helped, but she was in a constant battle with the pain and she knew she would lose. She did not want to tell the boy how bad it was, but she knew he suspected. Words were unnecessary between them and it was rare that they talked to each other. Not because she did not want to talk, but because she respected his silence.

She worried for him.

The sound of horses radiated into the home. Someone was outside and Llawela knew it could not be Geraint. He was long gone. She prayed silently to the Goddess that it was not raiders. Who would raid a single old woman who had nothing? The time of night made the feeling in her gut rise higher into her throat.

Shuffling to the door, she lifted the hide out of the way and stepped outside to face five men on horseback. Two of them carried torches. Around them and behind them were more figures on foot she could hardly recognize as anything more than fuzzy blobs, even though these others carried torches as well.

"What is it?" she declaimed to the mob. "Why do you come to an old woman in the middle of the night?"

One of the horsemen kicked his horse forward, obviously the ringleader. She could make out his brown wavy hair and the nasty red scar that ran from his forehead across what used to be his left eye and down to his jaw. This young man may have been good looking once, but the new scar twisted his features in a menacing way.

"We have come, old woman, to exact justice from you." The young man's voice was barely recognizable through its gruff countenance.

"What in the Goddess' good name are you talking about,

Huw?" She tried to straighten her curved back so that she could look up at him better.

"You killed my little girl!" cried a woman from behind the horses. Llawela could not make her out of the blurred figures before her. She could hear the woman break into tears.

Dumbfounded by the ludicrous accusation, Llawela responded. "Adyna, is that you? I have done nothing of the sort. Your daughter died because it was her time. Nothing could be done about that."

"Liar!" cried Adyna's husband.

"Is that what you have come here for, Huw?" demanded Llawela, bringing her attention back to the man on horseback. "If that is the case, then I am going back to bed and all of you can leave. We all know that Gwendolyn died of the wasting disease and I won't stand here and be accused of something I didn't have any hand in." She turned to go back into her home.

"Then what about our Chief's death?" countered the young man.

Llawela slowly turned around, menace filling her voice. "What are you talking about?"

"Do you deny that you cursed Geraint before he left to do battle for the king?" challenged the man on horseback. People around him murmured their agreement with his assessment.

"I do deny such ridiculousness! Now leave my home!" She turned to go back into her hut but stopped at the sound of the five horsemen dismounting in unison.

"I think not, old woman." Huw grabbed her by the arm, halting her escape. Turning her to face him, she could see how ugly the scar had made him. Or was that his rage?

"You cursed him and that is why his heart for battle was gone. And that is why he died," hissed the young man. "That is not all. We know you consort with the white devil. People have seen him come and go from your home."

Llawela could not believe what she was hearing. She knew she had never cursed Geraint. He was too much like a son, but the fact that some had seen the boy; it was her worse nightmares come to life. All she could do was stare dumbly as Huw pulled her away from her home.

"Here stands the witch that has brought us so much pain," Huw declared to mob. "She is the reason why our crops have failed, why our loved ones lay in the earth and why our Chief is dead. What say you for her punishment?"

Cries from the crowd called for her to be burnt, to be beaten, to be hanged. Every case was a death sentence. Llawela could not believe what she was hearing. These were the people she had helped all her life. These were her people she swore to uphold. Somehow she managed to find her voice in the growing noise of the crowd.

"I have done nothing of the like! You all know this!" she cried, and began pointing out all the good things she had done for the different people she recognized in the mob. She could not believe what was happening. Accusing voices resounded around her, drowning her protestations.

Suddenly, pain illuminated her sight and washed over her. Lifting her hand to her forehead, she felt the gash from a thrown stone and the warm stickiness of the blood that flowed freely down her face, into her eyes. The violence of the act had shocked the mob into a moment of silence before they attacked en mass.

Rocks flew and then it was hands and other implements. Her clothes were ripped as pain greater than what her own body could generate exploded with each new impact. Impotent tears ran down her face to mingle with blood and fear laden sweat. There was nothing she could do to stop the madness and was thankful that the boy was not here lest the same fate befall him. Twisting blurring orange and shadowed faces swirled around her. Each rotation brought new pains as she cried out for rationality, for help, but none came.

A blow landed on the back of her head and before she surrendered to the sweet oblivion of the Goddess she heard a familiar voice cry out, "Die witch!"

The walk through the forest at night was always magical to the boy. He stepped carefully, listening to the deadfall groan and crack under him and the dear's weight. The leaves shuffled out of his way. Autumn was a beautiful time even though he could not witness the changes of green into the rainbow colours of fire. The smell of mould and damp lifted to his nose with each footstep and he breathed deeply, gaining strength to carry the burden of the dead doe.

The forest never ceased to amaze him. Geraint had shown him so much that he never imagined could be found. All one had to do was look. The colours were gone only to be replaced with the silver and blue light from the moon and stars.

It was a magical world, one in which he had learned to enjoy even though he still missed the day. The night was a time of power, so Auntie had taught him, when those of the Otherworld would come and play. It was these creatures that he knew Auntie believed he shared a kinship with and maybe she was right.

He did not know, but there were times when he felt eyes staring at his back, sending the short hairs on his neck to rise. Tonight they seemed absent and he appreciated their vacancy in his life. They always reminded him how different he was. Auntie did not know he knew and he left it that way.

The knife's sheath caught on a bramble and he had to stop to give a gentle tug so that he could continue with his journey. It was then that he noticed the light; a sparkle of orange and yellow through the foliage that drew his attention ahead. Too early to be dawn and coming from the wrong direction, his breath caught as he realized that it had to be coming from his home. Leafy branches swayed in the breeze, staggering the growing glow. Sick fear washed over the boy as he moved forward to break through the forests edge.

Shock pummelled into him as he let the carcass slip and fall from his shoulders without notice. His mouth and eyes went wide at the sight of his home consumed in a conflagration roaring with greedy hunger. He could not believe what he witnessed. He *knew* that the hearth fire had been properly banked when he left that sunset. It had been done in the same way as every other night for the entirety of his life. He could not imagine what could have gone wrong. Surely Auntie would not have set it by accident. She was in bed when he left, with the promise to take it easy.

Oh my Goddess! thought the boy, realizing that Auntie must still be in there. Without reason, the boy ran to inferno that used to be his home in hopes that there would be a way for him to get inside and drag Auntie to safety. He had to get her out. She could not be dead.

The image of her burning to death in the blaze nearly choked him, or was that the smoke blowing down on him? Coughing in the black air, he cried out for Auntie. The heat from the inferno made it impossible to get within ten feet of the cottage. It was a useless gesture, but he called for her nonetheless.

Sparks and soot-laden air flowed around and upon him to the

point where he could not breathe and he had to back away. The sound of burnt beams cracking under the weight of the thatched roof gave a split second warning to its collapse, sending a new wave of searing heat, sparks and smoke flying. He had to back away, his face and hands sore and reddened by the intense heat. Tears left streaks of white on a face dusted with blackness. The sight of his home, his life, destroyed dropped him to his knees. His breath came in short gasps. All he could do was watch in numb fascination as the fire licked and ate hungrily.

A sound off to his left rang in the back of his mind, but he paid it no heed. Then it came again. This time, a little louder, forcing him to turn and face the intruding cause of the noise. Choking back tears, he pushed himself up to his feet, using the bow staff as support, and wiped away black wet streaks from his face with the back of his hand.

The sound came again and this time he recognized it coming from a pile of rags he had jumped over to get to the inferno. Could it be? It was too much to hope for, but he ran and slid to his knees beside the heap. What he had mistaken for a pile of rags was Auntie lying face down in blood soaked grass. Daring to hope, he carefully, gently rolled the old woman over onto her back so that her head and shoulders rested in his lap.

The sight of her battered and bruised face cut off any hope and his breath in a gasp. Bloody gashes had swollen her eyes shut and her mouth was twisted with teeth missing or broken. He had to take a deep breath with eyes closed in a failed attempt to recompose himself.

Opening his eyes, he took a look at the rest of the woman who had raised him. The illuminating light from their home aflame outlined the horror that used to be her body. Through the tattered remains of her clothing ragged wounds seeped life's precious fluids. Her right arm was bent in a way that no person's arm should be and he could see the wet glistening bone sticking out through her forearm. Her legs were not much better. This was not the result of the fire. An agony filled groan escaped her as she tried to move.

"Hush," he whispered, laying a hand lightly on her shoulder, afraid that even that would cause her more pain. "Everything will be alright. You will be better soon." He did not know whom he tried to convince.

Her left eye managed to flutter open and she coughed,

bringing blood filled spittle spilling over her ravaged lip.

"Boy," her voice rasped, pain evident in the attempt to draw breath. "Is that you?"

He nodded, too afraid to say anything and then realized that she could not see him.

"I'm here." Could she hear his voice tremble? "Shush. Don't try and talk." He brushed back a stray lock of grey hair from her face with a trembling hand.

She tried to shake her head and gasped at the pain the movement brought her. "I must," her voice thick from pain. "There is so much I never told you."

"It's alright. Everything will be alright." His long hair fell into her face as he gently rocked, soaking up her blood before he could push it out of the way. Red mingled with white and black.

"No," she managed. "I will not get better."

He stopped his rocking, eyes wide and fearful of the truth he could not deny. He had witnessed too many animals expire from wounds less severe than hers, but this was Auntie. She was indomitable, immortal. She was dying. They both knew it. Tears ran down her face to mingle with the red, her breath becoming more strained.

"I need you...to listen...to me, boy," she managed, words coming in between painful gasps. "Before Gwyn ap Nudd comes...to take me...to the Underworld." She sighed, looking up at the boy with a sightless eye, the light in it quickly diminishing. "Leave this place...Go. Do not be sad...I will come...again...Just live." She paused taking short quick gasps. "My only regret," she whispered, "is that...I never knew...your name." The light extinguished as her last breath depleted.

Overcome with grief, the boy fiercely embraced what once was his Auntie, trying in vain to hold onto her, to force her spirit not to flee. Tears flowed. She was gone. His life was gone and he was truly alone for the first time in his life, the shock of that realization still on the edge of his consciousness.

The sound of a snicker of a horse and the creak of leather drew his attention upwards. At first he thought the man on the horse was Geraint, but that could not be. Geraint was dead, too. The torch the man carried illuminated his scared face and the boy realized that there were others around, watching him in wide-eyed awe and fear. There was no fear in this man's eyes. All he could see was a familiar hatred.

"See here the demon!" proclaimed the man pointing the torch at the boy. "Even in death the witch has called him and he came!"

The boy could only stare in dumb shock. He was found! This was why Auntie was dead. They were the ones who did this to her—to them. This was what Auntie had feared the most and it finally came true. He could not believe it. It had to be a nightmare that he could not wake from. What disturbed him the most was that something about the man on the horse that reminded him of someone else, but he could not remember.

He could hear some in the crowd murmuring as they backed away, saying that Gwyn ap Nudd had come to take the old woman. Some prayed to the Goddess for protection from the Lord of the Underworld. Others prayed to the Christian God that Geraint had told him about. The men on horseback glared. Undaunted by the *devil* in their midst they drew their swords. Steel glittered orange off the mirrored blades as they dismounted, the scarred man before him the last to step down.

Vastly outnumbered and out armed, the boy slowly came to his feet, letting Auntie's body down gently, to stand well over a head taller than the man with the scar. He had to leave. He had to go now as Auntie had told him. She had known they were still there waiting to finish off their work, but it was too late. The trap was sprung and he was in the middle of their net. How could he be such a fool? He should have seen them, heard them, something.

The man's cry was enough of a warning that the sword was coming down to cleave him in two and he barely managed to side step the blow. Using his unstrung bow, he managed to strike the man across the face to send him flying to the ground. Without a moment's pause the boy turned and fled, praying to whatever spirits lingered in the woods to hide him as the leaves and branches engulfed him. The sound of jingling armour against creaking leather faded in the distance behind as he followed trails only he could see.

The trees and bushes caught and ripped as he ran through the forest, whipping at his face, his arms, his chest and legs, the flagellation a stinging reminder of the pain in his heart. His legs pounded on the ground uncaring to the sounds of cracking branches and crunching leaves. This time he did not savour the smell of the damp autumn. The only scent in his nostrils was one of smoke and death. His breath came in ragged gasps but he still ran on uncertain of where he was going. A stabbing pain in his side did not daunt him and he continued as he forced legs that became heavier and heavier.

He did not know how long he ran until he broke through a clearing in the woods. The full moon high above rained down blue light that illuminated the river before him. Too late to put a halt to legs grown accustomed to his flight the boy tripped over an unseen rock and fell into the river with a shocking splash.

Lifting his head out of the large stream, he spluttered and spat out water before standing on weak and wobbling legs. He stood with a hand on his knees and an arm around his chest letting the cold water rush about his knees. The stitch in his side throbbed in time with the pounding in his ears and with each gasp of breath. As he managed to get his breathing under control, the stitch gradually began to work itself out.

The water began to numb his sore feet and he stood straight, brushing his long dripping hair out of his face with one hand. Gaining the bank of the river, he carefully stepped up, nearly loosing his balance, before he stood once more on grass and breathed a monumental sigh of relief at the sight of his bow several feet from the large rock he had tripped over. Favouring his right foot, he limped over to the bow and sat down cross-legged, head in his hands. He recognized this place even though he had not been back since that day so long ago.

A chest-compressing sob tore out of his tightened throat opening up the floodgate he had held back. Tears flooded down his face and he let out a wail of despair, riding the convulsive waves of his misery. He did not have to know why Auntie had been murdered and his chest wrenched painfully with the guilt. He would never see her. Never touch her. Never be able to help her. After all she had done for him, caring for him, loving him, hiding and protecting him, he had brought Auntie her death as she had feared. The tears fell faster and he clutched and rocked himself, giving himself over to the waves of despair.

The sky seeped into a deep indigo signifying that dawn slowly approached and the boy wiped his face with shaking hands. The moon was far to the west and the trees cast silver shadows on the blue earth. Tilting his face up to the sky, he realized he had only a short time to find shelter from the oncoming day. Physically exhausted and emotionally bereft, the boy painfully regained his feet.

Looking about, he could not see anything that would be of help, and there was *no* way he was going to stay in this grove. The memory of his last day in the sun was too painful to bear and then he remembered.

The man who had killed Auntie and destroyed his home was the same person that had taken away the day!

The realization nearly made the boy crash to knees if not for the support of the bow staff now in both his hands. A groan escaped him and he felt as if he were going to be sick. Standing, shuddering at the truth, there was no choice, he had to leave this grove, flee the area, even if he were to be caught out in the sun. The pain of the truth was more horrible to bear than what pains the sunlight could cause him.

Not knowing where to go the boy did the next best thing, he guessed, and began walking upriver in hopes of finding a ledge or something in which he could curl up underneath. The pain in his right ankle slowly worked itself out to a dull ache with each step and he sent a silent prayer to the Goddess that he had not sprained or worse, broken his ankle. It was sore, but nothing he could not tolerate.

The sky ever so slowly began to brighten, but the trees gave him a little more time so long as he stayed under their shade. He made poor progress because of his foot and before he had gone far he realized he had no choice. He had to find a place to shelter him from the day. Looking around, he saw a large evergreen, its long branches spreading out from its base littered with brown needles. Maybe it would provide some cover. Something was better than nothing.

Crawling on all fours, the boy pushed under the branches to the trunk of the tree. The space was small and dark. He could not stretch out to lie down so he leaned his back against the rough bark, placing the quiver and bow beside him. Knees to his chest and arms around his legs he waited for the sun to rise, grateful at least to have something soft to sit on.

It did not take long to hear the stirrings of the daytime animals and for pinpoints of sunlight to come through his makeshift shelter. It would have to do. Closing his eyes, he made a pillow out of folded arms on his knees and fell into a bone-weary slumber.

VI

He awoke with a start, the terrible nightmare fading quickly into memory. He did not know what woke him until another plump drop of water landed on his face. Somehow, sometime during the day he had fallen over onto his side. His dagger, still attached to his rope belt, jabbed painfully into his side.

With the back of his hand he wiped the drop of rain off his cheek and realized that it was not the only cause of the dampness on his skin. Pushing himself up to a sitting position, he found that his lower legs were numb from being folded for so long, or could that be due to the leather boots drying and tightening? He tried to stretch out, but there was not enough room.

Gazing up through the boughs, the twilight of the setting sun was gone to be replaced with heavy silver clouds. The sound of sizzling told him that it was raining very hard and he was grateful that he had at least found a semi-dry place, but it was time to leave.

A grumble in his stomach reminded the boy that he had not eaten anything since waking the night before in his bed, in his home. What was he doing out here? Surely Auntie must be worried about him. He looked at the black smudges on his hands and shirt and the memory of the night before caught him, bringing new tears to his eyes. No, he could not go home. There was no home to go to, and Auntie... He closed his eyes in pain, letting tears escape. She was gone. He wondered who would bury her and say the prayers for the dead over her since he could not.

A few more drops penetrated the thick green branches to rain down on his head. It was time to go, but where? He sighed and ran his hands across his head and through his hair, releasing dead pine needles onto his lap. He ignored the tangles. Fitting the quiver onto his back, he took up the bow stave and got on all fours to crawl out from the shelter of the tree.

It felt good to stand straight and he stretched, feeling bones in his back click back into place. His ankle throbbed with the renewed blood flow to his legs, and he took a couple of careful steps to work out the tingling feeling.

More rain drops filtered through the canopy of the forest. There was still some light left and he decided that it was better to continue the way he was going, but before doing that he needed to quench his thirst even if he could not gratify his hunger. Limping over to the river, he knelt at its edge and dipped his hand into the fast flowing water, grateful that the rain had made it rise enough so he would not have to step down to its bed.

The cold water washed away his parched throat as he dipped handful after handful. Once he felt satisfied that he had fooled his stomach enough not to bother him until he could find real food, he stood up and looked into the darkening woods. Hopefully, he would find something soon. It was not that he had never known hunger, even starvation, but this time he was scared. This time his life was completely and utterly dependent upon his actions. Fortifying himself with a shuddering breath, he continued along the side of the river.

The ground was damp and muddy in many places where the trees were not thick enough to shelter the smaller plants from the rain. Dried up leaves, now soaked through, crumbled and broke under his uneven steps as he tried to keep the river in site to his left. At times, he had to pull away, only to follow the flow by the rushing sounds. Tonight the moon would not aid him and the darkness would be complete once the last rays were extinguished. That thought brought a sliver of worry to his mind in the midst of his thoughts about Auntie and the end of their life together.

He replayed the scene of the night before over and over as he walked. Maybe if he had not gone out hunting and had stayed home they would both be alive now? Or dead. He shuddered at that thought. He knew how much Auntie wanted him to live. Maybe if he had come home sooner he could have fought or scared off the people. Goddess knew many of them were fearful of him, except that one.

A knot of anger filled the boy, anger at himself for having let this happen. Auntie had always been worried that something like this would occur and she knew the reasons as he now did. He could not go and live among people who would do this. He could not live among people who feared him because he was different and he crashed down a wall between he and the world, choosing to isolate himself before others isolated him. It hurt less this way.

Again the thoughts repeated themselves. Too many what ifs plagued his mind until tears of frustration spilled from his eyes. This was killing him as surely as if that man had hacked him in two. He could not keep doing this if he were to survive. Living was not a consideration any more. His reasons were gone. Only survival was left and he would not let Auntie's sacrifice go undeserved.

He would survive at the cost of letting his past go. Closing his eyes, he brought the image of her battered visage to mind and banished it only to be replaced with the smiling, loving woman he knew, and then that too, with a heart wrenching sob, he banished. Walking through the forest, he was truly and utterly alone and accepted that fate.

The foliage thickened as he continued. He did not know how far he had walked in a daze of thought, but his mind had to come back to the here and now. The rain had stopped, but the thick clouds still blocked the stars and moon from shining down. At least that was something, but where was that thundering sound coming from? Hesitantly, he made his way through the dense brush, leaving the protective cover of the trees behind. Tall dead grass punctuated the spaces between smaller bushes stripped of their leaves. He walked a long time and though he could not see the river anymore, he was reassured by the rushing sound off to the left.

A few more steps and he entered into a large open area of short grass. He did not need moonlight to see the tall waterfall feeding the river. A cliff face of about forty feet rose above the grove. How was he going to get past that? His shoulders slumped at the realization that he had reached a dead end. He would have to turn back the way he came or he would have to turn north and see if he could walk around it. The river into which the waterfall spilled was as wide as the waterfall was tall and looked treacherous. Trees lined the face of the cliff, but they were not mature enough to be useful in attaining the height of the rock face.

To make matters worse the sky opened up, dropping a deluge that soaked him in icy water within seconds. The sound of the rain roared in concert with the waterfall. Perturbed, he looked up at the sky through the falling drops of water and wondered what else could go wrong. A flash of lightning accompanied by a crash of thunder resonated through his whole body and made him jump, his question answered. Somewhere behind him the crack and roar of a falling tree told him how close that bolt of lightning had hit.

The rain fell harder, plastering his hair and clothing to his body. He could not stay out in the open. It was too dangerous. Going back into the forest would provide some cover, but the second and third bolt of lightning and the sound of other trees and branches falling made it clear that it, too, was unsafe. Maybe he could find somewhere along the cliff face that would provide safe cover.

Stepping in soggy boots, he walked to the wall of rock. The few trees that were there provided minimal coverage from the rain, their leaves stripped by autumn. He could not stay under one; it was too dangerous. The thunderstorm raged overhead forcing him to continue north until he found a black gaping hole that indicated the entrance to a cave. Finally, something was going right.

Soaked, hungry and on weary legs, the boy bent and entered, revelling in the dryness of the place. He sighed in relief as he took off his quiver and laid the bow down on the ground inside the entrance. Sitting down on the dusty cave floor, he rung out his waist length hair, making a smaller puddle to the one his body had already made. He did not care. He was in a dry place and right now he wanted to take his boots off and feel how swollen his ankle was.

The leather laces, saturated with water, made it difficult to untie, but with persistence, the boy managed to undo the simple knots. He was not going to do anything to damage the boots Geraint had given him, and he breathed a sigh of relief once his feet were free. It felt so good to wiggle his toes. He felt his ankle and found it was not as bad as he had thought.

Halting in mid-examination, he stiffened at the sound of something off to his right, coming from deeper into the cave. He tried to see, but the blackness was absolute. A bubble of fear grew in his stomach. Something was in here with him! A whuffle and a growl that did *not* come from his hungry stomach proved the point as the sound came closer.

Unable to put his drenched boots back on fast enough, he decided to stand in bare feet. Whatever was in here with him made something of a coughing sound. It was definitely angry.

Taking no chances, the boy slipped his foot long knife out of its sheath from the small of his back, holding it ready as he moved slowly out of the cave. He was loath to leave his boots and bow and arrows, but he needed the room to move and run if need be.

Once outside, he was grateful that the cloudburst was mostly done. The grass was slick and wet under his feet as he continued to back away. He could not see what it was until a flash of sheet lightning illuminated the area.

The bubble of fear popped into terror and he found he could not move. Swallowing a suddenly dry mouth, he shuddered in fear, his eyes wide at the sight. Standing immensely tall before the caves entrance and nearly as wide was a bear. Its angry roar shook him.

There was no way he could out run this beast. It was he who trespassed upon its hibernation. He was not sure if he imagined or actually felt the bear fall to all fours to advance upon him. Not knowing what to do, Geraint or Auntie having never said anything about what to do when meeting up with an angry bear, but saying to avoid them at all cost, he stood still. Not because he wanted to, but because he found he could not make his legs obey him.

The bear lumbered up to him, its thick fat jiggled with each step. The next few moments became a blur. The boy could feel its hot fetid breath against his stomach before the bear rose onto its back legs and roared, front legs clawing the air.

He looked up at it, mouth open and knew it was too late, he was going to be with Auntie and Geraint very soon. Before he could step back and flee, heavy meaty arms covered in long matted fur came down and around him, pulling him into an embrace. Managing to get his arms up, knife still in hand, to protect his head from the large descending jaw, he felt his knife bite in.

Blood flowed down his knife and over his hands, onto his head. Then it was his turn to scream as hot knives of pain sliced through his back. The bear's claws tore into his flesh as it fought for its own life.

He could sense himself falling backwards, the bear taking him down to finish what it started. He had only one chance. His knife still in the bear's throat, the boy gripped the hilt as best he could with both hands and sliced to the left with what remained of his failing strength.

He was rewarded with a fountain of hot blood, spilling into his eyes and mouth before he landed painfully on his back, the dying bear on top of him. It took all his effort not to pass out at the impact.

Unable to breathe from the weight, the boy grit his teeth and slid out from under the creature, making sure to extract his lifesaver from the throat. The movement to free himself along the dirt and grass made his back ignite in agony, but the breath into his sore lungs was reward enough.

Slowly, achingly, he came to his knees and the world spun. He could feel warmth running down his back and legs and did not need anyone to tell him that he was losing a lot of blood. If only he could lie down he would feel better. Stumbling on rubbery legs, he made it back into the cave. Praying that there was nothing else living in there, he bent to enter, the act excruciating to his ravaged back, and collapsed unconscious onto his stomach once safely inside.

Fire and pain.

The nightmare slipped into oblivion leaving only the sensation of fire and pain.

Forcing his eyes open, all he could see was the dirt of the cave floor. A flash of cold ran up his body that made him shiver and was followed by a throbbing heat that in the next instant made his head swim and his skin break out in a cold sweat. He closed his eyes and took a couple of deep breaths in the hope that the nausea would go away. It did not, not completely, but he opened his eyes again wondering if the dry gritty feeling was because of the sandy floor he lay upon.

He did not know how long he had laid there on the floor of the cave, but the pressure in his bladder told him that it had been some time. He had to get up but the attempt to move his arms to his side so as to push himself up pulled at his damaged back causing him to cry out and abandon the attempt. Tears escaped his eyes as the world spun and a new flash of cold sweat beaded across his body. Black spots floated in his eyes, dragging him to unconsciousness. Having no choice, the boy lay there for what seemed to be an eternity, waiting for his body to recover somewhat before he would attempt to move again.

The next time he awoke the disappearance of the spots in his vision and the lessening of the nausea gave him another window of opportunity to try to rise to a sitting position. Gritting his teeth against the pain he knew would come, the boy moved his arms and pushed himself up on weak, wobbly arms. A roar of determination and pain echoed in the dark cave. A wave of queasiness threatened to topple him over and back to the cave floor. Black spots blossomed and broke in his vision making his head swim and then the shivering began in earnest, causing his teeth to chatter.

He was rewarded for the attainment to a sitting position by the sensation of warmth running down his back, the movement having caused the wounds to crack open and bleed again. Closing his eyes, once more he waited out the pull of oblivion knowing that if he succumbed again he would most likely die. When he opened them he was able to take a look at his surroundings as another flash of heat caused him to break out in a sweat. He knew he was terribly sick and he did not need anyone to tell him that the lacerations in his back were the cause.

The cave was lit with the reflected light of the afternoon. He could not see to the back of the cave, or even if it had a back. The ceiling was tall and it glittered, as did the walls. It was not a wide cave, but what it lacked in width it made up in length. If there were no other residents to this place it could make a pretty good home, if he lived long enough, but first he had to take care of the wounds the bear had inflicted and that meant he had to stand up and get some water to wash.

The thought of the cold water turned his shivers into shudders. With agonizing slowness, whimpering in pain, he gained his feet. He so wanted to lean against the cave wall, but the pain in his back told him how stupid that would be.

Looking down at himself in the minimal light he was surprised at the amount of dried blood that glued the dirt from the floor to him. His hair was matted with the colour of copper and sand, making it hang in ropy strings. Blackness of soot and brown of blood covered him. He had to get clean.

On unsteady legs he left the protection of the cave, finding a spot to relieve himself, grateful for the dark shade of the cliff in the mid-afternoon. Finished, he lowered his filthy kilt and made his way to the river, only stopping to stare at the carcass of the bear he had killed.

The boy could only guess that he had lain unconscious in the cave for the better part of two or three days. He licked his lips cracked from dehydration with a dry tongue. At least that explained his pounding headache, that and the reflected sunlight that brought the image of hundreds of flies enjoying their feast. The sight made him ill and he turned away to continue to the river.

The roar of the waterfall throbbed in harmony with his aching body. At the waterfalls edge the spray drifted over and onto him, mingling with cold perspiration as another hot flash from the infection over took him. He considered his options. He could either bathe in the river which meant he would have to leave the protective covering and support of the cliff or he could find a way to stand under the falls, letting the impact of the water wash him clean. Neither notion was something he relished, but he had to wash his wounds. In any case, he would be able to alleviate his thirst.

Mind made up to brave the falls, the boy agonizingly lifted his shirt but had to stop as a stabbing tug at his back told him that the fabric was stuck to the wounds. A flash of panic was quickly put down. The shirt had to come off. Building his resolve, the boy steadied himself with the feel of the shirt end in his hands and as quickly as he could he ripped the fabric off his body and over his head.

Blinding hot pain dropped him to his knees and onto all fours, the warm wetness renewing itself down his sides to drip brightly, dappling the green grass with red. His vision wavered as he fought to remain conscious, the remains of his shirt still clutched desperately in his hand.

Slowly, he kneeled, his sore ankle long forgotten to this new pain, and with shaking hands opened up the rag that was his shirt. If he could not see his back, then maybe the shirt could give him some assessment. Its once cream coloured wool was covered in dried blood and black smoke.

Turning it around to view the back, the boy blanched at the sight of five parallel slashes on each side where the bear had gouged him. Black blood and yellow ooze from the infection edged the rips. The back of the shirt hung in tatters, a testament to his ravaged flesh. His only shirt was no more than a well used rag and the only thing to keep him warm as winter proceeded. Resigned, he would wash it along with his kilt that was equally filthy.

Removing the rope belt that held his empty sheath and the stained kilt made from an old blanket, the boy regained his feet and stood naked, shivering in the cold to view the thunderous waterfall. He carefully picked his path to the edge of the falling water, making sure that each step was upon a secure rock.

Only once did his foot slip, causing him to cry out as he twisted painfully to regain his balance. The spray came down harder, cooling his fevered body. Glancing at a ledge under the side of the waterfall, he made his way to it. Sweat mingled with spray as he stood on the ledge, the pounding water only an arm's length away. The water was ice cold around his feet with a precognition of what he could expect. Holding onto the rock face of the cliff, he steeled himself and stepped under the water.

The impact nearly drove him to his knees if not for the rock wall in his hands, but it was the pain of the water washing over and into the wounds that made him gasp. He did not need to look down to see the river water turn red and black before swirling away.

Cold numbed the pain and when he was sure of his footing he let go of the wall to run his hands through his hair, releasing the tangles and filth into the undulating water. It did not take long for the water to run clear off his body and he drank thirstily in deep long draughts until he was cold inside and out.

Finally clean, his back throbbing numbly, the boy carefully made his way back to where he had left his ruined clothes and brought them to the lower part of the waterfall. Standing in the shade, cold water up to his thighs, the current pulled at him as he rinsed out the fabric as best he could, his back throbbing with the movements.

Getting them as clean as he could, he waded back to the riverbank and spread the kilt and shirt so they could dry. He sat down, hugging himself in an attempt to keep warm. The shadows lengthened and clouds skittered east, away from the sun. There was little time left before the sun set, leaving him in the darkness and the cold autumn night. He did not think that his fever would do much to keep him warm. What he needed was a fire.

A sense of dread blossomed in the pit of his belly. He did not have his flint!

Geraint had always told him to keep it on him because you would never know when you would have to build a fire. The boy had not thought much about that. He always came home and there would always be a fire waiting to thaw him. Panic grew and he ran his hands through his hair trying to think. What could he do? The flint was back home, or what was left of his home. Then a thought fluttered in the back of his mind, lending a glimmer of hope. Rising to his feet, he made his way back to the cave and picked up the quiver.

Please let it be there, he prayed as he carefully pulled the dozen or so arrows out before turning the quiver upside down. He groaned as the only thing left fell out…the bowstring.

He was without the ability to make fire.

Carefully, he repacked the quiver, making sure not to damage his only means of hunting, laid it against the wall of the cave and then sat with knees to his chest thinking about what to do.

He had to have a fire. He was foolish not to have taken the stone, but how was he to know. Geraint had told him, that's how he should have known. Without it he would not be able to keep warm. Without it he would not be able to cook. Without it he would not be able to cure hides or even preserve meat. The thought of food was too much; he was too hungry despite the illness.

He had to find a way to make a fire and the only thing that came to mind was that he had to steal it, and to do that meant he had to find people. A shudder of revulsion ran through him at the thought, but it was his only chance. Then he would be able to take care of the rest. In the meantime, he had to find wood. Standing up, he left the cave, his blood covered dagger in hand, and went to put his soggy kilt on after he had cleaned the blade in the river. The shirt he left on the grass. He wanted his back to have a chance to heal over.

He woke to the cold of night, trembling in an attempt to keep his body temperature up. He had only meant to nap for a short time, but the illness and the exhaustion of collecting deadfall had taken its toll. Not to mention the lack of food. He knew it was the same evening and counted himself lucky since had he slept through another day the sun would have roasted him alive. The wood was stacked inside the cave's entrance to keep it dry and he had slept face down on the soft green grass next to his drying shirt.

Rolling onto his side pulled at the healing skin and he sat up to drag the ragged shirt over his head. It was better than nothing. His breath came in soft white clouds to be dissipated in the slight breeze. If he was going to find fire he was going to have to do it tonight. The sky was clear with white moonlight illuminating the glade in unearthly silver.

Maybe he had died and was now in the Underworld. He instantly discounted that idea. If he were truly dead he would not be freezing in the middle of nowhere and Auntie and Geraint would be with him. The thought of the old woman and his mentor made him catch his breath. He needed to stop thinking about them, but he did not want to, and in a rush to his feet the agony of his back was enough to banish the pain of his thoughts.

The grass was frozen under his feet and sparkled in the moon-light; at least his feet would be warm once he put the boots back on. The cave was dark but he managed to find and tie on the leather boots. He thought at first to take his bow, but the idea of harnessing the quiver to his back ruled it out. The knife would have to be protection enough.

Freezing, he set out the way he had come in hopes to find someone with a fire. Geraint had indicated that there were people in the woods at night that had seen him and believed him to be the Horned God; people who hunted and could be very dangerous to him. Maybe he would come across someone. He hoped it would be sooner rather than later. His fingers and nose were already numb as he hugged himself for warmth.

He walked a long time, following the paths, always remembering to keep the river in sight or in listening distance. He did not want to lose the way back to the grove and the cave. The moon disappeared behind the canopy of skeletal limbs. The only sounds came from the river.

It was eerie not to hear anything, but he continued on, realizing what date it must be. A sense of dread overcame him. It was Noslen. Maybe he should go back to the cave and wait until the next night, he thought, but he could not. He needed the fire.

Quickening his pace out of fear, he searched through the dense sleeping forest for a light, any light, and prayed that he would not be led astray. Tonight was the night when the Fay would be out and the dead would come to visit the living. He shuddered at the thought as he continued.

He did not know how long he had walked when he saw the light and he prayed to Dôn that it was not a will-o'-the-wisp to lead him into a bog. Carefully, quietly, he approached. The light did not waver. It stood its ground.

Halting his progress, the boy took stock of what was around him. If that was really a fire, then there must be people around, and if there were people around then he had to be very quiet. Slowly, he picked out his steps so as not to make any sound. Tonight he hunted for fire and the animal that guarded it was more dangerous than a bear. He clenched his jaw to halt its chattering and focused on his task.

Branches and leaves made no sound under his well-placed steps. A sheen of sweat beaded his brow making him colder in the frosty air. Finally, he came up behind a bush, the branches of the thorn standing between he and the fire, but what stood between the thorn and the fire caught his breath.

A ring of five figures slept around the pit, huddled together to conserve heat. The metal of their leather clothes and sheathed weapons peeked out from under their blankets, glimmering in the orange glow. A pot hung over the fire from a makeshift tripod; its contents long gone to fill hungry bellies.

Unexpectedly, one of the men rolled over onto his back, grunting in his dreams before his sonorous snore caused the boy to jump back in fright. He had never heard such a sound, let alone coming from a person.

The hunters were fast asleep under their blankets, their warm breath puffing clouds into the air. Realizing that this was as good a time as any since the night must be coming to an end soon, the boy took a deep breath and held it to laboriously make his way around the hedge, making sure none of the thorns touched his back. Fear washed over him and he swallowed it down. If he was lucky, and Dôn was with him, the men would sleep right through his theft.

Clearing the foliage without a sound he let the breath go in a quiet sigh. The next and harder task was to pass over the slumbering men so as not to wake them. Gently, he placed one booted foot down beside the shoulder of the man closest to him and halted in mid-step as the man rolled onto his side. The boy's heart hammered in his head and his chest heaved in fright as he wobbled on one foot trying to maintain his balance. If the man had turned over onto his stomach he would have rolled right onto him and his quest for the fire would be over, as well as his life.

Placing his elevated foot down on the firm earth, he held his breath as he lifted his right foot to make the next step over the sleeping man and prayed that he did not turn again. Foot placed safely, the boy shifted his weight and lifted his other foot over the man allowing a brief sigh of relief to have made it past the circle of men. The pounding in his ears and the ache in his chest did not abate.

He could not remember ever having something feel so good now that the heat of the fire licked over him. The heat penetrated him, warmed him and he wished he could stand there and luxuriate before the flames. He knew he could not. To stay would ensure death. It had been pure luck that he had killed the bear and survived, he did not want to test that good fortune with five well armed men. Squatting down so as not to put too much of a strain on his back, he searched through the fire and found a large stick of wood, half of it in white coals that flamed. It would have to do. If everything went well he would be able to get it back to the cave and have his own fire.

The thought of being able to finally be safe, warm and able to cook ran a shiver up his back in anticipation. His mouth watered at the thought of a well-cooked piece of meat. Sifting the piece of wood out of the fire, the boy lifted it to his face. The flames licked the air and heated his skin, taking some of the numbness away from his nose. So far so good. He had the fire. Now he had to get away from these men.

Pivoting, he rose to leave the way he had come and the inflamed stick nearly dropped out of his hand. One of the men had awakened and stared at him in mute shock. Dark eyes wide and jaw agape. The boy could see the fear on the man's bearded face and he wondered if the hunter could see the terror on his. He was caught! His only option was to run and if they followed then he would have to run faster. This time his legs obeyed him and he jumped over the man he had stepped over, causing him to awaken, and ran into the woods, burning stick in hand.

Before he was out of earshot he heard the other four men

awaken and the one who had seen him cried out to his fellows, "Gwyn ap Nudd was here! I saw Gwyn!"

VII

His foot was stuck.

Gazing down at the mud, the boy sighed. The dark patch along the trail had not appeared to be that deep. The hooves of the deer he followed left obvious tracks for any hunter to follow, even an inexperienced one, and that was something he was not. He tried to lift his leather wrapped foot out of the mire only to feel the suction pull at his calf, keeping him from moving. He was well ensconced.

Dropping his bow to land on the grass next to the trail, he tried one last time to free himself from the cold muck and grabbed his leg behind his knee with both hands, shifted his weight onto his other foot and heaved.

With a sucking wet sound his foot was freed but the force caused his other foot to slip in the slime. Before he knew it he had landed on his backside with one bare foot and one clad foot. The mess of wrappings that were his footwear now lay as a bundle of rags in the mud.

Running a hand across his face, he shook his head against the ridiculousness of the situation and then reached to retrieve his footwear.

Clumps of mud dripped off of the wide strips of deer hide as he ran two fingers around each strip, cleaning them off as best he could before rewrapping his chilled foot. It was a laborious process, but it was better than walking along the forest paths without some protection.

He missed the boots that Geraint had given him. They had been turned into padding under the bear hide that served as his bed after he had outgrown the boots.

The gift had been a lifesaver that first winter. He had never known such hardship before. The snap turning of autumn to winter and the infection that had ravished him made it difficult to do more than maintain his precious fire and cook the bear into dried strips.

The fire was the only thing he put countenance to his survival that year, but getting it back home nearly cost his life. He had misjudged the time it took to find the men and in a fever he missed crucial turnoffs. By the time he reached the edge of the clearing the sun blazed, his eyes swollen and his head pounding painfully. Having no choice, he made a mad dash in the direct sunlight back to the cave. It took no time for his skin to redden, making his back flame in pain as it did the night the bear had taken those strips out of him. He had only enough time to build a fire large enough to keep him warm and to last a long time—he had hoped—before he passed out for the day, never knowing until that moment how good the cool earth could feel.

The next nights were excruciating as he fought his fever, brought in more and more deadfall to feed his fire, and skinned and butchered the bear. Thankfully, the cold preserved the carcass enough to be salvageable. With food and warmth and something of a bed, he allowed himself time to heal and to forget the past. The only thing that existed was the present and he dared not even contemplate the future. Each day was a constant struggle.

Foot now snug in its wrappings, the boy regained his feet, lifted his bow and continued tracking the deer. He was thankful for the spring thaw as it made the task much easier, but the rains that came with the turning of the seasons made the trails treacherous. Clouds flitted quickly across a ringed waxing moon, a sure indication that more rain was on its way.

He was relieved that this second winter was over. It had been brutally cold, bringing snowstorms that made it impossible to hunt. Foresight had taught him to store up, as he did not want to go through what he went through that first winter.

The back of the cave made a perfect place to keep the fruits and roots he had harvested, and the dried and smoked meats of the animals he had caught. Now he was almost out. Only a few apples and a strip of venison remained. He needed meat and tonight was the best and first opportunity.

Following the trail, he was careful to stay to the edges where there was less mud. The last thing he wanted to do was to stand in the freezing river cleaning his clothes. The kilt and shirt were long replaced by others made by his own shoddy workmanship out of the hide of a stag he killed last summer.

The kilt had been the easier of the two to make. The shirt required sewing and sewing required needles and thread, something he did not have, but with imagination and creativity he used his knife to poke holes along the places he needed and managed to use thin strips of hide as the thread. What he ended up with was something that looked laced rather than sewn, but it worked.

A wolf's hide hung from his shoulders to cloak him in extra warmth. That had been a fearful, yet lucky, instance; one that he had no desire to repeat.

Checking the position of the moon, he realized that it was growing late, and if he did not find the deer soon he would have to abandon the hunt until tomorrow night.

That was not something he wanted to do. He liked not being hungry and not having to worry about where his next meal was coming from. It was a hard life, but he accepted it. What he still had great difficulty accepting was the loneliness and isolation. He fiercely missed Auntie and Geraint, yet whenever those feelings bubbled to the surface he quickly squelched them.

The worst parts were the summers when he had to keep to the cave, sheltering from the blazing summer sun. It was then that he felt the desolation of his life. Summers offered too much time to think, to brood, but his experience with the contact of others was enough to keep him in his solitude. Being outcast from the world and feared by those who saw him did not engender him to seek out others. He knew it was a vicious cycle that he could not break.

The trail opened into a grove. The stag stood resplendent in the moonlight, munching on new shoots between its hooves. The boy crouched beside a budding bush and checked to see if he was downwind. Sure enough his position was fine. Tonight he would have this deer and tomorrow he would have fresh meat.

The thought of the fat dripping off of well-cooked flesh made his mouth water in anticipation. Reaching over his shoulder, he lifted one of the nine remaining arrows out of the quiver and placed it into the bow, notching it securely as he pulled the bowstring and arrow with his left hand to his cheek.

He angled the bow so he could shoot from a kneeling position and sighted along the shaft. Relaxing his shoulders, he focused only on the deer to the exclusion of all else. His breathing deep and even, his arm held steady as he waited for the perfect shot that would bring the beast down.

Silently, he willed the buck to lift its head and turn a little, enough to expose the vital artery in its neck. As if hearing his unspoken words the stag did exactly that. Without a moment's hesitation the boy let the arrow fly, the sound of its flight whistling, only to see it impact...

In a man!

The shock of the sudden appearance of the robed figure in front of the deer with his arrow in the centre of the man's chest drove the boy to his feet. He had shot a man! But where did he come from? One instant the deer was alone in the grove and in less time it took for the flight of the arrow a man appeared. And he shot him!

The deer bounded away into the brush in terror, his meal gone. The thought of having killed this person horrified the boy until he saw the short dark man pull out the arrow with a painful jerk and toss it to the earth.

Whatever this man was the boy could not begin to imagine. No one survives a bolt in the chest.

Jaw slack, the boy took a step backwards to flee, but before he could put his foot down behind him he was suddenly flat on his back, with the man on him, the quiver pressing painfully.

Agony erupted in his neck, sending searing pain down his arms and chest as lights popped in his vision. Panicked he tried to lift the smaller man off of him but the strength escaped him. He was rapidly losing consciousness. With one last hope to dislodge his attacker, he twisted his head and bit down hard on his attacker's neck. Blood gushed out and into his mouth. Having the choice whether to drown in the stranger's blood or to swallow, the boy choked down the hot metallic tasting liquid.

As suddenly as the attack began it ended, his assailant vanished into the night, leaving the boy to struggle for air in the cold. He painstakingly sat up. White lights exploded in his vision and he touched the side of his neck.

Blood smeared pale fingers, his throat sore at the site of the bite marks. The taste of the man's blood still in his mouth, the boy stood and righted himself before he could toppled over, and found he was having great difficulty breathing. Pain wracked his body, nearly driving him to his knees. Sweat beaded on his pale forehead. He had to get back home.

Bow forgotten in the grove, he could only think to get back. The fact he could not seem to take a deep enough breath brought him near panic, making matters worse. Staggering along, he fought the seizures his body inflicted upon him that threatened to fell him in his tracks. He could not stay out in the woods. He needed his cave, his fire and his bed. If he could survive a bear attack he could survive this.

He took the most direct route back and tried not to waste time. Each step became increasingly difficult. The spasms that cut off his air and twisted his guts became more pronounced, lasting longer each time and the times between them shorter and shorter. He could not keep the panic from his mind.

He tried forcing himself to cough just in case that would help his attempts at breathing, but all that did was send him through new wracking seizures. Tears mingled with drying blood on his face. The pain from the bear attack was nothing in comparison to what he was now going through.

Shaking between seizures he could finally make out the edge of the forest and the beginning of his grove. The sound of the waterfall drowned out by the irregular pounding in his head. Something was seriously wrong. Fear lashed through him as his whole body erupted into another seizure, this time dropping him to his knees.

He had come so far. His arms shook as they precariously held him from falling onto his face. This time the spasm did not dissipate. He gritted his teeth in pain as it intensified before abating enough to allow him to climb to his feet.

He panted as best he could to get even a little bit of air into his lungs and staggered into the grove. His eyesight dimmed, the blazing spots having turned into blotches of blackness that coalesced into a larger void. If he did not find his way back to the cave now he knew without any doubt he would die.

Stumbling on legs that he could barely feel, let alone control, he fell short of his objective when the world swirled around him and came up at him. Face down on the grass he wept, unable to cry out in pain, as another spasm crested taking his breath away and twisted his body. When it receded, enough to get to all fours, he crawled to his cave, gripping the new grass as if it could keep him attached to the here and now.

He could not see the fire when he finally entered his home. He could hardly feel its warmth touching his skin. Feeling his way across the cave floor, he was rewarded with the sensation of fur under his hands. It was a glimmer of hope that was eradicated with a paroxysm that blew away any remaining breath. Intense excruciating fire flowed through his body, twisting and contorting his muscles until the pain was too much and he surrendered the struggle.

The pain was gone.

    In the darkness the pain was gone.

    In the absence of all feeling the pain was gone.

    He did not know if his eyes were closed or open. The darkness was absolute. All he could do was float in the void. He did not want to do anything else.

Silence.

    In the darkness there was silence.

    In the absence of all emotion and thought there was silence.

    Nothingness buoyed him. The void supported him as he floated uncaringly.

    Time had no meaning in this place and nor did he care. Everything that he was he released into the invisible tides that carried him. He did not care where he floated. He just wanted it to continue forever. He accepted the comfort and succour the darkness gave him and embraced it as it enfolded around him.

    If this was death then he could accept it.

A star.

    In the darkness glimmered a single star.

    In the darkness the single star grew.

    Closing his eyes against the growing brightness, fear erupted through his being. Thoughts, memories and feelings slammed into him.

CHANGELING

The star grew into an orb that threatened to encompass and devour him and then he remembered.

Pain!

The brightness of the light warmed him.

The brightness of the light burnt him.

Opening his eyes he saw the Garden. It was magnificent to behold. Trees so tall the tops could not be seen. Flowers of every rainbow colour and hue burned his eyes. Tears ran from his eyes. It had been so long since he could see such colours, such beauty.

He remembered!

He remembered this place.

He remembered the last time he was here and fear clutched at him.

Before him, in the beautiful grove stood the three women. He could not see their faces. Gossamer veils the colours of their being covered them from head to toe. White. Red. Black. No sound could be heard except for their keening song. Arms held out to him. Handkerchiefs the colours of their veils dripped with shed tears.

He wanted to go to them. He wanted to be with them. He wanted to ease their suffering. Tears ran down his face and he held out his arms to them.

"No! He'sssss mine!" A voice exploded in the darkness, ripping him away from the light.

The keening of the three women turned into wails.

The wails of the three women turned into silence.

The light was gone.

He twisted and turned, fighting to get back to the light, back to the veiled women. His whole being crying out for the comfort, love and acceptance he knew only they could give.

"You would deny ussssss?" the voice resonated in the void.

Terror gripped his bowels.

He remembered this voice.

He had to get away.

He could not.

No longer the comfort it was in the beginning the darkness coldly supported him, keeping him solidly in place.

Tendrils of blackness licked over his body, tasting his fear, drinking his terror. He shuddered at the touch and closed his eyes wishing that it would go away.

"No, we will not go away," the voice slithered in one ear. Its frigid cold touched his brain before sliding out the other ear. "Choice wassssss made. Fulfillment hassssss come."

"Wh-what do y-you mean?" the boy tried to put his fear down. Maybe by confronting the creature it would let him go.

"Choice wassssss made. Fulfillment hasssssss come," it repeated. He could feel it thread along his body, stopping at the scars on his back. "The covenant issssss made. Now!"

"Wait!" he cried out in the darkness. "What covenant?"

It lifted the filaments from his body. Silence abounded in the darkness, but he still could not move. He was held solidly in place.

The sound of wind through leaf laden branches swirled about him. He knew it could not be what he was hearing as the sound increased. It was then he realized he had his eyes closed. Fluttering them open, he saw the silvery white mist swirling around him. Glowing ominously, silver and white wisps drew into a core that became increasingly solid, taking form. It was the same creature! Shaking in fear, he stared as this thing of mist coalesced until its partial human form became semi-solid. Misty silver rags fluttered in an unseen breeze. Red glowing eyes stared out of a skull ravished by decay. It's black maw open with pointed teeth.

"You chossse," it stated as it floated up to face him.

Its putrid face disgusted the boy and he tried to turn away. He could not. He was held firmly in place. The swishing sound continued and he could see a thicker mist developing, swirling around him and the creature. Faces peeked out, some as repulsive as the one that faced him. Others were more grotesque in appearance.

More and more of these creatures came from the darkness to watch, to participate.

Terror grew in the boy at the sight. All he wanted to do was get away.

"Good." It placed a silver tendril under his chin forcing him to stare into the creatures red glowing eyes. He whimpered in fear, completely under its power. "We drink deep. The covenant issssss made."

The boy screamed as it brought its gaping maw down onto his neck, biting deep. Tears sprung from his eyes as he saw, one after another, the other creatures come towards him. Their own sharp-toothed mouths open in greedy anticipation.

Pain exploded as each found a tender place, adding their own teeth to his flesh.

The boy hung there in the darkness, supported by the creatures and closed his eyes.

VIII

he scream he did not remember resonated throughout the cave and in his ears. The boy sat upon his bed having no recollection of sitting up. Head in his hands, he shuddered at the memory of the dream. It had been so long since the last one that he had forgotten how real they could be.

Wiping his wet face, he tried to get a hold of the fear racing through him. The pain of the bites still tingled but the one on his neck burned. With a shaking pale hand he touched the side of his neck and found no wound, only dried brown blood.

The colour of the dried blood was brown in the near pitch-blackness of the cave at night!

He tried to take a deep breath and found the pains in his chest gone. The memory of the attack the night before seemed surreal. Had he shot that man in the grove and had that man bitten him? The dried blood was a testament to the occurrence. Dream and reality swirled in his mind. He could make no sense of what had happened.

Swallowing back a knot of fear, he stared at his hands, then his clothing. Something dug into his shoulder and he swung the quiver off his back. The knotted serpents etched into the black leather seemed to come alive, and then it hit him. He could see the knot work when he never could without being close to the light of a fire. He ran his hand tentatively against the lines. A shudder ran up his spine. Something had changed, but he did not know what and he looked up at the cave wall opposite to his bed and gasped.

In the faint embers of the dying fire, the rock face glittered with colours he had never seen before. Pinks, yellows, golds and pure whites mingled and sparkled against the grey of the rock. It was a-glimmer as if the sun shown down directly on it, but there was no sun and there was no moonlight. The only source was a fire that threw off so little light that he should, by rights, not even be able to see the other side of the cave.

He turned to face the back of the cave, into the place where only darkness reigned and saw wood piled halfway up the back of the wall. He could make out the different colours of the different types of wood. Climbing to his feet, he went to the back and placed his hands on the pile. A flicker of movement caught his eye and he saw a black beetle crawl up between a pine bough and a thick stick of oak. He should not be able to see the bug, but he did.

Turning, the boy stared at the front of his home. Everything was changed. Well, not changed. Everything was the same, but different. Walking to the front, he trailed his hand against the cool rough wall and came to a halt before the opening, his jaw agape.

The night sky was littered with more stars than he could ever imagine, lighting up the night in a way that made it seem more like it was twilight than midnight. He could see individual trees, green and growing. Everything was green.

This was a gift, surely! Having lived so long in darkness to have the night open up like this was incredible and he stepped out of the cave and turned to face the deafening roar of the waterfall. White foam floated on the dark blue river. Silver mist filled the clearing like stars falling from the sky. Staring up to the top, he could see trees leaning over the ledge as the dark waters poured over. Overcome by the beauty he could only stand and stare.

Suddenly, a shaft of light exploded from the east, filling the glade with silver white light that ignited the colours all around him. He turned to find the source and over the budding tree tops rose the moon in Her splendour. The moon was so bright that he had to squint and shade his eyes with his hand. Then he truly saw and smiled in awe. Colours left only to be seen during the day were given back to him.

Removing his hand from his eyes, he drunk in the light and

extended his arms. He could almost feel the moonlight on the bare skin of his arms, legs and face. Everything was ablaze and his smile widened.

For the first time since coming to this place he felt alive. For the first time since that day when he was a child, losing the day did not seem a bad thing. Flowers of red, yellow, orange and purple blossomed in the taller grasses before the forest. The sounds of frogs and other night creatures slipped on the breeze to his ears and he laughed.

A weight lifted from him. One he never knew he had. The day was gone, but he was given the night and its beauty surpassed any memory he had of the day. He wanted to drink in every sight around him and so he slowly began to turn in place.

Spinning around and around the colours swirled, and all he could do was laugh in sheer delight when he finally lost his balance and toppled over to lie on the grass. The stars spun as he lay in place. His side hurt from laughing so much and his face was sore from smiling, but he did not care. He could not remember ever being so happy.

"Oh dear God, what have I done?" resounded a foreign voice in the glade.

At the sudden intrusion, the first ever of its like, the boy's joy turned into panic. Abruptly, he came to a crouched position, staring at the man from the grove the night before.

He was found!

Instinct told him to flee but he did not want to leave his home. Not again, and not to one man. Then he remembered the attack and absently touched his neck without removing his cold gaze on the man.

"Please. Do not run," the man implored, his open hands outstretched and took a step.

The boy did not trust the fact there was no weapon in this short man's hands, since last night he had needed none, and he tensed, readying to flee if necessary. He stared up at the man robed in brown wool with a white cord around his waist. Sandals covered with mud and debris indicated a good tromp along the trails.

It was with his newfound sight the boy could now clearly make out the strangers features. Dark and silver peppered curling hair hung to the man's shoulders. The stranger's soft-featured face was oddly clean-shaven, but it was his piercing hazel eyes that exhibited a profound sadness. The man's countenance confused the boy. This was not the appearance of a killer. Then again what would he know of what a killer did or did not look like. He tensed. If the man made one more move he would run.

"I'm so sorry what I did to you, my son," said the stranger, his voice full of sorrow. The term *my son* added to the boy's confusion. "What I did to you was reprehensible and I will forever be damned. It should not have happened. At the worst, you should have died."

That was it. The boy had heard enough. He bolted for the forest and ran as fast his legs could carry him. It was not fast enough. Without warning the little man seemed to appear out of nowhere. The boy tried to change direction, but the slippery muck made it impossible. Before he knew it his foot was caught by something in the underbrush and he was down on the ground rolling to a stop. Spitting out the mud, he shakily sat up and looked about. The man was nowhere to be seen.

Slowly, he recovered his legs, glancing about for any sign of the man. His heart pounded in his chest. Where was the stranger? The once dark forest glimmered in the moonlight, lending details he had never before seen. Every stick, every branch, every leaf stood out as if the sun were out. He no longer needed the sun. The moon was his sun now and he could see more clearly than ever before. What he could not see was where the man had gone.

Brushing off the forest litter from his shirt and kilt, the boy stepped out of the pile of mouldy leaves and cautiously made his way back to the clearing in hopes that the man was gone. Even if he were not, then maybe he would be able to get back to his cave and grab his knife, bow and quiver. Winter was past. Finding a new place to live, farther away from people, would be easier. All he would need were the tools to hunt.

The boy stopped in his tracks. Anxiety filled him as the realization hit. He had left his bow in the forest glen last night! He rubbed his forehead with the heel of his palm in an attempt to hold the reality of his situation at bay. The arrows were useless now and as such he was without a way to hunt. A single knife would not be enough; he would still need it.

Taking a deep breath, he let it out in a huff and proceeded back to the open glen. With each step he checked around him to see if the little man was anywhere in sight. Relieved at the lack of the presence of the stranger, the boy hoped that maybe the man had left. In any case, this place was no longer safe. He was sure that the man would go back and bring others to shatter his self-imposed isolation. He hated the idea of having to leave, but it was best. The last thing in the world he wanted to do was kill a person, even if in defence of his meagre home.

The forest parted and he entered the glade. A faint orange light sparsely illuminated his cave. So far, so good. There was no sign of the man. Gingerly, he headed straight for his home. One thing he would not forget to take with him was some burning embers for a new hearth, wherever that may be.

Before he made it to the mouth of the cave, he halted. Underneath one of the trees that bordered the entrance sat the little man, pouting in thought before looking up to meet his eyes.

"Please, listen," implored the man, his eyes moist in the moonlight. "I am not going to hurt you. Whatever harm I—" He broke off and stared at the grass in front of his feet and sighed before returning the gaze. "What is done is done. I cannot undo it. It must be the Lord's will. In any case I am damned."

He closed his eyes, and to the boy's amazement he watched a tear escape to travel down the clean shaven face. "Please accept my deepest, most humble apologies," continued the man.

The boy stared, thoroughly confused. He did not know what to say. Here was the stranger he had shot with his bow, who then attacked him, and now this man was apologizing to him? He shook his head trying to get a grasp of what was going on and could not. He backed a step away and swallowed.

At the reaction to the apology the man got onto his knees, hands pressed together in front of his face and stared up at the boy, into his crimson eyes. "Please. Please forgive me. If you do not have it in your heart to forgive me, please allow me to help you," begged the man.

The sight of the man's tears took the boy's breath away. There was a genuine air about this stranger. Something about him cried out that he was safe to trust, but it was so hard to do so. He wanted to forgive this man so as to stop his sorrow and what this man was offering seemed sincere. No one had ever offered to help him except Geraint and Auntie, and he realized that a part of him desperately wanted that type of connection again. He lowered his head and nodded.

He was rewarded with a large smile, deep brown eyes connecting with his. "Oh thank you! Thank you!" exclaimed the man and he began to frantically look around on the grass before settling himself down underneath the tree. "Please," he patted the ground next to him, hopefully. "Please sit. There is so much that needs to be said."

Still wary, the boy gnawed on the inside of his lip. If he were to sit, he would be at a disadvantage if he needed to flee again. Then again, the man was sitting as well, and he wore robes. Hesitantly, he half crouched half knelt down on the grass several feet away. The man seemed disappointed for a moment, but accepted the situation.

"First of all, my name is Father Paul Notus," began the man as he settled in his spot, as if this would take some time. It was hard to look at the young man crouched before him. He had never in his long life seen such a person as this. He was tall, taller than any other man Notus had ever known. Slim, yet muscular without looking skinny. Notus could see the well shaped muscles in the lad's legs and arms, indicating hidden strength, and the way the young man moved was distinctly predatory, like the large cats he had seen in other lands.

His long white hair and pale skin made the boy ghost like, but it was the blood red irises and pupils that made Notus shiver. It was those eyes that had scared him out of his wits, causing all rationality to flee and instinct to kick in. He would forever regret last night's mistake, but maybe, just maybe, something could be salvaged from his broken oath.

Notus stared at the tall youth before him. "My attack on you last night was unintentional and will be something that I will regret for the remainder of my existence. It was out of fear and surprise, not to mention the pain of an arrow in my chest."

The boy's eyes widened in shock. So he had hit the man! He had not dreamt it. But if that was the case, the boy lowered his gaze before bringing his eyes to stare incredulously at Father Notus, then the man should be dead!

Seeing the confusion on the young man's face, Father Notus continued. "Such things do not harm our kind. Hurt, yes. But not harm. If I had known you were there hunting the same stag as I; I would have let you have it. I do not know how you managed to come undetected by me and that too I will forever be repentant of, but what is done is done, and I am sorry for having attacked you."

He closed his eyes and whispered, "And I deeply and profoundly apologize to you that you survived the attack."

He could not believe what he was hearing. This man, this Father Paul Notus, was apologizing that he was still alive — again!

Crimson eyes widened in shock and horror as he regained his feet. He had heard enough. He was not going to let this man have any chance to finish what he started last night. Arrows and knife be damned, his life was not worth it. If necessary, he would find another way. He survived before. He could do it again.

Between the time it took for one heartbeat to run into another, Father Notus came to his feet. Fear and worry washing through him.

"Wait!" he cried as the young man took a step away. "That did not come out right. Please come back and sit. Please let me explain."

The tall young man turned to face him, his eyes almost glowing red with anger. Defeated by his clumsy words, Notus chose the simplest way, silence and lowered his head in shame.

He looked down at the robed man. At his full height, Father Notus only measured to about mid-chest and he could hardly believe that he had been afraid of this man. Without removing his piercing gaze, the boy crouched where he stood. He did not return the man's smile.

Notus let out a sigh as the slender young man knelt on the grass, albeit a little further away. He knew he was being given one last chance and he could not afford to ruin it. Sitting back down under the tree, Notus folded his hands in his lap.

Without gazing into the young man's eyes, he continued. "I had not meant to attack you. I was hunting the deer. It had been quite some days since I had sustenance and the stag was my first opportunity. I guess I was so focused upon the deer that I did not hear you enter the grove. As I was attacking, I heard the release of your bowstring and turned just in time for the arrow to hit.

"All I could see was your figure beside the bush, and—Oh dear God, please do not be offended—I was afraid. I had never seen anyone such as you. I feared I was in the presence of a devil and instinct over rode logic and I attacked. It was only when you bit me did I realize what I was doing and fled. But the damage was done—to both of us.

"I went back to my camp and began to worry. I was afraid I

had killed you. Worse, I was afraid I had broken my oath never to Choose another. Panicked at that thought, I came back to the glen and found you gone, but you had left a trail.

"I followed you back here. I could see you were in the pain of the transformation as you stumbled on. I hoped that you would collapse and let the sun finish my clumsy deed. God forgive me that I wished this so, but you did not fall. I have seen others go through the transformation. Many do not survive, even when it is intentionally done. I remember my own. Never before had I seen anyone do what you did. Never before had I seen anyone with such strength. God forgive me for my terrible thoughts. I watched you stagger into this cave and I prayed to the Good God that He take you instead.

"I waited as long as I could and then I went back to my camp to wait out the day. It was the longest day in my memory. I do not think I slept one minute. As soon as the sun was down, I was up and came back here to see what had happened during the day. My gruesome prayers were not answered. There you were in the rapture of your new senses and I could feel the connection between us.

"It was then that the full horror of my deeds implications hit me, and that I, Father Paul Notus, broke my vow to God never to make another alike unto myself."

Father Notus broke his gaze from the young man's piercing stare, too ashamed to look upon the results of his oath breaking.

Silence filled the space between the two. The boy could not believe what he was told. It seemed too much like one of the tales Auntie used to tell him. He did not feel like a character in someone's imaginings. This had to be real, but how could it? Not knowing what to say, he let the lull continue.

Father Notus scratched at his arm, beginning to feel uncomfortable as the silence stretched out. He was starting to think that this young man, strange as he seemed, was incapable of speech. The sounds of frogs and night birds mingled with the roar of the waterfall.

"This is the reason for my poorly worded apology," he whispered, his voice barely heard above the sound of rushing water. "It would have been better had you died rather than be brought into this hideous existence. An endless life where the slightest touch from the sun's rays will ignite your flesh, burning you, possibly killing you, and the requirement of the blood of the living as sustenance in replacement for the enjoyment of food and drink.

"This is the gift of being Chosen. This is the trade off to be immortal: to never see the sun and enjoy the day and to be always part of, but separate, from the world of mortal men." Father Notus sadly shook his head. "The Good God gave us His commandments so that we would live well in His sight, but it is difficult when the call of the blood rides us, as it did with me last night."

Again the silence drew out between them. The boy stared down at the grass silvered by a moon that was high in the night sky. He could feel Father Notus' eyes on him and he realized that he could not be afraid of this man. If what this man said was true, and there was no real reason to doubt it, then this man had given him a wonderful gift. It was not a curse. He had the day taken away so long ago it was hard to remember the land bathed in sunlight. If he had to drink blood to survive, well, he had done worse.

Notus watched the young man carefully. White brows tensed in thought, large expressive eyes averted to the grass. He had expected the boy to take this hard, as many did when they were Chosen without warning. Many went mad and were killed. Those that Chose another without consent usually did so out of selfish need, and to Notus, such an act was tantamount to rape. Would this young man see it as such? If he did, he could understand. Notus had been given a choice, but had not understood at the time. "Do you understand what I'm saying, my son?"

The boy sighed and lowered himself to properly sit on the grass. No, he did not fully understand the implications, but if the night was no longer fraught with unseen dangers due to darkness, then this man was the one who had gifted him. Gazing into those deep brown eyes, he found he could not say anything.

Concern crept up Notus' spine. Throughout this whole time the young man had said not a word. It was becoming increasingly difficult to keep up his end of the one-sided conversation, so he tried a different tactic.

Closing his eyes, he focused on the link that now bound the two of them, and followed it back to find a solid wall blocking him. He heard the boy grunt, but astonishingly the barrier remained. Giving up on attempting to read this young man's mind, Notus opened his eyes and saw the boy rubbing the centre of his forehead, obviously in pain.

This was unprecedented! Never before was there one Chosen who could not be read by their Chooser. Even Notus had been an open book to the one who had transformed him. It had taken decades and hundreds of leagues of separation to sever that link, and he doubted that if his Chooser came back he would be able to block him from entering his mind.

"Who are you?" implored Father Notus.

The sharp pain receded enough for the young man to see the stranger staring at him. The look on his face made him uncomfortable. It was the same he had seen on others. One of disbelief mingled with fear, and he turned his face away. It hurt too much to see that look.

It was not the reaction that Father Notus had expected to his question. Long straight white hair fell, masking most of the young man's face, but not enough to cover the fact that he could see the crimson eyes fill.

In the moonlight the young man seemed to glow, as pale as he was, and Notus could well see that many would see a very attractive, dare he say beautiful, young man. He tried again.

"What is your name?" he gently asked. "I already gave you mine—Father Paul Notus."

Not having spoken in over two years, he barely managed to whisper. "I–I don't have a name."

It was Notus' turn to sit confused under the tree. Everyone had a name, and he said so.

The boy mournfully shook his head, sending white strands of hair floating in the breeze.

Notus sat in stunned silence before asking, "Surely your parents must have called you something." He instantly regretted his words as the crimson eyes fell on him once again, this time the profound sadness made him close his mouth before asking his next question.

"I don't have parents," the boy managed, his voice becoming a little stronger with use. Before he could repress the feelings back down to where he had buried them for so long, he had to wipe the tears that ran down his cheeks.

"I'm so sorry to hear that, my son." Notus wanted to go to this young man to give him comfort, but respected the distance and the safety it provided. "How long have you been living here?"

The boy cleared his throat and answered, "A little over two years."

Stunned at the revelation, Notus blurted, "How old are you?"

The boy blinked. He had not expected such a question and he had to think about the answer. Truthfully he did not know for certain. "Eighteen or so."

"Dear God!" exclaimed Notus. "So young!" The full impact of what he had done to this boy finally hit. The boy may be a grown man, but he will never now be able to have a home and a family.

In one night's folly he had taken away the boy's future. Sure, many who are Chosen are young, but many had lived a life before choosing the transformation. Some had been old enough to have children. Some, like himself, had been well into their lives.

Here was a young man with no life experience. The weight of his responsibility to this young man grew heavier and the night was wearing thin.

Rising, he glanced down at the young man. "Come on now. We have a lot to discuss before sunup." He held out his hand.

Uncertain, the boy hesitantly grasped the outstretched hand, noting its coolness, and allowed Father Notus to assist him up until he stood over the shorter man. Brushing dirt from his kilt, he followed the little man into the woods only after he had ran back into his cave for his knife, just in case. He did not know why he trailed after the man called Notus, but it seemed the natural thing to do and hoped it was not some sort of trap.

"What am I to call you?" ventured Notus, his voice ringing in the night ahead of him. Brown wool robes caught in the underbrush, but were ignored.

The boy shrugged.

Not hearing an answer, Notus stopped on the trail and looked up expectantly at the white figure behind him.

After a moment of silence, Notus realized he was not going to be graced with an answer. Turning around, he continued along the path. "We'll figure something out, my son. In the meantime, walk beside me. I like to look at whom I'm speaking with."

The boy lengthened his stride and fell in beside Father Notus. He found he was starting to like this man, but trust was still a long way off. Listening in silence to Father Notus, he was fully aware that he had been called *my son*. No one had ever called him that and a part of him warmed at the thought that finally someone had.

"The bond between one who is Chosen and the Chooser can

be very strong," explained Notus as he moved a skeletal branch out of the way, allowing the boy to catch hold before moving onwards. "Especially if the two are in close proximity to each other. The connection will dwindle if they are parted by distance and will grow again once they come together. The only way the connection is severed is if one of the two, usually the Chooser, severs it, or if one of them dies."

Notus stopped, put his cool hand on the white flesh of the young man's arm and peered intently into blood red eyes. "Yes. Even though we are immortal, we can die, and only through three ways: immolation by sun or fire, decapitation or, and mind my words on this, drinking from the dead. Never ever drink from the dead."

The boy regarded Notus with disgust. *Drink from the dead?*

"We sustain our immortality by drinking the blood of the living. I do not know why this is so, but it is," said Notus in all seriousness. "It is their lives that uphold ours. Never forget that."

He watched Notus gaze at him from head to foot and back again before turning to continue down the path. Confused and a little more than disturbed by what was imparted to him, the boy hurried to follow.

They rounded a large tree, and the boy realized the speed at which they walked made the forest blur. Strangely enough, he did not tire from the pace, and he only half listened to Notus. "One of the aspects of a strong connection in our kind is empathy. The second is telepathic. I have a feeling we are going to have to work at that."

Again the pain grew in the centre of his forehead, forcing him to attempt to rub it away with the heel of his palm. Slowly, it dissolved into a tingling, until that too disappeared.

"Yes, definitely we are going to have to work on that," said Father Notus, none too pleased. "In time, I hope, you will be able to read my thoughts and emotions as easily as I will be able to read yours." Notus tromped along the path, and a sense of doubt as to whether this was possible began to grow. Along with that came worry.

"At this point" —Notus ducked under a large branch. The boy had to crouch to navigate the obstacle.— "I do not think it wise if we went our separate ways for some time. There is much I need to teach you so that you can live the life I unfortunately gave you.

"Ahhh, here we are."

The trees released their embrace and they found themselves in a small area surrounded with large oaks that blocked out the stars and moon. In the centre of the clearing stood a small domed hut covered in hides. Beside it, resting on its long arms, a cart stood with bundles carefully wrapped in oiled leathers.

"Welcome, my son, to my humble camp."

The boy stared, watching Father Notus shuffle through the desiccated leaves to the tent and bend to enter it. He could hear the movement of the man in the tent and then he saw the man's rear as he backed out with something in his hands.

Emerging from the tent, Father Notus stood with a bow-stave in hand. "I believe this belongs to you."

The young man could not believe what he saw, and carefully took the yew bow in both hands, examining it, feeling its smooth wood. It was no longer strung, but the string was wrapped neatly around the top of the stave.

"Thank you," he said, his voice barely audible. "I had thought I'd lost it."

Notus smiled and nodded. "You are most welcome." Then his smile faded. "I think we may have a slight problem."

The boy pulled his gaze from the expertly cared for long bow and cocked his head to the side, waiting for the man to continue.

"My shelter is too small for the both of us," continued Father Notus. "I do not like the idea of leaving you alone at this crucial time. I would not forgive myself if anything happened to you because you were ill prepared."

Uncomfortable under the intense searching gaze from those brown eyes, the boy studied his bow, feeling the unspoken request. A part of him still feared this man, but he had given him back his bow and had said nothing about the knife he wore tucked in his belt. He had also apologized.

Silently groaning, the boy knew exactly what he was going to do, and it went against everything Auntie had taught him. "The cave is big enough," he whispered, praying that this bit of trust was not misguided.

"Can sunlight enter it?" asked Notus, dubiously.

Clearing his unpractised voice, the boy replied, "Only for the first few feet. The back remains untouched."

"Good. Good," exclaimed the man and with a clap of his hands turned back to his hut to begin the chore of lifting the hides and folding them before placing them neatly into the cart.

Not liking to stand and do nothing while watching someone work, the boy walked over, laid his bow across the carts arms for safekeeping and went to help dismantle the tent.

The two worked silently in the night, each watching the other. As Notus smiled and hummed through the task, the boy began to doubt his own misgivings about this man and surprisingly grew more at ease in his presence, his shoulders relaxing their tension.

"You seem to be taking this well." Notus folded a deer hide in half so that it hung neatly over one arm before handing it to the young man.

Taking the hide, the boy folded it once again before laying it into the cart.

Notus noted the young man's quizzical look. "What I mean," he explained as he took the last hide from the tent, leaving the skeletal arms of the branches of wood that made up the tent's frame, "is that when I was Chosen I had many questions. I would imagine that you have at least one question to ask me."

The boy walked over to the tent frame, studying it, after placing the last hide in the cart. Did he have a question? He frowned, picking at one of the leather thongs that knotted vertical and horizontal branches together. The knot was well made and complicated. How was he to even come up with a question when he did not even know where to begin? He pulled out his knife and went to slip it under the thong to cut it.

"No!"

The man's hand on his own halted his cutting, and he looked down to see horror in Notus' face. Unaccustomed to the touch of another person, he let his hand drop away.

"Don't cut them. Untie them," explained Notus, picking and pulling apart the knot with deft fingers. "Cutting them would be wasteful. Time, patience and perseverance will allow them to be used again."

With a sigh, the boy sheathed the knife and picked at the knot, but only found he was entangling it even more. He glanced at Notus to see that five strings lay over his hand, when he could not even get one. Frustration grew at the simple task.

"So ask." Notus held up the sixth untied thong with a triumphant smile.

Distracted by the task of getting at least one knot undone, before the man finished the rest, the boy said nothing.

"Ask me a question. You must have at least one." He stood

with another one undone. He did not remark on the young man's inefficiency with tied things.

The boy stopped picking at the knot he had been working at and pulled his knife. "Why do you make these knots so difficult?" Deftly, before the man could stop him, he cut through the leather, and held up the string with the knotted ball in the centre before handing it to the man.

Notus' face fell at the sight of the leather string all bunched in its centre, sitting in the palm of his hand. "You did not have to that," he said, meekly.

The boy ignored the remark and proceeded to cut the rest of the leather strings that held the tent together. Creaking and cracking, the frame collapsed into a large pile.

Notus continued to stare at the little brown ball in his hand.

Ignoring the little man, the boy picked up one of the tent beams. "How do you want these packed?"

"What?" Notus glanced up, noticing the fallen poles. "Oh, yes. You can leave them. Others can always be found if needed. It's the hides that are important." He looked back down to the knotted string and with a sniff and a shrug he washed his hands of the thongs and the knotted ball, letting them fall to the grass.

Checking to see that the cart was properly packed, Notus took the bow from the arms and laid it on top of the folded hides before moving to stand behind the cart.

"Let's get going." Father Notus spat into his hands and squatted to get a grip under the cart.

Despite being unschooled in the ways of the world, the boy knew well enough that a cart was pulled, not pushed, so he stood there, staring at the man, his jaw slack.

Releasing the underbelly of the cart, Father Notus stood and noted the incredulous gaze on the young man's face. "No," answered Notus. He did not need to read his mind to see what this young man was thinking. "We are not going to push it. That would be ridiculous, especially over this terrain. We're going to carry it."

The disbelief in the young man's face grew to the point that Notus could almost hear the words asking if he was crazy. Sucking his bottom lip, Notus shook his head and drew upon hundreds of years of experience with people. "Yes. Carry," he authoritatively instructed, all humour gone from his demeanour. "Now that since it is your turn to lead the way, you lift the front, by its arms."

Finally, the young man put voice to his sceptical gaze. "You cannot be serious."

"I am. Now do as I say. The night is wearing thin."

The boy let out a huff, shaking his head dubiously and went to the forefront of the cart, turned his back on the man, and experimented with the best way to grasp the arms before he found what would be most comfortable.

A new thought popped into his mind as he looked back to see if the man was ready. *How did the man get the cart here in the first place?*

"The other path is much more manageable," answered the man. "It was quite easy to pull it along."

The boy whipped around to face Notus. *Could this man really read his mind?*

"Strangely enough I can't. I should be able to," explained Notus. "But, my boy, you are quite easy to read. An open book, one might say. Now, if you please?" He gestured for the young man to turn around to get back to the job at hand.

The boy grasped the extended arms of the cart and at the count of three, lifted it. He could not believe the ease at which the wheels left the ground, the cart supported only by four hands. A little push from behind was all it took for him to start moving forward. The weight of the cart was minuscule to what he had expected.

"Which way to the cave?" asked the man from behind.

"That way." The boy absently lifted the cart, trying to hold onto it and point at the same time.

"Whoa!" cried Notus, trying to stabilize the swaying wagon. "Do not do that again. Just start walking and do not let your long legs take large strides or you will be carrying this on your own."

Abashed, the boy, surprised by the lightness of his burden, lowered the arms in his grasp and made sure to take smaller steps. It was when he heard Notus chuckling that he realized that he had taken this man too seriously and a hint of a smile lifted the corner of his mouth, finally understanding that it was not meant as a reprimand, but a jest. He was surprised at how quickly he was beginning to like this Father Notus.

"I guess I should teach you a lesson or two." The monk let out a grunt. "The reason—Dear God! Try at least to keep it balanced!"

"Sorry," he muttered, the grin spreading to the other side of his mouth as he led the way down the track that would bring them to the grove.

"That's much better," continued Notus. "Now where was I? Oh yes. I remember. The reason why we can lift this heavily laden cart is that we have exceptional strength. It is another of the gifts that come from the transformation. I don't know why this is the case, but there it is. From now on you are going to have to be careful and watch your own strength, for you are now stronger than mortal men. Without thinking you could easily crush a man's hand into uselessness by a mere handshake. We cannot tire from exertion except if we are unable to find proper nourishment. And yes, we can starve, but not to death. I wouldn't recommend trying. We do, in fact, find our strength grows as we age over time. We do not grow old, but, in a sense, we grow in power. The last time I tested how strong I was, I bent an iron sword in half. Nevertheless the poor mercenary was non-too pleased and... well... that's another story. With the strength comes the ability of great speed. Our bodies don't work the way they used to, and if you are to pass for a normal human, we'll have to work on moderating these new found abilities."

The boy listened as well as he could, while at the same time, picking out their path back home. Ducking to avoid a tree branch tilted the cart dangerously. Notus lowered his end in response to the sudden imbalance and both straightened themselves once past the obstacle.

"That won't be possible," replied the boy, the smile long gone.

"Now don't underesti— oh. Sorry." The monk saw the boy's head lowered and realized he was right. He could help this young man learn to moderate his new gifts, but it was doubtful he would be fully accepted, even amongst the Chosen. Notus worried his lip at the thought of how to help the boy. He was caught off guard when the cart suddenly dropped to the ground, pitching him forward and almost on top of the pile of hides.

Straightening, he saw the boy, bent over in obvious discomfort and walked over to see what was wrong with his Chosen one. "Are you alright, my son?"

The deep ache that had taken away his breath diminished enough so that he could look up at the man. If he did not feel so rotten all of a sudden he would have noted the concern on Notus' face. Instead he let himself slide down to kneel on the ground, pressing his head against the rough wood of one of the wagon's arms.

A cool hand touched his cheek and then pressed against his forehead. It felt good. Then something was pressed to his lips and he was told to drink.

At first he choked on the thick liquid that ran down his throat, but the flush of renewed energy was enough for him to take the water skin from Notus. The taste was exquisite, unlike anything he had before. If pure energy could be turned into a taste this would be it. He gulped down the contents despite Notus' insistence to go slow.

When he had drained the container, he opened his eyes to see Notus take it away and loop it to a belt he wore between the layers of his robes. He felt much better and tried to stand. Notus motioned for him to stay where he was for a few more moments.

"I was wondering when you would need this," remarked the monk, his brows came together as he frowned. "Usually the need is instantaneous upon waking. If not, then shortly thereafter. Never before had someone Chosen gone most of the night without the need for first blood."

The boy wiped his mouth and glanced at the red smear on his pale skin. His first reaction at the idea of having gulped down a skin full of blood was nausea, but the lingering taste negated it. Licking his lips, he swallowed before looking back up at the man. The warmth and sense of strength permeated every part of his being.

"That was the hunger you felt, my son," commented Notus. "Mark it well, and consider it your first lesson. If you do not feed regularly and allow this to happen and go on, eventually the need for blood will encompass your mind and you *will* lose your humanity until you are satiated. The havoc you could wreak in such a state would be devastating, not only to others, but to yourself, and to your own soul."

He held out his hand, and the boy grasped it, allowing himself to be pulled with ease, to his feet.

"That was deer," explained the monk. "When I went back to the grove before finding you, the stag had come back. Little did I hope that you would need this before I. Tomorrow night I will begin to teach you to use what God gave us during the transformation." Notus tapped his own elongated and pointed canines and the incisors directly in front of them.

The boy ran his tongue across his own teeth, seeing if he had been given new teeth, but only felt the same ones he had always had since his baby teeth fell out and his adult teeth grew in. The sharp points of his own canines and two incisors still pricked his tongue. Did not everyone have teeth like Notus and he? The memory of Auntie and Geraint smiling answered that question. No.

"Are you ready to continue?" asked Notus.

The boy nodded and went to take up the front of the cart again as the monk took his position at the back. Again with a count of three they lifted and began their journey once more.

"These are the gifts that God has granted the Chosen," continued Notus from behind. "Simply put they are increased strength, increased endurance, nocturnal sight, superhuman speed, increased sensitivity of all the senses, and of course, immortality; if you consider immortality as a gift. The curses are extreme in comparison, for they will always separate us from all other living creatures. We are never to behold the sun and bask in its glorious radiance, for if we do our flesh will burn and we can die. There are others, of course, more that affect one on a personal level, but I am sure you will learn those in time. They tend to be in accordance to outliving friends and loved ones, and even family. To never having a family of your own. There are others of course. And for the strong ones, we learn to adapt, for it is adaptation that allows us to survive and live.

"I'm saying all these things again, so that the point is driven home. You are not what you once were."

Then indeed I have been given a gift, thought the boy.

The boy had not realized how far they had come as they broke through the line of trees and faced the clearing that led to the cave. Listening to Notus talk most of the way made the time fly by, but not fast enough for the first hints of dawn to subtly change the air around them. The sky was still dark, but he could feel a shimmering of energy that made his skin tingle and itch. Some part of him knew that the first rays of the sun would be peeking over the horizon very shortly.

Letting the cart regain its own weight on its two wheels, he rubbed his arms, not to alleviate any ache, for there was none, but to try and rid himself of the strange sensations of the predawn. A press from behind told him that his work was not done. This time he grasped the arms of the wagon and pulled it along new grass and flowers.

They halted before the cave. What remained of the fire was little more than almost used up coals, and the boy ran to rebuild his only source of heat. Grabbing several dry sticks from the back, he laid them on the coals and blew until the flames caught. Yellow light exploded into the cave, illuminating every nook and cranny like never before. It was then that he felt the man's stare into his home. He looked up to see Notus' nose wrinkled in disgust.

"I guess this will have to do," remarked the man, as he walked to where the food was stored. Bending, he picked up the strip of dried meat and the few apples and carried them out of the cave.

"Good food still smells good to us, but food that has gone bad... Well..." answered Notus after noticing the boy's look of surprise. "Well," clapped Notus. "Let's unpack, shall we?" He turned to the cart and began to take out the hides, one at a time, to make a pallet at the back of the cave.

After the first three, Notus turned back to the young man. "I would appreciate your help in unloading my cart before the sun rises. I do not wish to sleep on stone."

Rising from the warmth of the fire, the boy went to help. Silently, the two worked a short while until all the hides were placed at the back of the cave, and then the boy left the monk to arrange them however he wished.

The boy stood by the mouth of the cave, watching the colour of the sky shift into a deep indigo and then into a shade of purple he had never noticed before. The colours were magnificent and he stood enraptured by the kaleidoscope he was presented. The sky brightened, filtering to pink, preparing itself for the blue of the daytime sky. He squinted into the growing brightness. Leaning his hand against the side of the cave's entrance, he stood mesmerized.

The makeshift bed finished to his satisfaction, Notus flopped down on its soft skins and noticed the boy at the cave's entrance. "Get away from there!" he cried, bolting up.

At the sudden explosion from the monk, the boy turned his head around to see what was wrong and in that instance a faint beam of sunlight struck the mouth's edge, igniting the back of his hand in blazing heat. The shock of the burning pain forced a shout from his lips as Notus yanked him to the safety of the back of the cave.

"Stupid, stupid, stupid," angrily muttered Notus and forced the young man to sit on his pallet, taking the burnt hand in his own.

Tears streamed down the boy's face. He did not want to look at the blackened charred skin of his hand. Each movement brought more pain and caused the burnt remains to flake off. The sight of his ruined hand mingled with the agony made his head swim. Gritting his teeth, he tried to will the pain away.

Angry red blisters lay exposed where the charred remains fell off. Notus clucked while he examined the boy's hand. "Sit still," he ordered, and the boy ceased his rocking. The boy hissed in a breath as his hand was turned this way and that.

"This is most peculiar," remarked the monk, studying the burnt flesh. "This should be healing." He looked into the pleading pain filled eyes of the young man.

"Please," hissed the boy through gritted teeth. "Oatmeal and lavender." Taking another breath he managed in a rush. "It worked before."

"Before?"

"Please," pleaded the boy. He had never felt burning like this before. The whole of his hand was ablaze.

Notus shook his head. "Even if I had those things they will not work on you anymore."

Forcing a sigh, Notus knew exactly what would work. Uneasy at the prospect, Notus gently put the boy's hand down on his knee. Hesitantly, the monk brought his own wrist to his mouth and bit deep. Feeling the flow of blood, he held out his dripping wrist to the boy. "Drink."

The horrified look on the boy replaced the veil of pain.

"Drink," demanded Notus. "I'll not do this again. Drink before my wound heals."

Reluctantly, the boy took the dripping wrist with his good left hand and wrapped his lips around the self-made puncture marks. The taste of his Chooser's blood thundered through him as its energy shot through like lightning. The deer blood was nothing like this! Images and feelings not his own rushed through him; fears, loves, hates and ecstasies encompassed and moved through him at a blurring rate. He never wanted this to end. It was pure rapture and he wanted more. He sucked harder on the warm sweet nectar.

Notus' eyes went wide at the contact. Something was wrong, terribly wrong. He felt the connection between them solidify and then before he could do anything about it, feelings and images from the boy's short life poured into him in a swirling and confusing mass. This should not be happening. It could not be happening!

The intensity made him gasp as the images and feelings pounded into him, threatening to envelope him. Over and over the feelings of burning pain, solitude and loneliness threatened to sweep him over the edge; the images making no sense to his battered brain. He had to break this connection lest he be devoured completely.

Using all his strength, Notus ripped his arm out of the boy's grasp, feeling teeth rip flesh before falling backwards, gasping for breath.

All he could do was stare aghast at the white creature before him, cradling his rapidly healing wrist. The boy seemed not to notice. His closed crimson eyes opened slowly, the pain gone, leaving something else that made Notus shiver.

"Thank you," the boy said, huskily.

Managing a half smile, Notus regained a sitting position and went to slip into his bed for the day. "If you let it alone, it will be healed when we wake."

He watched the boy lay down, fully clothed, on his own pallet and waited until the boy's breath became deep and even.

Sleep eluded the monk.

Something was wrong with his Chosen. At first he had dismissed them, but now he could not. He should be able to follow the link between them and read the boy's thoughts and feelings. Instead, he encountered a wall, and when sharing his blood with the boy… He shuddered at the memory. He had never had *that* happen to him. He had felt the boy pull his life from him, if that was what he could call it, and replace it with confusing images and emotions.

Chosen could not do that. If he did not figure out what was going on, he knew he would not be able to resist being pulled into the boy's being.

This was something much more than he had expected and he played with the idea of just abandoning the boy, but he knew in his heart that he could not. He had received enough information from that one brief but intense connection to know that to leave the boy after promising to help him would devastate him. He did not know how he knew. He just did.

Whatever bond they had before had grown stronger with the sharing, and Notus feared that he, as the Chooser, no longer held the reigns. Closing his eyes, he fell into silent prayer, praying to the Good God to give him the guidance of what to do.

íx

LASH!

The winds rushed past him as he ran through the woods at night. Something chansed him. He did not know what. Blurred branches slapped and ripped into his skin. Blood flowed. He knew he was leaving a trail for whatever pursued, but he did not care. He had to get away before he was found.

Lungs laboured for each ragged breath. His legs pounded in rhythm to the throbbing ache that was his heart. The forest swirled about him. He could hear his pursuer crashing through the foliage in an attempt to catch up. Pleading with his body, he pulled upon rare resources and managed to put on a little more speed.

Tears ran down his face. He had to get away. Far away. A tangled root caught his foot, threatening his escape. Stumbling, he barely managed to regain his aching feet. His legs could hardly support him but he ran on. The whipping of the trees and bushes stung him in an attempt to slow him down. He could not let them. Pressing past he trusted what he could not see.

The sound of the crashing came closer.

Pain caught him in the side. He fought to breathe. His legs slowed down despite his insistence to keep going. His own body betrayed him. Stumbling forward, he forced his body beyond all reserves. His breath was gone. There was nothing left. The forest opened up to nothingness.

His foot caught air and he fell into darkness.

FLASH!

The bright day beat down, warming his supine tiny form under the giant oak. A concert of birds sat high above in the branches, singing their song for him. Lazily, he half-heartedly bat at a fly buzzing around his ear, hoping it would go off to find someone else to bother.

Suddenly, the birds halted their chorus. Something had disturbed them and in a flurry of wings, they all took off at once. He watched them go, saddened at the loss of their music.

Out of the sunlight a single feather fell, gliding down on the breeze, to land before him on the grass. A long tail feather from a raven glistened like midnight in the day. Tentatively, he reached a small white hand to grasp the feather. Its sharp edge glistened, reflecting nothing. White against black, the contrast astounded the boy.

A thundering called to his ears and he stood up. It did not come from the sky, but from the land. Following the sound with closed eyes, he could tell it was heading towards Auntie. Fear washed through him. It was Ninth day, but this sound scared him. Running, he left the oak tree in the hopes he would get home before the source of that sound could.

Skidding to a halt on a mound before the opening expanse that led to his home, the boy realized what the sound was caused by. There, beside the house, were what he could only assume were horses, and beside them were men. Leather creaked and metal jingled and the voices filtered through the air.

The boy flopped belly first onto the mound hoping he had not been seen, the raven feather in his hand. His heart hammered against the grass as the scent of horse and human sweat came to him. Could this be what Auntie was afraid of? If it waas, then he would be there to protect her.

He rolled away to hide behind a fallen trunk and stood, gazing at the men. Quickly and quietly, he ran to the side of his home, away from the men. He could hardly hear the conversation for the pounding of his heart.

"So Geraint, when are you gonna take Morwen for your wife?" chuckled one of the men.

"When she grows some brains," countered the thick set man with a long black moustache.

"Oh come now." One of the shorter men bustled up to Geraint. *"That's not a nice thing to say about my sister."*

"If your sister were nice to me the way she is to Geraint, I wouldn't want her!" laughed another. Others joined in.

The boy could see the man called Geraint did not seem pleased. Pulling his attention away from the company, he looked to see if the entrance to his home was clear enough to enter, and bolted through the door.

"Auntie! Auntie! There are horses outsi—" He stopped short at the sight of a large black haired man sitting at the table. He could not dismiss the fearful and shocked expression on the man. Slowly, the stranger pushed the bench away with the backs of his knees and stood.

The boy looked over to Auntie. He knew he had made a serious mistake. He had not thought there would be anyone in the house. He was wrong. Auntie's angry glare was proof of that.

"Get to the back and do not say another word," she ordered through gritted teeth. The boy had never seen her this angry, and meekly he obeyed.

Tears welled up and overflowed as he shuffled to his pallet. He could feel the man's eyes follow him, only to be cut off as he rounded the curtain. He sat heavily on his bed, crying silently, listening to Auntie pleading with the man for his oath of silence.

After what seemed a long time the man relented and swore to Dôn he would never reveal the presence of the boy. It was the slamming of the door followed by shouting and horses thundering off that indicated that the strangers had gone.

Auntie yanked the curtains open to glare down at him. *"What on earth were you thinking?"*

"I'm—I'm sorry." He tried and failed to still his sobbing.

"Sorry is not good enough, boy. You could have killed us both!" She shook her mane of straggly grey hair as she unfastened the leather belt that cinched her dress closed. *"I thought I had taught you never, ever to come out into the open. I hoped I would never have to do this, but you must be taught to stay far, far away from strangers."*

His crimson eyes widened in horror, tears forgotten, as Auntie sat down beside him. Grabbing his wriggling tiny form, she held him firmly face down on her lap and pulled up his kilt, *revealing soft white young skin.*

Stinging pain riveted through his body as the leather contacted flesh over and over. Howls escaped unbidden. He could taste tears.

FLASH!

Cold darkness forced shivers.

The rough bark of the tree felt unbearable to his bare flesh and he stood.

Night had fallen yet he could see everything, even the two figures steadily approaching him. At this distance he could only make out that it was a man and a woman and decided to stay put, waiting for them to come to him.

Closer they drew until the light of the full moon allowed him to make out the features of Auntie and Geraint. A bright smile formed and quickly fell from his face at the sight of their expressions. Anger and hurt filled their faces as they came to a halt before him. He was much taller than both, but he felt smaller.

"Why did you let this happen?" cried Auntie. "I told you to stay away from strangers; that they would kill us if they knew of you."

"It was because of you, that we were killed," stated Geraint matter-of-factly. "If you hadn't been so different I could have taken you and I would still be alive."

The boy could not believe what he was hearing. It was then that he noticed the bloody wound seeping from Geraint's eviscerated abdomen as bruises and burns blossomed on Auntie's face, her leg and arm turning crookedly. The two spectres stood in death and he tried to back away. The tree halted his escape.

In unison Auntie and Geraint pointed bloody arms and bellowed, "It is because of you that we are dead!"

FLASH!

The void surrounded him.

He knew this place.

"Sssseal the covenant," ordered the hissing voice.

"No!"

His shout rang through his body and pounded between his ears. He did not remember sitting up. Groaning at the remembered dream, he put his head in his hands and wept. The nightmares were back. Goddess help him, they were back. He had hoped they were gone for good, and this time they did not seem to disappear from memory.

He shivered in the damp cool air, as outside thunderous rain pelted down, not because he was cold, he was not, but because of the images from his dream that flashed in his conscious mind.

It was not the sound of the rain that pulled Notus out of his deep slumber. He always enjoyed the sound of water droplets striking leaf and ground. It always soothed him, giving him a cozy, comfortable feeling. He figured that it had something to do with when he was a child, but that was so long ago that that part of his life seemed more myth than reality.

No. Something else tugged him.

Sitting up, letting the hides that served as his blanket roll down onto his lap, Notus rubbed his eyes with the back of his hand. The sound came again. He had not heard it in a dream. It came from the other pallet. He could not mistake the sounds of the lad in the grips of a nightmare. Notus tested the connection between them and found it solid enough to traverse. Maybe, with the boy being asleep it would be easier to make the connection to read each other's thoughts, to find out what was going on with the lad. Notus did not like the idea to take advantage of the situation, but he did not think he would have a better chance.

Carefully, gently so as not to be detected, Notus followed the linkage. This time he was rewarded with a very slight opening. Taking a deep breath, Notus prepared himself to manoeuvre through this crack, but before he could enter he was snapped back through the link as the boy sat up and cried out. Notus' tearing eyes widened at the impact and he rubbed the centre of his forehead. In all his life as a Chosen he never had a headache. Now he did.

Serves me right. Notus pinched the bridge of his nose with thumb and forefinger.

A sound not caused by the rain, drew his attention back to the lad. In the darkness illuminated only by the glowing coals of their small fire, he could see the boy hunched over, head in his hands, and shoulders occasionally shuddering. Something was wrong. Notus doubted that he was the cause, but centuries of pastoral care dictated that he should provide comfort. Climbing out of his bedclothes, Notus walked over the few steps and knelt down beside the young man.

The boy did not notice his approach and started at Notus' gentle touch to his shoulder. In those blood coloured eyes, Notus witnessed a deep soul cutting sadness that took his own breath away. It took a moment for the lad to register the memory of the monk, before staring back into his lap.

Notus did not need the link to know what the boy was feeling and did not object when the boy pulled away as he stood. Notus wanted to ask what was wrong so as to help him, but instead asked, "Are you alright?" He did not want to press with too much of a personal question at this point.

The boy, hugging himself, turned and walked to the front of the cave, watching the pouring rain in the deep twilight of sunset.

"I killed them." The boy's whisper broke the strained silence.

This was not the answer Notus expected. He quickly rose to his feet and went to stand next to the boy, but not so close as to invade the lad's space. "Pardon?"

"I killed them," repeated the boy, his cracking voice barely audible over the sizzling rain.

"What are you talking about?" demanded Notus, aghast at the confession. Was this the reason why the boy was forced to live in solitude in this cave? Could it be that was why the boy had been so terrified of him at first? That he would take him to the authorities to suffer the consequences of his actions? Had Notus turned a killer into one of the Chosen?

Sure there were some Chosen who relished killing in their quest to satiate their hunger, but if they did it in a way to draw attention to their kind then he would be summarily dispatched. Notus chose not to associate with that kind. Only those of pure heart and ideals would be Chosen, or at least that was what he had been taught. Things were changing among the Chosen, but Notus was a consummate traditionalist. To have broken his Oath on a killer would be even worse than being judged and rejected by God when, or if, he finally died.

The lad took a deep shuddering breath and sniffed. "If it wasn't for me Auntie and Geraint would still be alive."

Notus did not know who these people were, and the boy's

confession made it all the more confusing, but he could not mistake the anguish in the boy's eyes. Something told him that this was not the visage of a killer, but he needed to be sure.

Clearing his voice, Notus asked, "How did they die?"

The silence grew between them once again. Notus stood patiently watching as the lad, still hugging himself, squinting up into the early night sky hidden by heavily laden clouds.

At last the boy spoke. "Geraint was killed in battle. Auntie was killed because they believed she consorted with a devil."

The boy was not a killer, but he had taken the guilt of one.

Notus grabbed the lad's arm and turned him. "Then why do you say that you killed them?"

Disconcertedly, the boy's crimson eyes landed on Notus' bewildered expression, his long white hair falling to brush against and hide his forearms.

"Because." It was obvious the lad was having a hard time catching his breath. "Because if I had not been different, Geraint could have taken me and...and—" Crimson eyes closed and his white face screwed up in guilt.

So this was it? Notus nodded to himself. "Listen to me, my son." He stared into the boy's now open eyes. "People die in war. Soldiers die in battle. To play these what if games do you and this Geraint no good. You obviously hold a great love for this man." The boy nodded as he stifled a sob. "Would you think he would hold you responsible when it was his choice—his duty—to go into battle? Would you not think that he would be happy that you were far away from such things and thereby live a fruitful life?"

Notus watched the boy's mouth open and then close a couple of times, searching for a retort. Not able to find one, the boy turned his head to gaze out of the cave. The rain was lessening its impact on the grass and trees. Notus could see the perplexed expression. It seemed that no one had ever brought this point to bear. He could almost see his words working on the boy's thinking.

"But it *is* because of me that Auntie is dead."

The boy's angry response through gritted teeth made Notus' eyes widen and before he could think, he blurted, "Now how could that possibly be?"

The bloody red glare sent a foreboding of dread through Notus' being. It was plain that the lad was angry, not at Notus, but at himself.

"I wasn't supposed to be seen." Notus could not be unaware of the sadness tingeing the boy's self loathing. "Ever." The monk's eyes widened at what was being revealed. "I was supposed to be kept hidden. She made it clear. If I was ever seen, they would kill us both."

Here the boy's voice faltered and he had to take a few steady breaths before he could continue. "I was seen once when I was a child. We were lucky that time, but I was punished. The second time..." The boy closed his eyes, his face betraying the pain of recollection. "I was hiding. But they found me."

His watery eyes opened. The faint glimmer of the fire made his eyes dance like flames. "I was lucky to survive—barely. The last time I had warning. I was told that I had been seen in the woods at night. They thought I was something else. I thought I was safe. I was wrong. They came on horseback and on foot, while I was hunting, and they killed her.

"They came because of me. They said so when I arrived. They burnt my home. They killed Auntie. They would have killed me, but I ran away. She had always told me that if I were seen we would be killed. Oh Dôn, she was right!" The boy closed his eyes, releasing a flood of tears, before turning back to stare out of the cave once more, his slender body trembling.

Notus rapidly blinked and closed his mouth. He had not realized his jaw had dropped. What could he say? There were no words of comfort ready to burst forth. No smart remark to help assuage the boy's guilt. Resolutely, he turned back to his pallet and sat down.

The slight cool breeze wafted into the cave, bringing with it the moisture from the easing rain. It went unnoticed by the boy, tears trickling down his face as he stood staring into nothingness. Beyond the cave, the night was shrouded in grey mist, the trees and bushes stood as silhouettes even to his changed eyes. A tear collected on his chin and dripped onto his folded arms.

Saying the words he had held buried within him for so long wrenched the wound, he thought was closed over, open. He could accept and partially understand Notus' argument about Geraint's death. He knew Geraint had loved him and knew that he would not be coming back from the battle, but it was his fault Auntie was killed and there was nothing Notus could say to change that.

He had not even tried.

The boy felt the man's eyes on his back. He did not know why he had told Notus what he did. Maybe it was because of the nightmare. Maybe it was because finally he was not alone. Whatever the reason, the boy knew that he had radically altered this man's perception of him. He could feel it as solidly as the stare. He would not blame Notus if he wanted to pack up and leave. If the situation was reversed, the boy would probably do just that.

The pain in the centre of his forehead briefly blossomed and then was gone. He was not one to have headaches, but he was getting them now. Maybe Notus was wrong about him being one of the Chosen. That would make Notus leave for certain. After all he was there only because he was accidentally Chosen. Even that may not be enough to keep the monk around.

A dull pain grabbed him in the gut and he hugged himself harder, recognizing the hunger, before it faded away.

He wished he could be with Auntie and Geraint, but that was no longer possible. They did not want him with them. That thought brought new tears down his cheeks and now Notus would undoubtedly leave and he would be alone again, so desperately alone.

A hand gently lowered on his arm and he turned his head to gaze down on the monk. There was worry and concern in those gentle brown eyes. "It has stopped raining, my son, and the sun is down. It is time for us to find some nourishment."

"You're—you're not leaving?" stammered the boy.

"No. Not without you." Notus shook his head, his salt and pepper hair glistening with moisture from the air.

He could not believe what he was hearing, and found he could not catch his breath.

"You and I are not too different," explained the man, quietly. "It is not easy to live among humanity and not to be part of it. For hundreds of years I have had to conceal my true nature, as have those of our kind."

This man had been alive for more years than he could count!

"To be caught has, and I imagine, will, cause the death of others of our kind. Mortal man fears us because they do not know us. You, unfortunately or maybe fortunately, have learned lessons that only the strong ones who survive learn. It may be that God has placed us in each other's path to help one another.

"I will not leave you, unless you want me to leave."

The boy found himself shaking his head. No, he did not want this man, who so readily accepted him, to leave. The realization astounded him.

"Then in that case, if you wish, I will teach you what I can." Notus patted his arm before lowering it. "And when it is time I can show you more about this amazing world that is beyond this little cave."

A smile lifted the man's mouth and set a glimmer in his eyes as he continued. "I can teach you how to read, how to write and I can teach you numbers. Would you like that?"

"What are they?" Curiosity piqued the boy's interest.

Notus smiled and nodded. "I will show you. But first we have to feed."

He followed his Chooser into the night mist. For the first time he had a sense of hope. Auntie had always said that the Goddess always provided for Her children and that if one path shut She would create a new one. It was highly possible that Father Paul Notus was sent.

"How's your hand, my son?" Notus continued along the muddy path, his sandaled feet squishing in the mire.

The boy inspected his hand. There was no trace of the burn. His skin was flawlessly white and soft as his fingers caressed the back of his hand.

"It's fine," he said, astonished.

Chuckles drifted in the mist to his ears and he hustled to catch up to walk beside the monk.

"See, I told you it would be well upon waking," Notus beamed.

Yes. Yes he had, and a hint of smile tugged at a corner of the boy's mouth.

They walked in silence without their preternatural speed, the darkness dancing with sparkles of floating light.

The silence between the two of them had drawn out, giving the boy time to come to terms with the changes in his life. He was not at all sure if he would be comfortable with everything, but he finally found the courage to ask, "How did you become Chosen?"

Notus halted for a brief moment, surprising the boy before he too came to a stop a few paces ahead. "That's a very personal question."

Abashed, the boy hung his head. "Sorry."

"No, do not apologize, my lad." Notus came to stand beside him and patted him on the arm once again. "It is usually considered indecorous to ask that to one of the Chosen as each person's story is very personal. In many instances it is tantamount to asking a couple what they do behind closed doors."

"What does a couple do behind closed doors?" asked the boy in all seriousness. He was rewarded with an incredulous stare and thought maybe that definitely was not the right question to ask.

The boy took two large steps and fell in beside Notus as they continued their journey to somewhere. He found that he quite easily trusted this man. It felt natural to do so.

Notus glanced up at the sky, not to look and see if the clouds were parting, but to find the distant threads of his memory. "I was younger than you are now, having recently passed my fourteenth autumn, when my father left Ynis Witrin to go to Mona. He took me with him on that long trek through the land. He would do this every seven years because he wore the mark and that time was to be my first.

"I was naturally curious about this place where my father had learned the old ways and became a Bard. I remembered the stories he used to tell me and my brothers and sisters. Out of the twelve of us, he chose me to go. I guess it was because I was the eldest.

"When we arrived, it was during the festival of Cofleu. Bonfires glowed upon the hills. It was the first night of my life in the training of the Way of the Oak. I spent the next twenty-five years or so on the Holy Isle before the Romans came and destroyed what we had.

"It was a joyous time for me. I learned the lore of our people. Some of the others taught me to read and write, but most of the teachings were oral. We served the Old Gods the way they had been served for thousands of years. It was a peaceful life. It was a fulfilling life until the Romans came.

"Hoards of them crossed the low waters and attacked. I remember I was wounded, but somehow I managed to flee.

"I was found by Seddewyn the Astrologer. He was the one who Chose me. No one knew that Seddewyn was Chosen. It was only after my transformation that everything he did made sense. I remember him asking me if I wanted to live. I did.

"I awoke whole the next night. I did not know where we were, but we were far away from Mona, in a cave by the sea. It was Seddewyn who taught me about being one of the Chosen. We were together for many years before he decided that the stars had heralded our parting. I have not seen him since. That was about four hundred years ago, give or take a decade or two."

Shocked at the unfathomable number of years this man had been alive, the boy almost missed seeing the large root sticking up from the ground. He was able to catch his balance and halt his fall that would have landed him face down on the muck and mire. His big toe throbbed for a couple of heartbeats, forcing him to hobble to keep up with Notus, and then the pain was gone.

It was hard enough to imagine living one year into the next. His mind could not comprehend so many years of life, and since he was Chosen he too could live long. The realizations made his head swim.

Mouth agape he followed Notus deeper into the lit up forest of the night.

X

ight flashed, igniting the sky in a sheet of iridescent colour before fading into nothingness. No thunder sounded. The storm was still very far away, but the frequency of the flashes belied the clear sky littered with stars. Wherever the storm raged it was powerful and the boy was grateful for its beauty and its distance. He sat underneath an ash tree where he had found the large stick he worked on with his knife.

This was his second attempt to make a wooden copy of a sword since Notus ensconced his presence in the boy's life. In the years since he was forced to flee his home he had not had the time to continue with the practice that Geraint had instilled in him. Now that he had the gifts of being Chosen the boy found he had more time on his hands than he knew what to do with when he was not hunting, or learning the strange symbols Notus called letters.

A sliver of bark popped off, landing on the ground a short distance away. Its silver grey outer bark lay face down on the matted grass. Its ends curled inwards in attempt to protect its coppery underbelly from the night air. It still astounded the boy how his sight had changed. Everything was alive and he loved it. Never before could he have been so precise with such work. He never had enough light. Now he had it in abundance, especially when the moon was out, and even more so with a full moon, like tonight.

It had taken the boy quite a number of nights to find the right piece of wood since the last time proved to be an utter fiasco. He halted his knife's work at slicing off another sliver of bark at the thought of what had happened.

He had not put much thought as to what sort of wood should be used for a wooden sword and had spent many nights working on it. It was painstakingly hard to take off all the bark, leaving the inner bark because it was so colourful. Smoothing it nearly made his hands raw had he not been Chosen. He could have stopped there, but he wanted to try his hand at carving designs into it. He thought himself pretty good at it. Even Notus remarked that his likeness for the forest animals engraved upon the wooden blade was quite impressive. That comment earned the monk a rare smile.

Then came the night he would finally try it out.

Notus stood by the front of the cave and watched the boy near the river. The mist from the waterfall caught the waning moon to sparkle up the night. Lifting the sword, the boy began the routines he had been taught by Geraint. At first he went slowly in an attempt to get his body to remember moves that had become so natural years ago. It did not take long for him to slip into the memories and then the world became a blur. Amplified by his speed and in the thrall of feeling the familiar and comfortable weight of a sword, even a wooden one, in his hand, he shifted into an offensive move that took him to one of the lone trees that grew beside the rocks of the waterfall.

The willow tree, with its long flowing withes, became the adversary and he brought his wooden sword into a horizontal strike to the trunk. The worst he expected was to be jarred. Geraint had had him practice against trees numerous times so as to get the feel of what would happen when he actually hit someone, or something. The boy had not expected what occurred.

In one moment what took many days to create exploded upon impact against the trunk. The shock resonated up his arm and his jaw before the hilt flew from his grasp, deeply slicing his hand. It was the large slivers of wood, both from his sword and the tree, which made him duck. Even still, a larger portion of the wooden blade smacked him squarely across his nose, making his eyes water, coughing and spitting blood.

Notus had been there in an instant, the concussion drawing

him to the situation. If it had not been for being Chosen the boy knew he would have suffered long with a broken nose and a sliced left hand. Instead, in a matter of moments, the pain of both was gone as well as the wounds. Notus only looked up at him after he had healed and shook his head before going back to the cave. The boy could have sworn the man laughed.

This time he would not be so foolish. He would take his time and he would not hit anything immovable with it. Notus had said that as Chosen they had greater strength. That night proved it.

Applying pressure to the bark with the edge of his knife, the boy worked to remove another slice. This wooden sword would be nicer than the last he promised himself. He enjoyed this kind of work. It made him feel useful since, with Notus around, his life had changed dramatically.

Gathering firewood was an easy and quick chore, and tending the fire was easier because they did not depend upon it for cooking. The warmth it provided was nice, but it was not absolutely necessary. He did not get cold any more. Then again the spring and summer had been quite warm, enjoyably so.

The biggest change was that he no longer needed his bow to hunt. The bow and arrows were now only used for practice as a skill he did not want to grow dull. With his new gifts he had to be extremely gentle with the bow and string lest he snap them in two. Hunting was still necessary, but the way he drew his sustenance was radically different, as was evident that first night after Notus had told him the story of how old he was. The number was still so large he could not fully comprehend it.

Notus had led them along the trail into the forest, but it was the boy who had caught the scent of the deer. Notus was been surprised, as he had not smelled them. Notus, at that point, let the boy take the lead. He could feel Notus' intense curiosity on his back as he took them off the trail.

What surprised him was the fact that Notus made noise in the woods when he made none. Several times he had to stop, turn and put his finger to his lips after the man would step on something that could alert the deer to their approach. It became frustratingly clear that Notus, despite his numerous years, was a horrible hunter. No wonder he had been so hungry that first night they encountered each other.

Closing his eyes, the boy took another whiff of the moist, still air and then motioned his Chooser further into the foliage. This time he would not allow Notus to make noise and had to stop and point out to the monk not to step on this or that. He could make out the man's exasperation, and ignored it. They were in his terrain now, under his expertise.

A sound up ahead halted him and he silently crouched. He had to grab the monk's robes and pull him down lest the deer see him. Notus was none too pleased with that and was about to say something when the boy placed a finger across his lips indicating Notus to be quiet. He then held up two fingers with his other hand and thumbed the direction in which the deer were. He did not need to see them to know they were there.

The pressure like pain in the centre of his forehead flared up momentarily and then was gone as Notus let out a huff of displeasure.

"What is it?" whispered the monk.

"Deer. Two of them," answered the boy in hushed tones. "Directly upwind and headed this way."

Mystified, Notus raised his voice. "I do not—"

A snapping sound followed by gentle hoof falls silenced the monk.

"How did you know?" whispered Notus almost imperceptibly, his awe apparent.

The boy touched his nose.

Quietly, both kneeling in the underbrush, they watched as a stag followed a doe to the cover of a budding hawthorn. The pungent smell of their heady musk filled the air. They did not smell like any deer before. This time there seemed to be more to the scent. In the humid air he could imagine that he could discern the distinct differences of their odours. What seemed the same was a metallic smell that fired his hunger.

A hand clasped his shoulder and he glanced over at his Chooser. Notus' eyes were heavy but his lips were pulled slightly into a smile, as though he were sniffing a bouquet of flowers.

The boy, about to ask what they were to do, halted before uttering a word by the man's fingers across his mouth.

"Watch and learn," came the whispered response. With heightened speed, Notus stood and ran silently through the brush to the doe and hit her with a closed fist squarely on her snout. The resounding smack echoed in the woods. Her big brown eyes rolled up as she fell with a thud. Before the stag could comprehend the intrusion to their evening meal, the monk whirled around, landing another strike between its eyes. Again the sound of flesh impacting flesh reverberated in the air. With less grace than its mate, the stag crashed to the undergrowth, leaving the monk standing between two heaving bodies.

The boy, stunned by the fluidity and grace, as well as the violence, stood, his mouth agape, and walked to the monk, carefully making sure not to step on the unconscious beasts.

"This is something you will learn, I believe, with ease." Notus lifted a half grin to the boy. "The hardest part is not to use too much of your strength that you kill them. Hitting with the right amount of force to hurt, but not harm, is also what I will show you. A dead creature's blood is no use to us."

Gazing down at the stag by his feet, the boy knelt and was drawn hypnotically to the steady rise and fall of its ribcage. His pale hand trembled ever so slightly in anticipation as he touched the soft warmth of the furred hide. He closed his eyes in pleasure at the new sensation of blood pulsating through veins and arteries. The fur seemed softer, more alive than ever before. The heat from the body was almost a solid, tangible thing he could grasp if he dared. Moving his hand slowly along the stag's side, he traced the flow of blood upwards, its heat guiding him and its intoxicating scent stirring a lust never before known.

He felt a hand cover his own, forcing him to pause on the great throbbing pulse on the side of the stag's neck. It jumped and danced to the heart's rhythm that he could hear. Its music fuelled his hunger. Sleepily, as if drugged, he opened his eyes to stare dreamily at the monk crouched before him.

"When you take him, be aware of his heartbeat." Notus' voice was thick with his own hunger-lust under tight control. "Allow his strength to carry the blood to you. Do not suckle or the creature will go into shock and die. Feel him give his blood, his life, to you. When you start to feel his heart struggle, release your grip. Let go. For it is at that point in which he can recover. We do not kill if we can avoid it."

The boy gazed down as Notus freed his hand, drawing his attention back to the stag. Tenderly, he caressed its neck, noticing how when he went with the growth of the fur it felt downy soft but when he went against the growth it stood up and was almost prickly. All he wanted to do was stroke the fur but his hunger wanted more. Bringing his face close to the pulsating vessel, he watched the quick rise and fall as blood sped into the stag's brain.

Without need of further instruction, his hunger leading, he opened his mouth and felt his sharp teeth puncture the soft furry skin.

Thick, hot blood spilled into his mouth. The force of it nearly caused him to choke on the volume before he could manage to allow the liquid to run down his throat, into his body. Instantly a rush of energy exploded within him, forcing a gasp and making him crave for more. With each pulse, more succulent blood filled his mouth. It was so incredibly difficult not to suckle and draw the life out of the stag faster. A hand on his shoulder steadied him, keeping him grounded as each swallow of blood fed the growing fire of his being.

After what seemed too short of a time, he became aware of a change in the flow of the blood to his mouth. The heart was starting its struggle to hold onto life. That was the moment Notus told him about. That was the moment he did not want to let go of. He could feel so much more life in the stag and he wanted to devour it all until the conflagration of energy consumed him as well. The hand on his shoulder tightened and with an excruciating effort of will he was able to release his grip on the stag, the taste of its blood still on his lips.

"Good. Good." Notus had nodded approvingly. "Excellent. We will do this each night until you are able to stop without guidance. At this point the stag will be able to recover. Now watch." Notus motioned with his chin for the boy to look back at the stag.

The four puncture marks on the deer's neck slowly began to close, cutting off any trickle of blood. Within a matter of moments the marks had completely disappeared. Astounded, the boy gazed back at his Chooser.

"I don't know how it works," explained the monk, "but there is something about our bite that allows them to heal quickly."

The boy looked back at the unconscious deer and licked the remaining blood off his lips. Its breathing had slowed, as well as its pulse. His hunger had been satiated, but he still felt the strong desire for more. Oh so much more.

The hand on his shoulder left him and he watched enthralled as Notus knelt and fed off the doe.

That first night of feeding was repeated every night for two full months before Notus felt secure enough to let the boy go off on his own one day out of seven.

Tonight was one of those nights.

The wood was almost completely cleared of its outer bark by now. The stars had a veil of clouds coming in from the west, foretelling the storm's approach. Flashes of lightning were distantly followed by the low growl of thunder so far off he doubted he would have heard it with normal ears. Looking up at the night sky, he figured the storm would come with the dawn, and that was still some time away.

With a last flick of his knife the complete under bark of the ash lay exposed. A pile of slivers littered his lap and the ground around him. Standing, he batted his kilt and shirt free of any shavings that chose to stick, and sheathed his knife in the braided hide belt that held his plain deer hide kilt closed.

The ground under his bare feet was warm in the late summer night and the uncompleted wooden sword in his left hand felt just about right. Stepping into the middle of the small glade, he held the sword out. It was far from completed. It still needed smoothing and he wanted to decorate it like the last one, but more than anything he wanted to feel that wondrous glow when he practiced the forms. This time he would not hit anything, he promised himself.

With both hands on the end designated to become the hilt, the boy deliberately and slowly took his time as he moved from one position into the next. The wooden sword cut the air with a swish.

One night in seven Notus let him off by himself for the whole of the night, and the boy relished the freedom. He could not fathom the reason why his Chooser, or anyone for that matter, would voluntarily starve himself and sit outside on his knees for the whole of the night muttering incomprehensible words. At first the boy thought it was some form of magic, but Notus had explained that God had made all life in six days and on the seventh He rested. On that seventh day, Notus devoted himself fervently to the worship of his God.

Notus had tried to get the boy to join him, but it seemed a strange practice and an even stranger belief. A God could not create life. That was solely in the realm of the Goddess. It was females that gave birth and so only a Goddess could give life. Unwilling to budge on that, Notus begrudged him that single day off from learning how to read; by Notus drawing images he called letters in the sandy cave floor, and by learning basic numbers through the same means.

The boy was happy to finally get back to what he wanted to

focus on. The wooden sword cut the air as he made an oblique strike at an imaginary assailant. Sure he enjoyed the stories of Notus' religious mythology, but it seemed strange in a fascinating way. It was when he managed to get Notus to tell the stories he had learned on the Blessed Isle that truly interested him. There were many nights in which, after hunting, he had sat listening to stories of the Ancient Ones and the Gods and Goddesses of the Cymraeg. Sometimes Notus would favour him with a story of a God or Goddess from Iwerddod or from the people called Romans who once ruled over the land, but were only recently gone. Those stories he thoroughly enjoyed.

A quick turn, followed by a downward vertical stroke brought him lined up for another horizontal strike. The air swished as he sped up his routine until he had to fully focus on his task.

Flashes of lightning seemed to come less frequently and when they did they lit up the glen for an eternity. Thunder rolled and grumbled closer, but he paid no mind. Soon the light from the moon became completely enshrouded by heavier clouds and even the faint glow that the stars gave off blinked out of existence.

The storm approached. He gave it no care. Nothing else existed but him and his sword. Fluidly, he moved from one position into the next. The air rang as he sliced the night. Slowly, he realized a breeze brought thick moisture with the promise of heavy rain and he came to a stop, exhilarated by what he had done. If only Geraint could have seen him.

Lifting his head to contemplate the time remaining to the night, the boy realized his prediction of the weather timed to the rise of dawn was only a little off. He had to make his way back to the cave now if he did not want to be drenched. Holding his newly made waster in the palms of both his hands, the boy smiled. It would do very well.

The walk back home was pleasant. He was grateful that he did not have to wear the foot wrappings and enjoyed the feel of the earth and Her plants under his feet. He could have easily used his gifts to get back faster, but because of those same gifts he chose to take things slowly. The night became an enjoyable time with new wonders to discover.

Wooden sword in hand, the boy followed another trail than the one that had led him to the glade. Not because there was anything wrong with that one, but because he wanted to stay out as long as possible. He knew Notus fretted over him when he entered the cave with only moments to spare. Sometimes the monk came so close to yelling at him about what would happen if he got caught out. Had he not learned what would happen since that first day when he burnt his hand? Chagrined, the boy would always apologize, but secretly he enjoyed forcing these reactions because it showed him how much the strange little man cared for him.

Hard packed mud cooled the soles of his feet as he took the right hand fork that he knew would lead very close to a cart track. He never saw anyone on it or even near it, especially this late in the night so he paid it no mind when he walked the short ridge next to it. Even if there were people on it, it was highly unlikely they would even see him up there.

Trees and bushes grew thickly in places and he carefully manoeuvred himself around them. The way became a bit more treacherous as a heavy mist descended. It was a sure precursor to the oncoming storm. Even with his gifted vision the mist would still block his sight so he trod carefully.

Lightning flashed, eerily illuminating the forest in frozen images that would halt the heart of a living man. To the boy, the pictures the light created seemed to evoke the true spirits of the living foliage about him, and brought chills when haunted faces exposed themselves from the dead and dying trees. Everything was so alive, even those that were dead danced in the light of the storm. Faces caught in expressions of horror, sadness and on the occasion, joy and laughter. When the grumbles of thunder followed, the boy could almost make out words, as if the sky talked to him in some secret and sacred language he was not privy to know. He wished he did.

Another series of flashes flared in the night sky. Expectantly, the boy waited for the roll of thunder as the storm closed in. What followed was not thunder. A high-pitched scream penetrated the night, giving voice to the petrifying tree spirits caught in the grips of pain. Only when the scream fell off and ceased did the deep resounding boom follow.

The boy stopped in his tracks. Following the direction of the sound, he looked down through the greenery to the cart trail. Had it not been for all the leaves in the way he would have been able to see clearly, as it was he could make nothing out. It was very possible that his imagination worked over time. It was also very probable that whatever made the cry was some sort of forest animal turned into dinner for a predator. Dismissing it with a shake of his head, the boy returned his attention back to following the trail that would lead him home.

"No! Please!"

That definitely was not an animal.

Coming to an abrupt halt, the boy crouched, his heart hammering in his head. Whoever cried out was very near and he had no intentions of being caught—again. Gazing from underneath leaves cupped in anticipation of rain, he took a couple of careful crablike steps in the direction in which the cry had come and was able to see the tracks of the cart trail. Someone was on the road at this late hour.

The high piercing scream cut the night again, this time coming closer. Every instinct yelled at him to flee, but something about the voice held him fast, something plaintive and panicked. Lightning flashed and he saw the source of the terror stricken cries.

A girl ran down the track, her rough grey woollen dress torn and stained with mud and blood. Her dishevelled chestnut coloured hair gleamed like fire as lightning flared in the sky. Tendrils that made its escape from her long braid down her back gave her a haloed appearance. He could clearly make out the dark bruise swelling the side of her mouth and the tracks the tears left down her face. Holding up the ragged ends of her skirt as she ran, the boy could see and even smell the blood on her legs.

The girl was obviously in distress and had been attacked, but the boy stayed frozen to his hiding place. Whoever did this to her could very well do this to him if he were caught, and he pivoted so that he could quietly make his departure from the scene.

He felt for the girl, he truly did, but he was not going to risk his life. In any case, she probably would turn and attack him for what he was, whatever that was.

With a last glance back he could see the girl turn and look down the path. He could not see what followed her, but whatever did caused her to gasp aloud and she tried to hasten her escape.

It did not take long to see what she saw. Coming around the bend four men in heavy leather armour strode along the track, the chains linking their protective coverings jingled with each forceful step. They did not have to run to catch her. Their steady full-length strides were enough.

All were filthy, as if they had been out in the wilds for a very long time. What caught the boy's attention was that each of them carried, on their hips, a sword. They were dangerous men. The type who had killed Auntie and thus people he wanted no part of.

One of them, one with a large protruding stomach, held a torch that lit up the night, making the boy's eyes water at the sudden brightness. The other three laughed as they caught site of their prey. The one with the long tangled light brown hair and moustache pointed to the girl as she stopped, trapped along the trail.

"Darlin' don't run. We're not finished with you, yet." The implied threat was clear in his husky voice.

The other three laughed. The one with the torch picked at his nose and then proceeded to pick at his teeth. The boy recoiled at the disgusting act, but found he could not move from the prime place to watch the scene before him play out. He knew that what he witnessed was frightening but he could not tear his eyes away.

Panting, the girl stood defiantly, but the tears gliding down her face and her trembling stoic form ruined the image. The boy could see very clearly that even in defeat she still defied them and a part of him admired her while part counted her a fool who should run as fast as she could.

With a nod of his head the man who was obviously the leader pointed with his chin for the others to go and grab her. The one with the torch stayed where he was, too interested in feeding himself with what he found in his nose. The two others, as filthy and dangerous looking as their leader, lecherously smiled and ran to the girl.

The girl turned to flee, but not fast enough. One of the two made a grab at her, missing by only a hair's breath to land on his stomach with a whoof. The leader broke into guffaws at the sight of his man bested by a girl. Not to be outdone, the second man lunged for her legs and with a shrill squeal the girl landed hard, the impact with the ground cutting off her cry.

She squirmed and tried to kick and punch her assailant, but it was plain that her efforts were completely ineffective. The man caught her two thin wrists in his meaty hand and with the other closed in a fist, punched her across the face. Her efforts to free herself came to an abrupt end as her head bounced with the impact.

The boy, never having seen such violence, except to himself, had to cover his open mouth lest he make a sound that would deliver him to these men. He felt for the girl, he wanted to do something to help her, but he knew that it would only mean his death if he did.

Lightning flared, quickly followed by a thunderous crash and a wash of wind blew through the trees. The storm was nearly there.

The tableau illuminated by the lightning was terrible to the boy. The man on top of the girl pulled her by her hands to stand before the leader.

"It's a shame that you decided to run." The man rubbed a grimy hand—knuckles covered with thick calluses stained with dried blood—and grabbed her delicate chin in his vicelike grip. "What I don't understand is why such a fine young thing like you, who managed to hide from us for so long, would stay around and not run away."

The girl spat in the face of her attacker and said nothing.

Stunned by the girl's brazen defiance, the boy could not believe that she would encourage them to cause her more harm. He had never witnessed such courage in the face of adversity and a part of him felt silently ashamed of his own lack of courage. Even though she was captured she still fought, something he never did. Now, more than before, he wanted to see her survive this ordeal.

Wiping off the globule of spit, the man, his face red with fury, hauled off and punched her in the stomach, knocking her from her feet. It was all the second and third man could do to keep her upright on her knees as she vomited from the impact, coughing up bile and what little food she had managed to scrounge. Once she was done, the man who failed to catch her grabbed a fist full of her chestnut hair and yanked her head back, forcing her to gaze up at them from her kneeling position.

"So, are you going to tell me what was so precious as to stay and hope to get past me and my men?" The man glared down at her, while the other two stood behind, forcing her to remain upright. With another nod, they hauled her to her feet, her arms pulled painfully behind her back. She moaned and panted in pain.

"You were with the caravan, so you know what's there." He leaned his filthy and blood splattered face close to hers. "Tell me and I will kill you quickly."

Gasping, she matched the stare. It was plainly obvious to all that she was not going to say a word.

The man clicked his tongue against the roof of his mouth and shook his head. "So much the worse for you, darlin', but I do promise you I plan on enjoying every moment and so will my men."

Taking a step closer, he pressed his large muscular body against her thin frame and kissed her. When he released her she gasped for breath. His eyes were clouded with lust. It was obvious to the boy, who had never seen such a thing, that the man wanted more and was thunderstruck when the man grasped the top of the girl's woollen dress and tore it. The sound of fabric ripping preceded another bought of thunder.

Her chest heaving in the firelight, the men leered at her high full breasts, but it was the man in charge who would take his first taste of her. A licentious smile pulled at the man's face and he pressed up against her, kissing her ruined mouth, the side of her face and down the side of her neck while his men held her in place. His large muscular hand squeezed her left breast and she cried out in agony.

Normally such a reaction would have encouraged the man, but this time something unexpected happened. Pulling away, he stood staring at his hand as if something had bitten him and then he glanced back at her exposed chest. White liquid dribbled down from large dark nipples, staining what was left of the front of her dress.

The shock of realization washed over his face. "Find the baby!" he screamed.

The man with the torch, finished with his pickings, snapped to awareness and without another word ran back down the path in which they had come.

"No!" screamed the woman, beginning her struggle in earnest.

Without the torch, they were plunged into darkness, illuminated only by lightning. The boy could still see everything and wished for once he did not have the gift. Frozen in his hiding place, incapable of taking any action, he could see as the man slapped her hard across the face. He could see her fall onto the ground and the two other men pin her arms down. What followed made him blanch.

Roughly, without thought or care to the woman, the man hoisted her skirts above her waist while the other too snickered, obviously looking forward to their turn with her. Ignoring his underlings, the man lay on top of her, brutally kissing and biting her. He followed the line of her bruised jaw, down to her neck and then down to her chest. She cried out as he found a sensitive nipple and bit hard.

Her squirming seemed only to entice him more and he lifted the front of his leather kilt as he placed his knees between hers, forcing her long thin legs apart. Leaning up on an extended arm, he lifted his other hand and squeezed her full breast until the milk dripped through his fingers. She bit her lip, moaning as she stared blankly up at the sky.

"I'm going to enjoy this," the man whispered huskily as he brought his milk covered hand down and rubbed the fluid along his erect member. Without another word, he positioned himself and with a thrust jammed himself deep within her. His satisfied grunting drowned her cries of pain.

Tears ran down the girl's eyes as he drove himself deeper with each violent thrust. The man, who had missed her in her flight, panted at the sight and with a free hand fondled himself in anticipation that he would be next.

The boy could not believe what he was witnessing. Nothing could have prepared him for the brutality of what he saw. He wished he could stop it, but it was too late and he thought that maybe it would be best if he leave now, while they were engaged in their act, but a mewling sound and the returning light of the torch pinned him to his spot.

In the bright light of the fire, he could see the man's pale hairy rear as he thrusted repeatedly into the girl, his heavy groaning pants becoming more insistent, more urgent.

The fat man with the torch appeared with a small squealing creature. "I got it, Cadwallader," he said, completely unawares of Cadwallader and the woman. "I got the baby. She'd hidden it in a trunk in one of the wagons."

With a shudder and a groan, Cadwallader finished and laid his full weight on the baby's mother, panting his release. Turning his head to glare menacingly at the man, he said, "Good for you, but your timing is lousy."

He disengaged himself from the girl, looked down at his now partially erect member covered in blood and let his kilt down.

Hearing her baby, the woman rolled onto her side and tried to crawl to the man holding the infant, weeping with effort.

"What do you want to do with it?" The fat man lifted the howling naked infant by a single leg.

"Beti!" screamed her mother, horrified at the site of her daughter hanging in mid-air, twisting and turning.

Cadwallader snapped his head around and noticed for the first time that his prisoner was no longer under his control. Without further ado he took two strides and brutally kicked the woman in the abdomen, causing her to roll away and removing any chance she could have to obtain her daughter.

"That's what you were staying around for, wasn't it?" he sneered, spittle flying out of his mouth. The woman lay on the ground panting, clutching her stomach. "Answer me!"

The storm in his voice cut through her pain and through the rain of her tears she nodded, sobbing.

"Slit its throat," he ordered the man with the torch and he turned back to stare down at the woman. "There may not be anything of worth in what we raided, but I promise that you will wish you had died along with the rest." With a nod of his head, he let loose the other two men to take their turns with her.

Clutching his ash wooden sword, his long pale fingers squeezing the fibres hard enough to leave dents, the boy realized he could no longer remain a bystander. They were going to kill the baby for no other reason than it was a baby while they took their perverse pleasures with its mother. Anger long repressed and deeply hidden swelled within him.

Jaw clenched, his teeth grating, he shook his head in denial of everything he had experienced at the hands of others and in denial of seeing it done to another. All his life he was told to remain hidden, that being different would cause him his death. It was no lie, but what Auntie and Geraint had failed to teach him was that people would hurt and even kill others just for the sake of it. The pleasure he saw that man take in the brutalisation of the baby's mother was the epitome of how evil people could be.

Then a horrendous thought crossed through his mind. What if the men who had killed Auntie had done this to her? The thought captured his breath, threatening to never return it. It took several gasping breaths to make him breath evenly.

He had no choice. The Gods had placed him there for a reason and he prayed to them for their protection for what he was about to do.

Time shifted. Lightning flared in a white wondrous sheet that seemed to go on forever. He watched the man with the baby slowly pass the torch to Cadwallader and went to slip the long knife from its leather sheath attached to his leg. Through it all the infant's howls seemed protracted and no longer human. His first concern was the child.

Stepping from his dark hiding place beneath a short elder tree, he ran to the fat man holding the baby. He paid no attention to the shocked expressions as he stopped, and using his wooden sword, sliced down on the man's outstretched arm with the baby dangling from his vice-like grip.

With howl the man dropped the baby and his knife as he pulled back, gripping his shattered forearm. The boy took no notice or care and let Geraint's training take over as he redirected the downward stroke for a horizontal one landing in the middle of the man's chest.

A sharp crack like thunder from forked lightning snapped and the man was flung off his feet, flying down the path in which he had come to land with a sharp thud on the hard packed earth.

Turning to face the other three, he noticed that the leader, Cadwallader, stood back, his face white with shock and horror before turning red with rage. The boy felt, rather than heard, the man's orders to the other two to come and attack him.

Pivoting in place, he stepped clear of where the infant lay screaming for her mother, and met the two men. Years of rage fuelled by fear he never knew he had, bubbled and exploded to the surface. In his mind, these were the people who had brutalized him when he was a boy. To his heart, these men were the same ones who had crippled and killed Auntie, destroying his home. For the first time in his life he let loose his anger, revelling in the thrall of revenge.

His wooden sword that had shattered upon impact with the fat man was still useful. He ran towards the other two, closing the distance before they could even draw their swords, let alone a breath. Using the stick, he slashed one across the face with the broken ends, exploding an eye. He could feel the wash of spray across his arms and his doe hide shirt.

Ignoring the screams of the incapacitated man, he turned the wooden dagger and thrust it deep into the chest of the man who had missed catching the girl. Holding him upright, he glared down into the man's brown eyes, noticing the whites were yellowed. Bright red blood spluttered out of the man's mouth and the light went out of his eyes. The boy let the corpse fall to the ground.

There was one man left, and he turned to face him as the first drops of the rainstorm fell.

The horror on the man's face did not upset the boy. For the first time he enjoyed the terror his appearance caused in others and used it. Slowly, methodically, he took a step towards the man.

That was all that it took. The man fled back down the road in which he and his followers had come.

The boy stared through the curtain of pounding rain, his chest heaving not with exertion, but with the release of years of pent up anger. He had not expected the man to run and a part of him wanted to go after him, but he knew it would be foolish to do so. Fighting to gain control and put down the rage, the boy's body shook.

Lighting cut through the storm. Following on its heels, the crackling and resounding boom shook the ground. The boy paid no attention to the sound, but stared at the shattered ash sword as the rain washed red blood and human offal down around his white hand to drip onto the ground. Raindrops of blood swirled into oblivion with the crystal clean water from the sky.

He had killed.

He did not know what to feel.

He did not know what shocked him more.

Fulfill the covenant.

The voice of his nightmares resonated through the woods and throbbed in his mind. Never before had he heard Them when awake. His breath caught as his eyes shot around in panic, expecting that somewhere in the darkness they were watching him.

Fulfill the covenant, came the voice more urgently.

Spinning around, sodden white strands of hair whipped his face. Ruined wooden sword in hand, his gaze fell upon the injured woman sitting on the soaked earth, clutching her baby to her bare breasts. She rocked as she tried to sooth her child, ignoring her own hurts, kissing the top of the baby's head while staring up at him. Fear and awe peered at him through summer green eyes.

It was then he realized they were all soaked to the skin in the pounding rain. Even through the metallic odour in the air he could smell the sweetness of the blood that oozed from her cut lip and swollen eye. Its scent intoxicated him, pulled at him.

Fulfill the covenant! The voice urged.

He had fed well tonight but something drew him, calling him to take her, to end her pain by drawing it within himself.

Yessssss.

It was the creatures from his nightmares. They were the ones who pulled at him. He shook his head in denial as he stared down at mother and child. He felt the ash in his hand compress and crack under pressure. He knew what these creatures wanted from him.

Fulfill the covenant, the voices cried out angrily, urging him to do the unspeakable.

He would not take this woman's life or the life of her child. Throwing the blood-splattered ruin of his wooden sword, he heard it splash in the wet grass and slide. He turned away from the woman, shuddering at the effort it took to do so. He would not kill her as the creatures demanded and he took an unsteady step away.

The itchy tingling feeling along his skin was back. Dawn was not far off. He had to get back. In this world he knew he had control, or at least hoped so. He would not do what the creatures wanted.

Noooooooooooo!

The voice faded in defeat, but left its imprint on the boy's soul. They had come while he was awake and that terrified him more than the thought of doing their bidding.

He did not want to contemplate the meaning of their intrusion into his waking life. Every night he dreamt them, waking in cold sweats. He knew Notus was aware of these almost daily occurrences. How could he not when he cried out? He never told Notus the nature of the nightmares. Notus never asked. What was he to do now that they were in his waking life?

Closing his eyes and taking a deep breath, he managed to calm down. He had killed and They were now in his waking life. Everything had changed in the blink of an eye. He wondered what new nightmares he would have come morning. He did not relish the thought, but it was high time he headed home.

The rain made it difficult to see where the path was to lead him back to the cave, but a flash of lightning revealed the muddy track. Scratching at his arm, he walked over to it. Despite the thick clouds pouring down on him, he did not want to get stuck outside when the sun finally rose.

"Please."

The plaintive cry came from behind him, from the woman with the baby. He halted. He had almost forgotten about her.

"Please, my lord," she sobbed.

He turned around to face her. She still sat, a pool of water surrounding her. The infant lay nuzzled against her. Stray chestnut strands were plastered against her pale and drawn face. Her green eyes glimmered in pain and desperation.

"Help me, if not for me, but for my daughter?" Tears mixed with rain.

He gasped. Her pain and her need confused him. His beaten in instinct about strangers drew his back up straight, afraid of what she could possibly do now that she knew about his existence. Maybe They were right, but what could she do? He had to get back now to escape the oncoming dawn.

"I don't want to die out here."

Her pain pierced his heart as surely as her green eyes touched his soul and he knew he could not leave her here. He took the few steps towards her and tentatively held out his hand. The touch of her warmth on him electrified him as he gently pulled her to stand, but before she could fully make it all the way up she cried out and buckled. Without a thought, he scooped her and the babe at her breast into his arms.

Surprised at his own boldness, her head leaning against his shoulder, he could only stare into her liquid eyes. Her warmth flowed over and through him, and her scent beyond the blood that washed off her face was clean and intoxicating. He tried to imagine what she would look like without the injuries to her face and thought she could be beautiful, but he had no real point of reference. Having her so close and touching him brought more feelings he never realized he had to the surface.

A sad smile flittered across her ruined face. "I'm ready to go to your fairy realms, my lord." She sighed, closed her eyes and snuggled in closer against his shoulder. Her baby hugged to her breast.

He watched her breathing deepen into the steady rhythm of sleep. Disturbed by her assumption of his nature, he fleetingly thought to place her back down on the cold and soggy grass.

The tingling along his arms grew insistent and he could feel the same along the exposed parts of his legs, feet and face. He had to get back, and having chosen to help, he found the path that would lead back to the cave.

XI

The glade opened up beyond the trees. He could hardly make anything out through his sore and swollen eyes. The sun had come up behind steel grey clouds. He had tried to get back as fast as he could, but he did not want to risk slipping on the mud-churned trails and dropping his charges. Even under the heavy rain soaked leaves of the thick trees there was enough light to make his skin redden.

The cold rain did nothing to halt the burning of his flesh and nor did the water give any relief to the pain. It did not take long for his skin to blister and crack, peeling to reveal more bright red skin already burning at the faint touch of sunlight. Every part of him was aflame. All he wanted to do was get into the cave and, if the Goddess was merciful, die.

Now he stood at the edge of the open expanse with the woman and baby still cradled in his burning arms. The rain pounded down, the lightning storm fading in the distance. Goddess help him, he could not see well enough where to go. Everything was a blind wash of light that brought stabbing pain to his eyes. Shuddering, he tried to swallow the rough dryness in his mouth and took a step from the shelter of the trees.

He gasped. Light flared around him, scorching his skin, literally cooking the meat off his bones. He could almost believe that the rain sizzled against his flesh, impotent in providing relief.

The rain lashed his hair against his ravaged face and shoulders, making it feel as though they were slicing into his skin. It was all too much.

Through squinted and inflamed eyes he looked down at the woman in his arms. He knew he could not carry her any longer. His strength was going. He had come so far only to fail just mere steps from his home.

"Please wake up," he whispered hoarsely, his voice almost unrecognizable to himself. If she could wake up and stand on her own, maybe then he could make it to the cave.

She stirred and attempted to stretch. It was enough to unbalance him and he dropped to his knees, splashing in the cold wet grass. Miraculously, he still managed to hold onto mother and baby, but the lightning pain of the impact brought an involuntary gasp.

There was no way he could make it back to the cave.

A cold hand gripped his shoulder. It could not be the woman. She was still in his arms. At least he thought she was. He could no longer feel his arms. Panting in pain, he could hardly make out the hooded figure before him.

"Dear God," whispered Notus, "I've been so worried about you."

If it had not so painful, he would have laughed in relief.

"Take her," he croaked.

"I already have her in the cave."

He shook his head and thought better. His skin cracked and peeled at the movement. When had Notus done that?

Strong arms lifted him to his feet, and then supporting him around the waist, Notus brought him in out of the brutal faded sunlight and the torrential rain.

The relief of the dark cave was glorious and he collapsed onto his pallet, panting, his eyes closed. He was so incredibly tired. All he wanted to do was sleep. He did not care that he soaked his bedclothes with rainwater. The agony would not let him sleep. He had healed from the other burn he would heal from this one too— he hoped.

Through the haze of pain he could make out voices. He prayed they were not from his nightmares. Then he recognized Notus' calming tones. It seemed that the woman was awake and Notus was discovering her story as he checked her injuries and those to the baby.

He could comprehend some of what they said to each other, and only made out her name when Notus addressed her by it. Tarian. He also heard that she and her baby, Beti, were traveling from the coast after her husband fell to raiders. She had hoped to flee the horrors on the west coast by going inland. It was on her journey with the others that she gave birth. That was only a fortnight ago. He could hear her sobs as she told of how raiders came and cut down the caravan she travelled with. He could not make out how she managed to survive. Everything was slipping from consciousness. Trusting she was telling of how he found her, he sighed, surrendering to the quiet of sleep.

A gloved hand touched his face pulling him to the twilight between wakefulness and sleep. He did not bother to open his eyes. He doubted they would respond. Every part of him felt heavy and incapable of movement.

"I'll be back as soon as I can," he heard Notus whisper close to his ear. "I need to take Tarian and her daughter to someone better versed at healing. You did well, my son. I'm proud of you."

But was not it daytime, even with the rainstorm?

A flutter of panic caught him, comprehending that Notus was about to go out and be burnt as well. He tried to push himself up so as to stop his Chooser. The hand moved down to his shoulder, pinning him to his bed. He was too exhausted to resist.

"It's okay, my son. I've done this before," stated the monk as if sensing his concerns. "I will be alright. Just sleep."

The hand disappeared to be replaced by a soft cool gentle touch.

The feather soft touch disappeared and he snuggled deeper, finally surrendering to the oblivion that called to him, content that he had chosen right.

It felt so good to stand under the raging waterfall. The cold water poured over him as he scrubbed his skin raw with handfuls of sand. Dry dead skin sloughed off, leaving sensitive red flesh that quickly faded to his natural whiteness. Scooping up another handful of rough sand beside the precarious ledge he stood on, the boy worked the abrading earth into his scalp and long white hair. He had awakened at dusk itching all over, his skin peeling. Scratching his arms had broken off flakes and he knew he had to do something about it. Now he luxuriated under the waterfall as he allowed the sand and water to wash him clean.

It had been quite some time since he had enough privacy to bathe. Notus' time away worried the boy, but he also counted it a blessing. Now he could finally get clean. Lifting his head so the brunt of the waterfall's force surged down his face, he brushed back his hair with his fingers then tilted his head forward to let the water shower down his back. It felt so good, so contrary from the burning agony he had experienced that morning. He shuddered at the memory and quickly dismissed it. He hoped that Notus was all right.

His memory, spotty at best, told him that Notus had been able to go out during the day before, but the boy could not fathom how that was possible. The flakes of blackened and burnt skin was testament enough of how even a little bit of sunlight could cause damage to his kind. He smiled at that thought. Now he was part of something more. He was not different anymore.

Carefully stepping from the waterfall, revelling in how clean he finally felt, the boy made his way back to the grassy bank where he left his dirty clothes under the ancient willow. He did not have enough time to clean and dry his shirt and kilt, but at least something was better than nothing and he sat down beside the clothing to let his body dry. Scooping a thick handful of hair, he began to pick and comb through the knots. Runnels of water ran down his chest and abdomen from his waist length hair. It would take time to get the bulk of the tangles out, giving him time to think.

Images of the woman he had rescued flittered to mind. Visions of her attack played through. She had been badly hurt and that was why Notus had to take her to someone else, but that brought up the question of whom Notus knew in these parts. They had been together almost constantly since the night he was Chosen. A flutter of worry crawled up from his belly. What would Notus say to those he took the girl to? Then a more horrifying thought: what would the girl say?

His hair forgotten, the boy stared into the clear summer night, his heart beating rapidly. She had thought he was some fairy lord. What would she think now? And not only that, she now knew where he lived! For the first time the possible repercussions of saving her slammed into him. Gathering his straightened hair at the nape of his neck, he let go, allowing the wetness cloak his back before reaching over to his stained and ratty tunic to pull it over his head. A new worry caught hold of the boy as he stood to wrap the kilt around his slim hips. He had to find Notus.

Stepping out from under the sweeping willow withes, he saw a familiar form enter the glade that was their home. Relief flooded over him. Notus was safe. The boy quickened his pace to meet up with his Chooser; a true smile ignited his eyes.

Notus halted mere paces from him, a shocked expression swept across his face that made the boy frown.

"You're alright?" asked the monk.

The boy nodded. "You?"

Notus' brows furrowed together. "What?"

"I was worried." The flutter gathered more fuel. Notus seemed distracted about something.

Confusion flickered across Notus' brown eyes before the light of understanding took hold and his mouth made a silent O. "I'm fine," Notus said absently shaking his head. "Solid gloves, boots and hood give me enough protection during such rainy days. I wouldn't dare try it when the sun is out. And you? There doesn't seem to be a mark on you."

A small smile pulled at the boy's mouth. "I'm fine."

"That's good." Notus patted the boy's arm and grinned. "I was worried about you too. Have you fed yet?"

The boy shook his head and realized he was famished.

"Good. Perfect." Notus glanced back at the direction he had come. "Just what I was hoping." He regarded the boy for a moment, his face expressionless. "Tonight I think I had better teach you a new lesson."

He watched Notus turn and head back down the path he had come. It took only a moment before he realized that Notus wanted him to follow. Lengthening his stride, he easily caught up with the short man. It was strange to see Notus so uncommunicative, but the relief of going out hunting together was enough to give the boy a sense of security that everything would be all right.

They walked in silence beneath trees weighted with leaves. Night birds sang to each other, punctuated by the occasional hoot of an owl. Scrabblings and scrapings from the flourish of nightlife filled the air with nature's music. It probably would not take them long at all to find something in which to feed upon. A snap and a crash off to their right were followed by the sounds of screaming animals fighting for their territory or the right to mate. The boy noted the sounds and continued along the path with Notus.

"You didn't ask me about Tarian or her baby girl," Notus said, breaking their silence.

Caught off guard by the question, the boy remained silent. The pressure in the middle of his forehead came back and as quickly dissipated.

Notus halted and sighed. Perplexed, he turned to face the young man. "The polite thing would be to ask how they are doing. After all, you were the one who killed their attackers, thus saving them both."

"How—how are they?" He felt uncomfortable under the scrutinizing gaze of his Chooser. He also did not like how Notus seemed to point out that he had killed. The girl must have told him that. For some strange reason it had not bothered the boy that he had killed the three men. Part of him regretted being unable to go after the fourth one – the one who had hurt the young mother.

"Mother and baby are going to be fine, thanks to you."

The praise surprised the boy, but he could not discount the dark undertone to Notus' voice and followed down the trail once Notus turned and continued walking.

It did not take long for them to find suitable prey. Between long thin tree trunks a doe stood chewing on green succulent leaves.

Notus touched his arm and then pointed, indicating that it was the boy's turn to take down the doe. He did not need to be directed twice, his hunger gripping him, driving him. Swiftly, silently he left Notus' side, and as quick as lightning he was at the doe's side and tapped her firmly between her big brown eyes. She dropped, unknowing of what hit her.

Pleased with how well he did, the boy stood, waiting for Notus. The monk made his way through the undergrowth, his brown robes momentarily sticking to small branches and twigs before releasing him as he moved forward. For the first time, the boy had a sense of foreboding at Notus' approach. He could clearly discern Notus' stern expression.

Hunger calling him, the boy knelt down beside the graceful neck of the deer; the pulsing of the carotid artery mesmerizing.

Notus' hand fell onto his shoulder. If he noticed the dampness caused by his still wet hair, he made no mention. "I know what I taught you about feeding, but I feel it important for you to know what it is like to feed freely."

Stunned, the boy looked up at Notus, searching the man's face for the truth. All he saw was sadness mingling with apprehension, making his worry grow. He looked back at the doe. He did not know if he could do what Notus wanted and why should he if doing so created such a reaction in the man.

As if sensing the boy's worry, Notus gave the boy a gentle reassuring squeeze before letting go. "Go ahead. You need to know what this is like. Just let go and let instinct guide you."

Steeling his resolve, the boy took a deep cleansing breath. Goddess he was hungry. With one last glance up at his Chooser he moved closer, bringing his face an inch above the throbbing vessel. The scent beneath the skin was intoxicating. It had taken him so long and so many times to control the hunger so as not to kill. The thought of letting go of that control was more than enough of an impetus. Biting down hard, hot blood erupted into his mouth. The taste fuelled his hunger and his first reaction was to just let the heart bring the sweet life giving liquid to him then he remembered what Notus wanted him to do and he surrendered to his hunger.

Succulent blood ignited within and he sucked, forcing the blood into his hungry mouth faster than the heart could handle. Each pull threatened the life of the deer and he had to hug the beast in a deadly grip to keep it from thrashing. Its own instincts for life created a tug-o-war, one that she was quickly losing with each swallow of her blood into him. Sucking on the wound to pull more precious fluid into him, he could hear the heart begin to skip beats and falter. The doe's terror of its imminent death forced greater thrashings, but he held her still in his grip. He continued to nurse, suckling as her attempts for escape diminished. Her heart fluttered once, then twice more and then stopped.

At the instant of the doe's death, the boy abruptly pulled back with a gasp, his eyes wide as he licked his lips. He felt euphoric and he closed his eyes to luxuriate in the feeling of the deer's life within him.

"Did it feel that way when you killed Tarian's attackers?"

The question shocked the boy out of his reverie and he spun around in place to stare up at Notus' stern expression. He did not know whether to be offended or hurt. Those men had deserved what they got. Did they not? Slowly, he rose to his feet, the dead doe forgotten, never leaving the monk from his sight.

"Well, did it?" pressed the man, a hint of anger tingeing his voice.

Placed on the sudden defensive, the boy's eyes narrowed, his anger growing. He could not imagine what would make his Chooser demand this from him. No, it did not feel the same as killing those men. The satisfaction he gleaned from that experience was completely as a result of feeling he had done something right. Was not that what Notus had said? What did Notus expect?

Shaking his head in disgusted disbelief, he turned around to head back home.

"Don't you dare leave this spot until you answer my question," ordered Notus.

The boy halted. He could feel the man's hazel eyes boring into his back and then the pain in the centre of his forehead came back. His own anger grew. Why Notus was brewing for a fight he did not know, but if he was going to be drawn into one he wanted to know why. Turning around, his eyes met the monk's.

"Why do you deem it necessary to know how I felt when I killed that woman's attackers?"

The pain vanished in an instant as Notus' eyes went wide and then rubbed his own forehead before pinching the bridge of his nose.

With a sigh, Notus looked up. "Because I need to know why, in God's green earth, she would think you to be a fictitious Fairy Lord who came out of the mists to rescue her. If she had seen you feed, we would have a problem."

The explanation shocked the boy. He did not know whether to yell at Notus for being stupid or to laugh. Instead, he held out his arms open at his sides. "Figure it out for yourself," he said before turning to leave. He was still angry.

"Wait! Boy!"

He heard Notus calling from behind him, but this time he would not stop.

"Stop!"

He felt a firm grasp on his arm and he halted to glare down at the monk. Was it his imagination or did the short dark haired man cringe?

"Look, I'm sorry," explained Notus. "But I need to know how you killed those men."

"Why?" spat the boy.

"Because mortals aren't allowed to know that we exist unless they are about to be Chosen. If they find out about our existence it could cause us trouble, more than you can imagine. That's why I need to know. Because if she even suspects then something will have to be done about it."

The boy stiffened.

As if reading the boy's mind Notus continued, "I wouldn't harm her, but we do have abilities I have yet to show you that could change her memories."

He shook off his Choosers grasp. "You could have said so in the first place."

Abashed, Notus stared at the undergrowth at the base of a tree ahead of them.

Glancing up at the umbrella of leaves, the boy let out a sigh. For someone who was supposedly so ancient and learned, Notus still needed to learn tact. "No," he answered, his voice soft and melodic in the quiet of the night. "I did not feed on them. I used the stick I was making into a sword. If you have any more accusations make them now."

"Then why would she think you a Fairy Lord?"

The boy could not believe the naïveté of his Chooser. "Why would anyone in these parts think of me that way? Yes, she saw me move faster than a mortal. Yes, she saw me burn in the light of day. But even if she hadn't seen those two things she would still think of me as such."

"Not everyone thinks of you like that," said Notus, incredulously.

Shaking his head, he stalked away, leaving the monk standing alone in the suddenly quiet forest.

xii

"ome on," urged Notus. "Let's go. We don't have all night."

The boy scowled. They had fed, this time killing their prey, and now the dead buck lay across his shoulders as they wound their way through the woods. He did not know where they were headed, but Notus seemed to be in a hurry.

They had not talked much in the last couple of nights. Mainly because he was still angry with the monk and Notus sensed it. He was grateful for the silence. He had expected a rift to form between them, but surprisingly, one had not developed. Notus was willing to wait until the boy cooled, whenever that would be. Even the boy did not know. Now he followed the monk through the forest and once on a well-worn track they were able to move fast enough that the world around them became a blur of green and shades of grey.

Notus had not said where they were going or why, but seemed anxious to get there. A couple of times Notus had tried to broach a subject of conversation, but quickly squashed the attempt when he saw the look in the boy's eyes. It became quite clear to the boy that Notus did in fact find his eyes disturbing to behold. That was not a shock. Neither Auntie nor Geraint could withstand his intense gazes for long.

He followed at a respectful distance, the corpse of the dead buck hardly a bother to his new found strength. What he also did not understand was why Notus wanted them to bring it along. They could not eat it. It would make them very sick, or so the monk had said. So why did he carry it? And where were they going?

Long minutes passed in a blur. Trees and bushes became a wash of vibrant greens in the near moonless night as he passed down the track. He did not know where they were going. This was a new part of the woods to him. The path opened up wider until he could distinctly make out the ruts in the mud. They were on a cart track. A sense of foreboding gripped the boy and he nearly stumbled over the monk as they reduced their pace to a mortal one.

He wanted to ask where they were going, and the words were on the tip of his tongue when the forest suddenly relinquished its comforting hold on them. He stopped, the words dying unspoken as his mouth dropped open at the sight of what could only be a village.

Under a canopy of stars veiled by fast moving wispy clouds, round houses made of stone and thatched roofs, not unlike the one he grew up in, speckled the landscape ahead. Smoke from hearth fires floated upwards before being caught and blown away by the cool breeze coming from the west. He did not need to focus to hear voices in states of laughter and argument. They mostly seemed to come from one of the larger structures in the centre of the array along the cart track.

Heart pounding a torrent of fear between his ears, the boy tried to swallow and found his mouth dry as fluff. He could not believe it. Notus had brought him to a village where there were people! People who, if they saw him... He terminated that thought, shuddering at the implications.

Notus brought him here! How could he?

He glanced around to see where the monk had gone, but Notus was still walking ahead, oblivious to the fact that the boy had stopped. All of a sudden, Notus halted and turned around to face him, his dark brows drew together as he came back.

"What's the matter?" queried Notus. "Why did you stop?"

"I'm...I'm not going there," said the boy, huskily, shaking his head. Lifting the buck off his shoulders, he let it drop with a dull thud to the ground.

Notus stared down at the corpse and then back up at his

Chosen, a contemplative frown pulling at the corners of his mouth. "I thought that you would like to visit Tarian and see how she and her baby are doing since you are the one who rescued them."

The boy's eyes met the monks, but it was his turn to look away. Did he want to see Tarian? He did not know. A part of him was concerned and would like to visit, but not if it meant going to this place of strangers. Strangers equalled harm. He shook his head.

Feeling exposed as if many eyes were upon him, he glanced back at the village and saw a figure staring in their direction. A new wash of fear rolled over him and he turned to flee back into the safe embrace of the woods. It was only when he noticed that Notus had not followed that he stopped to turn around. Beyond the trees he saw the robed man huff, shake his head and follow, obviously annoyed by the situation.

He waited until his Chooser caught up before turning back the way they had come but the hand on his arm arrested his movement.

"Alright, you don't want to see Tarian and her baby," commented Notus. The boy opened his mouth to protest, but Notus' raised finger making the words disappear before a breath could be taken so as to speak them. "But we do have business that needs to be taken care of, and that means going to that village there."

"Wha—what business?" Horrified the boy could barely speak.

Notus walked to stand under a lone oak and motioned the boy to follow. "Sit," he commanded and the boy did so, worry washing over him. Notus knelt down before him. "Did you think I was traveling these parts just for the sake of it? Did it never occur to you where I came from and where I was going?"

The boy shook his head. White tendrils of hair floated in front of his face to be pushed back with a pale hand. It was never something he really gave much thought to.

Brown eyes bore into his. "I was on my way to Ynis Witrin, to the new monastery there, delivering the beginnings of their library. Now, since meeting you, I have to go to Londinium and you are going to have to come with me. I cannot have you meeting the Elders in that." Notus tugged at the worn doe hide kilt the boy wore. "You need some proper clothing and to do that we have to go into the village."

At first the words made no sense, they did not seem real, almost as though spoken in another language and then the meaning seeped in. Notus wanted to take him away! He wanted to expose him to others! Panicked, the boy slowly rose to his feet, his back against the rough bark of the tree, shaking his head over and over. It went against everything Auntie had taught him.

A cool hand grasped his trembling arm as if to calm him, but he brushed it away as he turned to find the path that brought them here, but stopped at the pressure on his forehead.

"I can't," he panted over and over.

Then Notus was there, suddenly standing above him. Somehow he was on his knees.

"Breathe." Notus' cool hand touched the back of his neck. "Just focus on your breath."

"I—I…can't." The sense of panic grew. His heart beat thunderously in his temples.

"Oh dear. Listen to me, my son." Another cool hand guided his face and it took a moment to register Notus' worried expression. "You can't live in that cave alone for the rest of your life. And a long life it will be. It is your choice whether you choose to simply exist or to truly live. You've existed for too long. It's time to live. I hope you choose life for life is magical, mysterious and a never-ending adventure.

"The world changes and grows and to live in it, you have to change and grow. If you stay, to exist alone, one day you will be discovered. Existence alone is not living. You cannot let your fears rule you. Not everyone is a bad person. There are many good people out there."

The boy could only shake his head and glance away for a brief moment before Notus brought him back to face him.

"Yes, there are good people out there. After nearly five hundred years I would imagine I have a pretty good grasp on such things." A smile lightened Notus serious expression. "And I do know that you have the courage to face your fears or you would never have stepped up to save Tarian and her baby."

"That was different," said the boy in a shaking voice, trying to excuse himself.

"No. It wasn't." The boy could tell Notus was adamant in his belief, if only he could have even a partial amount of that belief. He managed to swallow down some of his anxiety.

"Now, come on." Notus lifted him to his feet and on wooden

legs went with him to the edge of the wood. "Do you see that house on the furthest edge of the village? The one in front of that large pen? That is where we are going. Alright?"

The house in the distance was a little larger than many of the others, but its location marked it as being separate, yet part of the community. It was definitely much larger than the home he grew up in. Heart pounding in his chest, the boy worried his lip and glanced down at the monk. "I don't know."

"It will be alright. I'll be right beside you," Notus said with a comforting smile.

The boy looked back at the village and the home. If Notus believed it was safe… He took a deep shaking breath and realized that he was willing to take this leap and finally solidify his trust in this man who seemed to care so much for him. "Okay."

The wooden door to the stone house was weather worn. In the centre, near the top, hanging by a single nail, sprigs of green accented the colourful array of picked flowers, bringing a sense a beauty to the dingy grey door.

The boy stood back and off to the side. He could not believe he let himself be talked into coming and he hugged himself in an effort to get his trembling under control. Every instinct in him told him to run, to escape. Instead, he watched Notus raise his right hand to knock three times. Each knock thundered in his ears. The sound alone was enough to make him take a step back to flee, but he caught himself in time to hear a faint voice welcome them to enter.

Notus turned his head to face him with a small encouraging smile. "Ready?"

A new bolt of terror washed over him. If there was ever a time to back out, he had passed it. The single nod of his head was lie enough. Catching his breath as Notus opened the door, he bent and followed the monk out of the night and into another world.

His first sight was of the stone fireplace nestled along the northern wall. Its warm yellow light near blinded him as he stood to his full height inside the house, knocking his head on one of the lower beams of the rafters. His eyes adjusted quickly and he could see the opulence of the place. He had never seen a fireplace before, and the cauldron and other cooking utensils were all blackened iron. The posts arranged throughout the home were decorated in colourful paintings of hart and hind, raven and heron, salmon and frog, bear and boar. Green serpents undulated their way between them, enlivening the home with a pulsating energy that cried out of the sacred. Overhead beams hung with every manner of herb and flower and root.

The eastern wall was home to a large round table and curved benches to match. The polished wood gleamed in the dancing firelight, giving the wood a reddish glow.

The western part of the home was blocked off with rich tapestries of woven wool. There were no distinct shapes, but every colour the boy had ever seen was woven into the drapes that divided the sleeping quarters from the living ones. Blues mingled and melded into green. Reds, yellows and oranges clashed magnificently with the purples and browns. The whole home was alive and the boy could feel it thrumming through him the same as when he had worshipped the Old Gods with Auntie.

He caught Notus glancing at him, a smirk lifting his thin lips. "We're here, just like I promised," Notus called out.

"I'll be right out," came a soft feminine voice behind one of the tapestries. It was a voice that carried the implied strength of silk. The hangings fluttered at the homeowner's movement. "I was just feeding Beti so that Tarian can rest when you knocked." The drapes parted. "I hadn't expected you so—Oh my dear Goddess!"

The woman before the tapestries stood in stark reflection to the boy as they stared at one another.

The boy closed his mouth and swallowed audibly. He had never before seen such a beautiful woman, but then again, he had very little to compare against.

In the gloaming firelight, her raven black hair hung long and straight, down over her full rounded breasts outlined in the cornflower blue tunic, to hang over a slim midriff. What captured the boy were her large, intense dark eyes in a face as pale as milk. The brown of the irises were so dark as to almost make it impossible to make out where the pupils started and she did not avert her eyes. There was something oddly familiar there and it was he who finally looked away, suddenly embarrassed at her scrutiny. He ignored Notus confused expression.

"By the Gods, I don't believe it," she said as she approached, intent on examining him.

Uncomfortable at the attention, the boy took a step back only to have the rough stone wall press against his back. This time he did look to Notus, his eyes crying out his panic, and this time the monk came to his defence.

"Eira," stated Notus as he slid smoothly between the two, "this is the young man I told you who saved Tarian and her baby."

As if snapped out of a dream, the woman shook her head, blinked, and then did something that nearly made the boy melt—she smiled.

"So, you are the one." Her brown eyes danced in the firelight as her smile brightened. "You are most welcome in my home."

Not knowing what to say in response, the boy glanced to Notus.

The monk, who stood a half head shorter than the dark haired beauty, touched her lightly on the elbow. "Thank you. Your hospitality is greatly appreciated."

"We follow the old laws of hospitality. Of course you are welcome." She turned from Notus and took a couple of steps to the hearth where the cauldron hung from an iron hook, sending wafts of something cooking through the air. "Would the two of you like something to eat or drink, perhaps?"

"Thank you. No." replied Notus with a warm smile. "We have already supped."

"So it's down to business, then?" The graceful arch of her dark eyebrow lifted.

"If you do not mind, my dear, we do not want to keep you up too late."

Eira nodded and then held out her hand to the boy. "Come here to the table."

Confused and uncertain as what to do, the boy looked to Notus for guidance. At the monk's nod, the boy hesitantly stepped away from the wall of the house but did not take the offered hand. He was very aware of her sad smile before she nodded. It was then that he noticed the strands of multicoloured wool that were laid out on the round wooden table.

Noticing the concerned look on his face, Eira picked up the longest one, a piece of yarn the colour of dark oak. "I'm going to take your measure for the clothes Father Notus wants made for you, and by the looks of it, you are in sore need of them."

The boy quickly glanced down at his doe hide tunic and kilt. A rush of warmth ran to his face at the sight of their stained and shabby appearance.

"If you don't mind, Eira, my dear, I'd like to check on Tarian while you measure the lad." Notus walked over to the draped off section of the home.

"No, please. Go right ahead," replied the woman, her attention momentarily diverted from the young man standing tall before her. "I gave Tarian a sleeping draught earlier so I doubt you'll disturb her. I know she would have been happy to see you, but I felt it best for her to get as much rest as possible."

"Thank you, my child," Notus said with a smile and a nod of his head before disappearing behind the fabric and before the boy could protest at being left effectively alone with Eira.

Eira's brown eyes turned back onto the boy and the corner of her mouth lifted in a smile. "Shall we begin?"

Trapped and unknowing what to do, the boy stood there making every effort not to look into her deep, dark eyes and started at her touch.

"This won't hurt one bit." She brought her strings to work, first taking his height from neck to foot, then from clavicle to waist. Her proximity lifted her scent to his nostrils. He could smell the essence of flowers mingled with the sweetness of milk and sweat. Her touch on his skin burned and it took every ounce of resolve not to flinch or move away from the process, but for some reason he did not want to disappoint her.

"Have you ever been measured for clothes before?" she asked, bringing the yellow coloured string to measure him from the nape of his neck to his wrist. She was pressed close to him, standing face to face, or nearly as possible since he was well over a head taller than she. Her breath smelled of beef, wild garlic and herbs, but underlying it all was the spellbinding scent of her blood coursing through her veins.

He shook his head.

She took her hands away and stood back, making a knot in the string before laying it back on the table and picked up the orange length of yarn.

"You don't say much, do you?"

He gasped as she knelt before him and wrapped her lily-white arms around his waist. Her body's heat radiated into his and he began to feel himself stir.

"Steady." She held him firm and quickly took his measure.

Still kneeling, she drew her arms back, made a knot and

glanced up. "I guess you don't," she said, a twinge of sadness marking her voice. Looking back up, their eyes locked and he saw her brow lift again as she half smiled. "Now don't move. I need to measure your legs."

Snow white brows drew together then rose in alarm as Eira used the same orange thread to first measure the length from his hip joint to his foot. He nearly fled the house when she held him in place and measured him from crotch to foot. Mortified at what she must be able to see, he turned his face from gazing down at her and noticed his Chooser standing by the multicoloured curtain, a big goofy grin slicing his face in two, obviously enjoying the torment placed upon his Chosen.

Eira stood and placed a hot hand on his arm. "One last measurement and we are done," she smiled. "Though I do have to admit it's been quite some time since I've received such a complement from one who has come to me for my arts."

Slowly, her words dawned on the boy and he felt another heat rush to his face as he looked away. Her laughter tinkled through the air. He stepped away, embarrassed but was again halted, as her grip on his hand became firm before falling away.

"Oh, no, you don't," she said slyly. "I have to measure you for boots."

She turned away and brought over a worn piece of hide and knelt before him. She patted his slender hip in a manner to comfort and reassure him, and asked him to place one bare foot and then the other on the hide as she used a piece of charcoal to draw a black outline around each foot onto the hide. The measuring completed, she stood gracefully and tilted her head with a half grin on her face.

Notus pulled back the kaleidoscopic tapestry that separated living and sleeping quarters. "I have never met such a fine healer as you, Eira." Tension flowed as he suddenly felt the intruder up- on an intimate interlude and he raised a questioning brown brow.

The boy took the opportunity to step safely away from the woman who stirred up unknown emotions, refusing to take his eyes off his Chooser. He did not have any desire to see what reaction Eira may have to Notus' entrance and not knowing whether to be grateful for the interruption or furious at having been placed in the situation, red eyes bored into brown.

"Well, um—" Notus broke off eye contact chagrined and turned to face the lady of the abode.

Saving everybody from the unusual awkwardness, Eira moved away from the table as she laid the boot measurements on it, wiped her hands and smiled.

The door to the home burst open, allowing a gust of wind to sweep across the carefully swept floor and into the fireplace, enticing the flames into an ecstatic dance that flamed the room in vibrant light. The unexpected intrusion turned all three's shocked and surprised attention to the figure consuming the opening.

The lumbering figure in the doorway stepped into the light. "I *knew* it!" he slurred, pointing accusingly at Eira, before bringing a hateful eye upon the white youth standing by the hearth. A sneer lifted to reveal yellow rotted teeth, which accentuated the slashing scar across his face.

"Huw, get out!" Eira met the man's venom. "Get out, NOW!" The house reverberated with dark and foreboding energy.

The whole scene seemed to play in slow motion. He could not believe whom he saw. Memories from the night of Auntie's murder and the man across the blaze flared into his mind, evoking the old fears to flee, but there was nowhere to run.

Ungainly, Huw stepped further into the home, sneering at Eira, his face twisted and ugly with hatred. "When Garem came running into the Hall, frightened that he saw Gwyn ap Nudd at the forest's edge, I knew that you had something to do with this, woman."

"You're a buffoon, Huw." Eira stepped forward to intercept her cousin from his attempt to get to her guests, but was stopped by a young girl darting out from behind the tapestry to clutch at her mother, crying up for comfort. With a whisk of her arms Eira reached down and settled the child on her hip, hugging and patting the girl in an attempt to sooth and calm, all the while glaring at Huw.

Red eyes flickered from intruder to mother, fear trickled into a transformative fire, igniting a long past memory. Here was the man that not only killed Auntie, but he was the boy who had wielded the wooden sword in the glen. Notus had brought him into his worst nightmare, one he could not wake from.

His eyes sparked with anger banked by the all the injustices he had suffered—the loneliness, the hunger, the desolation—caused by this man's, and his ilk's, hatred.

Time became protracted. The sound of a baby's wail became a siren song.

Flickers of light from the hearth no longer danced, but rather stood stationary as if expectant to the next moment.

Yesssss...NOW!

The boy agreed, uncaring of the fact that the voices came again while awake and in the presence of Notus. Before the flames could shift position for a better view of the scene unfolding before it, the boy held Huw against the stone wall, white hand pinning him under the chin so as toes dangled and scratched the earth.

"Murderer," hissed the boy as he angled the man's head to the side, exposing a rapidly pulsing artery. The smell of terror and sweat mingled with, but did not over power, the intoxicating effervescence of the blood beneath the unwashed skin. Ignoring the incessant pulling of his side to dislodge his childhood tormentor and the strange elongating shouts, the boy slowly brought his mouth to his immobile feast.

Fulfill the covenant! The voice cried out victoriously.

"GWYN!"

The sound of the name pushed into his mind and snapped reality back, and the boy jerked away, his revenge incomplete.

Noooooooooooooooooo!

Before him stood Huw, hacking and holding his bruised neck, a pitiful excuse for a living creature. The fear had evaporated. The anger subdued. All that remained was disgust that such a creature could be allowed to exist. Turning away from the nauseating sight, he found Eira staring in shock, and worse, Notus fumed. Before anyone could say a word, the boy turned and departed the warm hostile house to the cool inviting forest.

Quick to cover up and clear the disaster the night had turned out to be, Notus went over to the injured man and laid a hand on his hunched over back. "Are you all right, my son?"

"Of course not!" cried Huw, his rough voice bringing upon another bought of coughing. Brushing off Notus' concern, Huw managed to stand up, his face full of fury at having been humiliated in front of the woman he always wanted and the priest.

"That creature is DEAD!" he exploded in venom. The wails of the children ignored. "Tomorrow morning I'm going to get a hunting party together and we'll scourge the whole area of its kind!"

Notus blanched and quickly blocked the doorway before Huw could leave. He had to do something, and fast, before the situation became even more unsalvageable. Despite his own fury at his Chosen, he had to protect the boy. Making contact with bloodshot heavyset brown eyes, Notus locked their eyes together and spoke to the man's heart and soul, pressing his own energies along the rivers of blood into the man's mind. "You will do no such thing."

All thought and will escaped Huw as he was forced to do the priests bidding. Some part of him cried out in defiance, but that too succumbed to the power of the Priest's will until all he could do is stare slack-jawed and round eyed at the Father.

Noticing his complete capture of Huw's attention, Notus pressed his advantage. "You will leave here, Huw, and remember nothing of tonight's transgressions. It will only be a blackened out memory of a night filled with too much drinking. Go back to your bed. Forget everything after you left the hall."

Notus cleared the door as a yawn split the man's head. Huw stumbled from Eira's home without looking back.

When the intruder was out of sight, Notus slowly and carefully swung the door closed and went to sit at the table, exhausted from all that had transpired. He watched as Eira settled her daughter back into the bed they shared and then went over to the crib where two huddled masses mewled for comfort. Placing a long fingered hand upon the two babies, she shushed them back into silence and stood up. Notus could see the toll of the conflict in her drawn face as she came to sit opposite to the Priest.

"I'm so sorry, Eira," apologized Notus as he ran his hand over his face to land his chin on his palm supported by the table. "If I had ever thought to bring such discord into your home I would never have come."

Eira reached out to touch her friend's hand lying limply on the table. "It wasn't your fault, Paul. It was ours. No...I don't mean yours. I mean mine and Huw's." A sad smile lifted her lips.

"That doesn't make any sense." Notus pulled his hand back and straightened up. "If I hadn't asked you for the clothes, and if I hadn't brought the boy..."

"No, Paul," said Eira firmly, "we can play all the what-if's we wish, but in the end the Goddess brings about the truth no matter how much we wish it to be buried in the past."

"I don't understand your meaning."

Uncomfortable with the idea of breaking a decade's old

secret, Eira stood and began to pace. "I've seen him before, Paul. A long time ago when I—we were still innocent, Huw, Rhys, Glenys and I. Rhys and Glenys have long since passed into the Summerlands, but Huw and I remain with our horrible secret."

Something from a conversation he had with the boy early on in their partnership rushed forward into the present. "He mentioned something about being found when he was a child. He barely came out alive. Was that you?" Notus could not believe that Eira could be capable of such violence.

Long straight dark hair swished back and forth in confusion and she looked into Notus' eyes, her own sad and imploring. "Huw was the one who wouldn't let him go when he was discovered and ran. Huw was the one who hit him. Huw was the one who used his waster to hit the side of his head. But it was all of us who left him there to die; a secret to take to our grave." Tears ran down her soft, flawless cheeks.

"But how could you know the boy is one and the same?"

She sighed and sat down opposite to Notus. "Because, there is no one like him, Paul. No one. I recognized him the instant he came over my threshold. I'm just glad to see he survived."

"No matter that, my daughter, he shouldn't have—"

Eira cut Notus off with a slash of her hand. "You're right. The laws of hospitality were broken, but Huw had no right to do as he did either. In any case," she brought her hand back down to the table and stared at both of them, "I do not begrudge him his reaction."

Silence filled the void between them until Notus stood up. "Are you still willing to make the clothes for the boy?" he asked hesitantly.

"Oh, yes," Eira looked up, nodded and smiled. "It is the least I can do for all that I have brought upon him."

"Thank you." A weight relieved itself from Notus' shoulders. "When will they be completed?"

"At the first harvest festival after the first harvest full moon. I believe it's what you call the autumn equinox."

"That soon?"

Eira nodded her head.

"What do you wish in payment? You know I do not own possessions or carry money." Notus opened his hands palm up.

"I know," stood Eira as she moved to stand beside her friend and took his cool hands in hers. "Just two things."

"Just two?" Notus smiled inquisitively.

"Just two," smiled his friend. "Tell me how you met him and anything else you can, and, if he's anything like what the people here are saying about him, meat to last the winter."

Notus nodded in agreement and then grew confused. "What are they saying about the boy?"

Eira's eye's shown with excitement. "That he's the Horned Hunter, Gwyn ap Nudd, returned to us at the time we need Him most by heralding the return of the Old Ones."

Taken aback at the bluntness of her belief, Notus realized that it was Eira who shouted the God's name, and it was that name that broke the boy away from feeding on Huw. Taking a deep breath, Notus licked his lips and realized a new burden upon his shoulders. Without another word he left Eira's home and entered into the dark of midnight, wondering what he would find when he got back to the cave.

XÍÍÍ

he warm rainfall had plastered long ivory hair to his face, neck, bare shoulders and back as the young man walked, heedless of where he went. He stalked the woods far enough away from the cave and the hamlet so as to hopefully not be noticed by anyone.

Fuelled by anger still smouldering after nearly two turnings of the moon, he ignored the sounds and sights around him, ones that normally he would have been in awe of with his newfound abilities. Tonight, as with all the previous ones before it since being brought to Eira's, the resentment exposed him raw to the elements.

It was easy to be angry with the monk who had changed and subsumed his life, but it was being confronted with his past and the blatant evidence of why he had always been hidden by Auntie, that did not allow him to forgive the man who now called him son.

Meeting Eira had been the only highlight of the event. She was beautiful with her long straight nearly black hair and eyes large and brown to match. Her touch intoxicated and confused him, and a part of him was still upset with Notus for having left him alone with the woman to check on Tarian, but it was being brought into direct contact with the man who killed Auntie and recognizing him to be the child who had changed his existence in the glade that sparked the anger afresh.

Oh how he wanted to take his revenge, to sink his teeth into Huw's neck and take his life. Even all that was denied to him with the snap of the God's name. Never before had he felt so relieved to be out of anyone's presence as he fled Eira's home.

It took no time with his new abilities to find himself back at his cave, and he remembered that it was *his*, not Notus'. Seeing the monk's bedding, it reminded him of the trap he had been led into it and without further ado started throwing the musty hides out of his cave with every intention to stock them in the cart. He did not care about what Notus' wanted anymore. That strange man had not improved his life, only complicated it and brought him into more danger, regardless of the excuses Notus seemed to come up with.

He had been so focused on his fury and the clearing out of Notus' things from his cave that he had not noticed when Father Paul Notus appeared at the entrance. The shorter man's cough spun the younger around and they faced each other across the darkened space alight with reflected moonlight off the inner walls. Enraged crimson eyes matched hazel until the shorter broke away, allowing the boy to return to the removal of Notus' possessions.

With an armful of hides, the boy rudely shouldered past the monk and dropped his bundle on the grass outside. Ignoring Notus' query about what was going on, he turned, without acknowledging the man's presence, and returned to the back of the cave for another armload. It was only when an unyielding hand grasped his arm, freezing him in place, that he heard the words repeated.

"I asked you: what you were doing?" It was unmistakably clear that Notus too was more than annoyed.

Shrugging out of the grip, the young man glared down at the monk, allowing more of the bedding to fall forgotten to the sandy floor. A tense silence filled the cave with promised violence as they glared at one another. Jaw tightening, he realized that he was shaking with unspent fury and turned to leave. If Notus would not leave, then he would.

"Are you just going to keep running away?" hollered Notus, following quickly.

He spun around to face his maker. "Just leave me alone!"

"So you can sit in your cave forever?" Notus came to stand almost a hair breath away, glaring up at the one he had broken his

Oath on. "Afraid of life, forever? Is that what you truly want?"

This time the intensity of the monk's piercing gaze made the young man's eyes drop as he turned away to flee once more.

"Oh no you don't." Notus grabbed the younger man with the force of strength his centuries provided him and spun the boy around until he was forced to sit on the ground. Without releasing his grip, Notus crouched in front of the boy. "Listen to me."

The boy tried to pry the iron grip of his maker off his arm and failed. The pain was a warning of the fact that had Notus wanted to he could snap the boy's arm in two with just a little more pressure if he tried to move. Realizing defeat, he could only glare at the man.

"I'm sorry that things turned out the way they did at Eira's," stated Notus, remorse mixed with the firmness of anger checked. "How was I to know that Huw was going to come calling and that he was the one who beat you when you were just a child?"

Shocked at the knowledge Notus held about him, the boy hissed, "I never told you that."

"No, you didn't," angrily replied the monk before his Chosen could fabricate another reason to fault him with. "Eira did. She was also at the glade that day, and after you left she told me about it as if to excuse your behaviour for breaking the Guest laws and attacking Huw."

Eira had been there too! That's why she looked vaguely familiar. Notus had brought him into his nightmare, but Eira had been so nice to him, had she not? Realizing that Notus' grip on him had lessened, he managed to yank free and stand up.

"And did she tell you that it was Huw who killed Auntie?" he hissed, anger flaring.

At least Notus had the wherewithal to look startled and then his face softened, as did his voice. "I'm so sorry."

It was the heartfelt apology of his Chooser that halted the boy from attempting to leave again. He wanted to blame this man for everything that had gone wrong, but found it difficult for all the good things he had brought. The anger, lessened, still simmered, but this time at himself.

"Do you still wish to be alone?" asked Notus, quietly.

The question cut him more painfully than a knife would have. Shoulders slumping, he shook his head, the realization brought unshed tears to his eyes.

Notus came to stand next to him and offered a sad smile. "I'm glad. We will leave here come the fall. When we do you will have new clothes. Eira still wishes to make them for you, as her own apology for the past—I think. In the mean time, dawn is approaching and we best be safe out of its touch."

Notus led them back to the cave where he sighed and began remaking his bed with the help of his Chosen. Once it was completed and the first turnings of the sky that promised another hot summer day began, they snuggled into their respected bedding and prepared to sleep. It was then that Notus explained the payment for the clothes and how it was to be delivered. The boy inwardly seethed at how he was being forced into the rest of the world.

"One last thing, my son," said Notus, "You are to *never* ever feed in front of a mortal. If you think that your past differences have caused you such turmoil in your life, doing such will end it, understand?"

The boy felt a sharp pain centred on his forehead and nodded, glaring at the monk as he rubbed away the pressure.

Two moons passed and he was still angry at himself and at Notus, but mostly because his life was changing and it scared him. Soon the clothes would be ready and Notus would take him back to Eira's to face her once again, but this time with the knowledge of who she was. No longer could he hide from her. Not even the animals they hunted and killed in payment brought him in contact with her when they deposited them either in the slaughter shed, or, if he were without Notus and someone was coming out of their home, wherever he dropped it, before returning to the forest.

He did not relish the idea of having contact with anyone from the village. He did not understand why he and Notus could not stay in the cave and not travel to unheard of places.

The rain turned to a light drizzle, changing rivulets into pregnant beads of water across his body. Wearing only the kilt due to the late summer's heat, he ignored the slapping of the branches across his skin as he traversed an ill-defined animal track into a bramble filled with gorse.

Cursing his mindless heeding of what the forest had been telling him, the boy found himself pricked, head to sole of foot as he turned around to escape what he should have never gotten into had he been paying proper attention. The smell of his own blood winked in and out of existence as each thorny branch jabbed holes through alabaster skin, creating ruby jewels before the wounds quickly closed, allowing for others to take their place.

Almost out of the thicket, the sound of a stick cracking halted him to stone stillness. It was the sound of a deep-throated snort that brought a new fear and tightened the boy's chest as he reached for the hunting knife that was not there. Damning himself for a fool, he searched the night for the source of the sound, but even with his new gifts of night vision he could not penetrate the dense foliage.

Cautiously taking another step out of the gorse brought a grunt of pain as he stepped onto another fallen bramble. A squeal and the crashing of leaves and wood responded. Too late in the realization that he had blundered onto a boar's nest, the boy felt himself crash to the ground. A cry tore from his lips as the boar tore into him, ripping the skin and rending muscle of his thigh.

Panic gripped in the waves of blinding pain, the boy barely managed to catch onto the fleshy folds behind the boar's ears and with the strength imparted to him by his new nature he grasped the enraged beast. With a sobbing heave he yanked the creature out of his ruined groin, pulling another bellow of agony from his being. A sudden twist of the great beast's head and the night filled with a popping sound that was rewarded by presence of the boar's dead weight on the boy.

In pain, all he could do was lie there, suddenly grateful that he was now Chosen otherwise he would be dead. Agonizingly, he heaved himself up onto his elbows so that he could finally take a view of the creature as he tried to extricate himself from its corpse.

The boar was huge, heavy and judging by the length of the bloodied tusks and how they curled into spirals, it was old. It had lived long on its strengths. Pushing the beast off of him with a grunt, the boy's head swam in pain as he contemplated the deep gash in his inner right thigh. His own blood smell filled the night air.

As if by magic, he watched as muscle began to knit together with muscle, sinew to sinew, and gradually skin to skin until all that remained was a redness and tenderness to the area. Pain diminished into a dull ache until the only evidence that remained of the attack was the tattered kilt that left more leg exposed to the elements and the dead boar beside him.

At this rate, he would have nothing to wear and he sighed, reminded of the clothing Eira was making for him and his payment due. Tentatively, he bent his legs to get them under him. Rewarded by only a slight twinge, he stood and breathed a sigh of relief that he did not topple over.

Gazing down, he welcomed the sky as it released its torrent, heavier than at any other time in the night. Broken leaves and sticks washed down and over him, mingling with red to pool around his bare feet. Pulling his fingers through long tangled hair released more debris until his hair provided a cloak to his back as he carefully crouched to take stock of the boar laying prone in the path.

He could not consume its blood. To do so would be his death sentence. Grateful that he had fed earlier he could ignore the light hunger pains his blood loss caused, but he did not revel in the thought that he should take the meat to Eira's hamlet. He preferred to go with Notus or not at all. Unfortunately, it would be a waste of this great beast's life to be left to decay in the forest when so many others could benefit from its meat.

A flash of distant sheet lightning illuminated and exposed the yellowed curling tusks. The boy stared at them and at the boar. If it had not been for being Chosen he would have been dead to his own self defeating anger, and the strangest of feelings came unbidden.

Did our paths cross so that you could teach me a lesson? he thought and was answered by a prickling at the back of his neck accompanied by the low rumble of thunder. For the first time in two months the boy felt ashamed for having placed his anger upon a man who obviously cared deeply for him, and upon himself for his continued allowance of old fears to drive him. He allowed his angers to wash away in the downpour until all that was left was himself and the gift of the boar.

With two fingers to his lips and then to the boar's brow he gave a silent thanks to its spirit for the lesson learned and the self-forgiveness it had given him. Lightning flashed again, this time giving the tusks an iridescent glow and he knew that the spiralled bones were a gift to him. Without his knife, but with his strength, he carefully ripped them out of the skull so as not to break them. Thunder met as the final tusk was released.

Under the brilliance of the night, the boy could see they made natural bracelets and with great reverence to the gift he was given, placed one onto each wrist before hoisting the boar onto his shoulders. He would go to Eira's and give it as a gift so that the boar's wisdom would be carried to others, and not just to himself.

The clap of thunder far overhead masked his first steps towards the village.

The thunderstorm had mostly past by the time the canopy of dripping trees relinquished the night to expose the boy to the hamlet in which Eira lived. He had not seen her since that first meeting, and even though a part of him now wanted to see her again, there was still a larger part that was glad he lived in the night. Silence reigned over the village, to which he was grateful. All he could see was the heavy silver smoke lifting out of the chimneys of the roundhouses, only to fall to the ground and mingle with the rising mist. Burnt wood, ash and the metallic scent of the rain washed earth mingled in the smells of night, over riding the deep earthy fragrance of the woods.

Noticing the stillness of the village, and of Eira's home in particular, the boy easily picked out the round shed that was for butchering, which happened to be connected to the covered pen where several cows sleepily chewed. If he could get to it, drop off the boar and be welcomed back into the embrace of the forest before anyone could take notice, he would be pleased, and he headed out of the protection of the foliage.

He crossed the open expanse without incident and stopped next to the shed. Easily hoisting the carcass off his shoulders, the boar landed with a heavy thud, leaving him feeling naked to the sky without the protection of the foliage the woods readily provided. Pleased with his benefaction, he turned to leave and go back to the cave, and to Notus.

"Don't go," implored a small voice from the covered pen.

The smell of the night mingled with the scent of the boar must have prevented him from noticing the young girl in the separate shed. Tension encircled his chest as she stepped out into the light rain. Not well equipped to guess the age of others, he could only imagine she was about four or five. Her long brown wavy hair glistened with pearlescent raindrops as she stared up with large brown doe eyes ringed with thick long lashes.

"Where's Father Paul?" she asked, looking around into the night, seeing nothing but darkness. "I thought he usually comes to leave the meat."

Mouth dry, he replied huskily, "He's praying," and turned to leave. It unnerved him that even a young child could make him feel so self-conscious.

"Oh," she replied softly, obviously disappointed, and then hesitantly, "Will you stay with me while I milk the cows?"

Stunned at the request, he turned and took stock of the little girl before him. For the first time in his life, someone he had never met offered no fear nor trepidation at his presence, nor the threat of violence. Eyes ephemerally touching, he was more comfortable gazing at her mud encrusted bare toes peeking out from the bottom of a grey woollen robe obviously too large for her slim frame.

He so desperately desired to disappear into the late night where the darkness would be his refuge, but the hopeful look on the girl's face obliterated his fear and he nodded.

"Oh, wonderful!" Her voice took on the air of singing bells as she brightened, obviously having expected the worst. She grabbed his pale hand in her sun darkened one as she led him into the pen where a single lantern gave off a bright yellow glow, illuminating the brown milking cows chewing their cuds.

With a stumble at being pulled by one so much shorter than he, he barely managed not to hit his head on the edge of the slanting roof before finding a safe place to sit in the straw. For the first time he was amazed at how a little girl evoked his long hidden desires for acceptance and how much relief he felt in its reality.

A faint smile traced across his face as he watched her pull out a small three-legged stool and a wooden bucket to the nearest cow and began her expert milking. She commenced a litany of the goings-ons' of the little world she participated in. Most of her stories were of her annoyance with a boy named Tegyr.

With the nights becoming longer, dawn was still some time off, and finding a pile of clean hay by the entrance, he took off one of the boar's tusks and began to clean it.

Milk squirted past her strong small hands, filling the bucket slowly. "...and he just started learning to use a sword," she continued. "Of course his Da won't give him one until he can learn not to slice off a toe. Can you believe it?" Her giggle brightened the pen more than the lamp. "Yep, that's what Tegyr did. Took his Da's sword and tried whirling it about. Ma said Tegyr's lucky he didn't slice off something more important than a toe." She broke into peals of laughter that slowly dwindled when she realized no one laughed with her.

At the halt of her delicious giggles, he brought his attention away from his cleaning job, only to bring it quickly back to the straw bed at the sight of her staring at him.

"You don't say much, do you?" Her question was more a statement.

Suddenly uncomfortable with her directness, he continued to buff the tusk so that it would shine. Only the rhythmic beat of milk splattering into the bucket made him distinctly aware that the little girl with brown curly hair observed his every motion in great detail.

"Is that a boars tusk?" she inquired without stumbling in the rhythm of her milking.

Without looking at her, he nodded as he continued to clean the tusk that already gleamed. He started to become uncomfortable at her scrutiny.

She exhaled in amazement. "Wow! Ma says that tusks from a boar are powerful and are to be treasured. Only Chiefs are allowed to wear them. The more they curl the more the power. Did you get it from the boar you brought?"

Splash. Splash.

Again he nodded into the pause, wishing she would return to her narrative rather than focus on him.

"Did you kill it all by yourself?" The milking ceased as her expectation of a possible story caught her young attention.

Quickly glancing up at her, her brown eyes beamed with excitement and he dropped his gaze back down without so much as a nod. He had to get out of there, but was surprised that he did not want to hurt her feelings.

Taking his silence as affirmation, she continued her exuberant story telling as she picked up the milking beat. "That must have been scary. Weren't you afraid—"

"Bronwen, who are you talking to?" came a voice approaching the pen.

Attention snapped away from the polishing, panic rushed in his ears to be followed by a loud crack and pain accompanied by flashes of light and momentary nausea. He could not remember rising quickly to his feet, but it did not matter now that he was crouching and grasping the top of his throbbing head. What he did remember a little too late was that the pen was made for much shorter people.

A hand lighted onto his shoulder. "Are you alright?"

Taking his hand away from the crown of his head, red jewels glittered darkly on his milk white hand before he rubbed it away in the straw.

"Here, let me take a look."

Before he could so much as utter a single syllable of protest, the woman began looking for the wound.

"That's strange," she mumbled after finding none.

Carefully this time, he stood up to find himself staring down at Eira. She was as beautiful and as intimidating as he remembered. He forced himself to swallow as he looked around for an escape, finding it blocked.

The repetitive splashing of milk into the bucket stopped as Bronwen watched in fascination the dynamic unfolding between her ma and the tall, white young man people in the village believed to be Gwyn ap Nudd returned.

Silence thickened the air between the two adults as Eira took stock of the young man's appearance. She had not expected to see him here with her daughter and was not too sure how she felt about that. She had not expected to see him at all until Father Paul said they would come at the harvest celebration. Noting every detail, she frowned at the kilt shredded at the right thigh and the pinkness of new healing skin. Healer's instincts taking over, Eira's face relaxed into concern as she stepped closer for a better look at the once wound and stopped when the tall pale youth stepped back with a thud against the wattle and daub wall.

Heart pounding in his ears, he realized too late the trap he found himself in. This time one of his making, but at least the path to escape was now cleared. He noted the slight tingling, the precursor to dawn, and knew he had to leave, now.

Mistaking his trembling, Eira explained, "I'm not going to hurt you. I just wish to examine your wound."

Quickly taking his gaze off of Bronwen's mother to look down at his thigh, he found it a ragged and red. It felt perfectly fine and thought it was completely healed, as it did not pain him. The sound of her kneeling in the hay was the only precursor to her warm gentle touch on his thigh. Closing his eyes in abject embarrassment, he rested his head against the thatch as he felt her light touch probing the afterthought of the wound.

With years of experience as the area's only healer, and having seen several of similar types of wounds, Eira quizzically commented, "It looks as if you were gored not long ago, but in this placement, you would have died." Brushing her long flowing hair back from her eyes, she stood up and stared into his. "I know Paul well enough to say that he would have brought you to me for healing as this is out of his range of expertise. He doesn't know about this does he?"

Mouth gone dry, he could only stare back, fear flashing, and swallowed. Notus told him what would happen if those not Chosen found out about them, and he had enough experience to know the truth of it.

"What are you?" Her voice fell to an intense whisper, her eyes boring into his.

The question hit too close to a nerve he thought was well walled up, and he turned to escape the pen and those it contained. His progression came to a halt as she grasped his forearm and he turned to face her once more.

Noting his frightened crimson eyes flickering to the wide expanse past the pen to gaze into the forest, sympathy filled her voice. "I'll let you go if you answer my question."

Allowing her to continue her grip on his arm, he searched this tall beautiful woman's eyes for any hint of maliciousness and found none. Still, he could not bring himself to trust her.

"One question," Eira pleaded.

Appraising her, he cocked his head, milk white hair flowed off his back, and he nodded, inwardly hoping that it was the right decision. He would answer her question.

The faint hint of a smile twitched at the corner of her full lips and she breathed a sigh of relief. Maybe she would not have to extract the second half of the payment from Paul. Ever since that time in the grove a lifetime ago, this young man captured her attention like no other and she wanted to know why. "Who and what are you?"

Removing her hand from his arm, he replied. "That's two questions." Relief washed over him as he took a step out of the pen. Sunrise was still a little time away. If he hurried he would make it back with moments to spare.

"Please," she pleaded, following him out into the pre-dawn,

once again catching onto his arm.

Something in the tone of her voice caught him, and he turned. Maybe it was the hurt, but there was a longing easily read even by him. "Why do you want to know?"

This time Eira broke the gaze to land on her hand resting on his arm. In the silence, she moved her hand down his muscled arm, and reaching his hand, and lifted it in hers. Long delicate fingers, belying a greater strength, lined up one against the other. Two hands similar except hers were smaller and sun touched. Intertwining her fingers with his, she tightly clasped his hand.

The warmth of her grasp surprised him. Large ruby eyes shifted from their interlocked hands to meet deep brown eyes. He found himself speaking without realizing. "I do not know what I am." He halted, disturbed by the truth finally spoken aloud. Frowning at their hands, he continued, "As to who I am? I am whom Llawela raised. I am whom Geraint trained. I am whom Notus has made. I am *crimbil* made Chosen."

The litany of names bit at Eira as surely as if he had and she pulled back her hand with a cry of surprise. Half remembered memories, snatches of conversations and reasons snapped into place, revealing the truth her soul felt but never gave thought or feeling to.

"A real changeling!" exclaimed Bronwen.

Having realized they had both forgotten the child in the pen, they both quickly turned their attention to her. Ignoring her inquiry, the young man looked down at the cleaned boars tusk in his other hand and gently placed it into Eira's.

"For the girl," sadness consumed his voice and he turned to leave.

Eira ogled the rich gift, her mouth slack with dumb shock. When she looked up to thank him he was nowhere to be seen. Heart beating faster than it ever had before, Eira clutched the curling tusk to her chest and sank to the ground, allowing tears to flow.

XÍU

The orange moon hung over an eastern horizon clear of clouds and bespeckled with brilliant stars. The light from the heavens illuminated the forest and the village beyond it in a spectacular display of vivid colours to the two standing at the wooded edge. Greens, yellows, reds and oranges of the new turning trees promised a winter not long in coming. Everything was awash in a cold fiery light.

He stood beside his Chooser, staring at the village bustling with the exuberant celebration of a successful harvest. Orange shadowed figures flitted in and around the round houses carrying trays of food, musical instruments and other items to share. The bonfire in the centre competed with the sky in its brilliance. The sound of drums carried the higher pitches of flutes and voices in song. Laughter rang out, filling the night. The noise did nothing to cheer him. Mouth gone dry, he rubbed his hands on his ratty and stained homemade doeskin shirt and let out a huff into the cool, clear night.

It had only been that morning since seeing Eira and her daughter, and he wished more time had passed. Having never been to a harvest, or even a festival, he had no clue as to when such an event would take place and was surprised to find upon waking that Notus would be taking him back for the promised clothes. That would also mean they would soon be leaving his cave for a world unheard of to him.

So many changes in such a little time threatened to crush his chest to take away his breath. Unfortunately, feeding tonight had not provided the sense of freedom it usually did and took away none of the trepidation he felt. He looked down at the monk.

Keenly aware of his Chosen's fear and why, Notus patted the young man's forearm and smiled.

"Just like the first time," he commented jovially, "but this time we go to meet friends."

Giving a curt nod, he audibly swallowed down his fear and desperately hoped that this time would not be like the first. He watched Notus noisily step from the entanglement of the woods, brown robes brushing at his ankles, to make his way to Eira's home. Moving silently out of the wood, the boy quickly caught up to him.

Firelight flared from the huge bonfire, casting dark undulating shapes moving rhythmically around it to the cascading sounds of the musicians. Consumed in their own enjoyment, the villagers were unaware of the two strange outsiders coming to the home of their healer.

"Let go of my arm," whispered Notus.

Not realizing he had grasped his Chooser's arm, he let go with a muttered apology.

"That's okay," replied the monk, rubbing his upper arm. He did not need to see the boy's face, nor read his mind to sense the tension borne from fear, and silently prayed to the Good God that this visit would not end as horrendously as the first.

With the second knock on Eira's old weather beaten door, it opened on hinges squeaking in the humidity of the night air. Eira smiled and bade them enter. The tall young man was more than pleased to be out of plain view of the villagers and was even more surprised to be pleased at the being welcomed back.

The sight of Eira captured his breath and threatened to never release it. Her fine cerulean gown embroidered in white delicate flowers clung tightly on her slim frame, accentuating her soft round features. Abashed to find himself staring, he quickly looked down to the freshly swept and new threshed floor. Her smile was not lost on him as she closed the door behind them and motioned the two to sit by the blazing fire.

Well versed in proper etiquette, Notus graciously accepted the offer from his friend, bowing to her generosity. The boy, on the other hand, continued to stand and played with the single boars tusk on his wrist in the hopes he could disappear.

Noting his discomfort, Eira sighed. A slight frown marred her features for a brief moment before she turned to take the other chair by the fire and flashed Notus a glowing smile. "I'm so please that both of you were able to come. I was afraid that after this morning you wouldn't have. I'm glad that I was wrong."

Notus turned in his seat to glower at his Chosen.

The young pale man had hoped that this morning's incident would remain in the past and had wished not to share it with anyone. Conscious of Notus' disappointment in his secrecy, he abashedly dropped his eyes back to the floor.

With a sigh and a shake of his head, the monk faced their hostess and smiled. "My dear, nothing you could ever do would drive us away." Whatever had transpired between the two of them that morning could be discussed in private with Eira. If the boy had not told him, given the opportunities throughout the early evening, Notus doubted that he would be told now, knowing the young man's predilection for long silences.

Having the good sense to know that he had been chastised for not telling Notus what had gone on that morning, he squirmed uncomfortably, shifting his stance from one leg to the other, gazing only at the dirt floor. He was not used to be accountable to anyone else since Auntie died and the monk made him feel even more self conscious in Eira's home.

Aware of the growing tension, Notus decided a change of topic was necessary. Glancing around the brightly lit home he noticed the tapestry separating living from sleeping quarters were pulled back to make the roundhouse appear more spacious. It also revealed that the three of them where alone except for Eira's sleeping infant son.

"Where is everyone?" asked Notus.

Cheerfully, Eira replied, "Tarian took Beti and Bronwen to the bonfire. I thought it would be best for all concerned." She glanced up at the boy with understanding in her eyes.

Her smile returned and with a clap of her hands the sombre mood dissipated. "But enough of that, you came here for your end of the agreement, though I must admit that you have more than kept up your end of things."

Confused and concerned that there was more going on here than he knew about, Notus asked, "How so?"

"We agreed to an exchange of services, clothing in exchange for meat for the village, not the whole entire region." Her laughter brightened the mood even further. "The extra meat we traded and I think you will like the results."

She stood up and gracefully walked to the back, the white flowered embroidered hem floating around her ankles. "I will need some help here."

Since all of this was for the boy who had nothing, Notus caught his Chosen's eyes with his own and mouthed, "Go help her," and sighed in frustration. He really needed to be able to communicate with the boy as other Chosen communicated with their own.

Glowering incredulously at Notus' order, but daring not to incur anymore of Notus' disappointment he moved reluctantly to join Eira at the back of the roundhouse between the two beds. Beside the wicker cradle housing the sleeping infant sat a large wooden chest, finely carved with knot work and stylized animals similar to the ones carved into the posts of the house. Eira stood beside it and smiled and with some direction they lifted their ends of the chest and brought it before Notus.

Placing it gently on the ground, Eira came over to her helper and whispered her thanks under the surprised whistle Notus let out. Shocked at her sudden closeness the young man tensed and moved away as she turned back to the monk.

"My dear child, this is the most exquisite work I have seen in a very long time," proclaimed Notus.

"I'm glad that you like it," she beamed with pleasure. "It's now yours, or rather his." She brought her smile to the shocked young man.

"What? No. That cannot be." The chair groaned and squeaked as Notus sat back, astonished at the generosity. "This is by far too priceless an item."

"Nevertheless, it is yours, otherwise how else do you expect to carry all the clothes." Unlatching the elaborate lock, Eira lifted the lid. Inside, carefully folded, lay richly tailored clothing fit for a king.

"My goodness," exclaimed the monk as he stood to take a better look at the finery. The boots lying across the clothing were black as night, yet mirrored the flickering light from the oil lamps. Picking them up, he could feel the well-worked cow hide before placing them back down so he could lift up the spectacular indigo shirt embroidered with silver ivy. Amazement filled his eyes as he turned to Eira. "My undying gratitude, my dear, but—"

"But nothing," she interrupted, picking out a pair of dark brown trousers. "The village has accepted your fine gifts of meat, ensuring for the first time in a very long time, that we and the children will not starve for lack of meat this winter. In return we hold to our end of the bargain."

"Eira, my dear friend, I can only thank you for your generosity and bless you in the Good God's name," said Notus, flabbergasted.

"I will gladly receive both." Eira bowed her head reverently then looked at the young man gawking at the clothing made for him. "Come, it's time to change."

Gazing down at his dilapidated kilt, he shyly took the pants and boots from her outstretched hands. Instantly, he recognized the high quality at the feel of the soft leather. Respectfully, he took the shirt from his Chooser, very aware of hazel eyes beaming at him. The silver on the deep purplish blue was stunning and upon examining the stitching he found that it was indeed very thin silver wire held by thread.

"You can go to the back and change." Eira broke his concentration at the fine details.

Never before had he had anything so beautiful. Clothing was meant to be practical, made from whatever materials were easiest to find, at least that was what he and Auntie had to make do with. The richness of the apparel astounded him and made him wary to even wear it for fear of ruining such craftsmanship. Keenly aware that the other two watched him, he took his new raiment to the rear and pulled the tapestry closed, providing a false sense of privacy.

Silence reigned in the house, as Eira and Notus waited patiently for him to change, only to be occasionally broken by sucking sounds coming from the cradle. Slipping out of his stained doe hide shirt, his long milk white hair splayed against his scarred back before being replaced by the soft fine woven wool shirt.

The fit was perfect. Taking off his ruined kilt to be replaced by the trousers was a relief. Though he had never worn clothing such as this, he found them exceedingly comfortable, yet somewhat more restrictive. Using the edge of the bed, he managed, with a little struggling, to pull his boots on before standing to pull back the tapestry, leaving the tattered clothing of his past on the floor.

Eira's eyes widened as she let out a gasp followed by a brilliant smile matched by Notus.

"My son, you look stunning," grinned Notus, before turning to Eira. "My dear, you have out done yourself."

Tearing her eyes off of the transformed young man, Eira sombrely replied, "No, not yet."

She returned to the side of her bed and pulled out from under it a large swatch of heavy cloth with a large glittering bronze clasp lying atop, its artwork of intricate knot work standing out. Gently placing the clasp onto the table, she unfurled a long cloak so deep a green that it was almost black, and at night it was as good as such.

He tried to take a step back as she flourished the cloak to land heavily upon his shoulders, and swallowed at the close proximity of his benefactor standing on tip toes to reach his height. Their eyes locked for the barest of moments before Eira turned to pick up the clasp.

"This used to be my father's," explained Eira as she hooked the clasp through the fabric, linking them at the young man's collarbone and fastening the cloak firmly on his shoulders. "He wore it up until his death a couple years ago. My mother had it made for him when I was just a little girl, before the madness took her." She gazed up into ruby eyes. "I want you to have it now."

Dumbfounded, he tilted the clasp. A double headed dragon connected by a complicated braiding with a pin woven around the dark fabric stared back at him. Something was familiar about it. He had seen it before, but that was not possible. Neither he nor Auntie had anything like this. The only person he had seen wear such as this was—Geraint! The pin belonged to Geraint! His eyes widened at the realization and at the discovery that the woman whose generosity astounded him was Geraint's daughter. Her sad smile blurred through the wash of unshed tears.

"Thank you," he said, hoarsely.

She nodded, her own eyes swimming, and she caressed his smooth cheek. It was the first touch he did not flinch from. "You will always have a home with us."

Unexpectedly the door opened with a crash, dispelling the connection between Eira and the tall pale young man and caused the baby in the cradle to cry.

"Mama, c'mon out, you're missing all the fun." Bronwen bounded into the roundhouse followed by Tarian carrying her swaddled daughter. Tarian halted at the sight of Father Notus standing closest to the door.

"Oh, you came!" Bronwen exclaimed, running to hug the monk.

Tarian's eyes widened at the sight of her saviour and Eira standing between the beds at the back. Closing the door, she had thought she had dreamed that night of the attack and the fairy lord that saved her. Seeing him here in the home of her benefactor, regally dressed, captured her breath. When she remembered to breathe, Tarian found her heart rapidly beating.

Surprised by the intrusion, the young man found he could only stare at the transformed woman he had saved a few months ago. She was shorter than he remembered, but with her face healed from the lacerations and bruises, he could see the soft rounded beauty of her slightly freckled face. Loosely curled chestnut hair floated around her head and past her shoulders. Eira's beauty was borne out of his lack of experience, Tarian's captivated him. Even with her daughter held at her chest, he found that everything and everybody had disappeared in the home except for the two of them.

"What's wrong with them?" Out of the mouth of babes, Bronwen was quick to pick up on the buzzing energies.

Embarrassed and feeling overly exposed, he nervously dropped his gaze to the floor.

"Nothing, my sweet," saved Notus, reading the looks between his Chosen and Tarian, and ruffled Bronwen's thick brown hair. He was pleased that the young man was more at ease and obviously allowing himself to connect to others. It was a good first step. Though what had transpired between his Chosen and Eira was a mystery to him.

Sticking out her tongue as if sick, Bronwen pulled herself from Notus' embrace and declared, "I'm going back to the festival."

"Bronwen," exclaimed Eira, stepping forward to her daughter, Llyr quieting in her arms. "Please remember your manners."

"Sorry mama," muttered Bronwen, abashed.

Crouching down to face her daughter, Eira brushed an unruly lock from the girl's face. "Thank you, sweeting. We'll be out soon." With a kiss on the girl's forehead, Eira patted Bronwen's bottom as she turned and headed out the door.

"Did you want me to watch Llyr?" shyly ventured Tarian once Bronwen had left.

"Thank you, dear." Eira stood and placed the sleeping baby back into his cradle. "That's okay. Father Paul and I have some things to discuss. I can watch Beti and you two can go to the festival." Her eyes swung from Tarian to the pale man.

"That would be nice." Tarian smiled and placed Beti in the same crib as Eira's son. Taking in his full measure, she stated, "Those are the clothes we made for you. You look nice."

Dumbstruck at the number of people around him, and by Tarian's appraisal, he glanced at Notus wondering what to do beside follow his instinct to flee. He was greeted by a smile. Obviously his, Chooser was enjoying himself.

"Would you like to come to the festival?" asked Tarian. She hoped he would say yes. He had said nothing so far and she feared rejection for the first time since she thought her husband would not propose to her. That had been another lifetime and he was buried. He had been a good and gentle man. Not very good looking, it was his heart that mattered to her, but this fairy lord took her breath away and the thought of going to a festival with him was something born of a dream.

Before he could decline, a grinning Notus piped up and answered, "Of course he is, and he will be happy to accompany you."

Eyes widened in surprise, he glared at his Chooser. This had not been in the plans. They were to go, get his clothing and go back to the cave. There was nothing mentioned about going to the festival, let alone without Notus. He opened his mouth to object.

"Then it's settled," declared Eira. "You two, out. Go. Enjoy the festival."

Before he knew what was going on, he was ushered out the door with Tarian. The sound of the door closing with a thud made him distinctly aware of the presence of the villagers. Fear staggered him to a standstill as he watched children darting in and about the festivities. He wanted to run, but was too afraid to move. A touch on his forearm caused him to jump.

"If you put up your hood no one will notice you," Tarian quietly suggested.

Confused, he stared down at her, not exactly sure of what she had said until the words finally sunk in. Pulling the cowl over his head, he found he felt a little less exposed hidden beneath the fabric.

Tarian moved to follow the sounds of boisterous activities around the fire. Realizing that he did not follow, she halted and turned back to stand before him. For someone who was able to fight off several raiders intent on murdering her and her daughter, seeing fear in his large eyes scared her.

"What's wrong?"

Unable to tear his view of the multitudes in celebration, he absently shook his head.

"I can't," he barely whispered, his heart pounding in his ears. "Too many people."

Glancing over her shoulder to the fire and then back to the tall, frightened man before her, Tarian wondered anew at her saviour. There had been such strength in him, but now she only saw vulnerability. She reached and took his hand in hers, causing him to break his trance and look down at her.

"That's okay; we can sit over here, out of the way and watch the festivities."

He allowed himself to be led to a bench set against the side of Eira's home. It was far enough away from everyone that he did not feel conspicuous, but it was still close enough for Tarian to enjoy the night. The bench creaked under their combined weight as they sat, and in the reflected firelight he took full notice of her beauty. Her gown was green and plain, fitting snugly to her young curvaceous form. The flickers from the fire lit up her long hair to a fiery red that brought out the summer green of her eyes.

With a sigh Tarian leaned her head and back against the stone and mud wall, allowing silence to settle between them.

Catching himself watching in fascination at the gentle rise and fall of her chest, he quickly turned his gaze to the festival when he realized he was staring.

"I want to thank you for coming to mine and Beti's rescue," she said quietly, breaking the silence. "I don't remember much of that night, but I do remember how you saved us and for that I am completely in your debt."

He did not know what to say and so said nothing.

"It's been hard. My husband has gone to the Gods. My parents, if they still live, are far to the north. If not for Beti, I would be alone. If not for you, I would be. Now we have a chance for life. Thank you."

He wanted to tell her that he was sorry he had not been there sooner and found that he still wanted to protect her. Hunching over so that elbows rested on his thighs, he stared at his clasped hands and the boar's tusk dangling from his right wrist. Not for the first time he felt the guilt of having watched for so long before stepping forward to help her.

He could feel her eyes on him, but did not return her look, instead he gazed upon the distant blaze allowing the silence to overtake them again. After an unknown time of watching the play between children—Bronwen in the middle of it all, the banter between friends and the passion between lovers—he spoke without realizing and found he could not stop the fall of words.

"All my life I have been hidden away. I could not even watch without repercussions. I don't understand how I can be here now and be accepted."

He felt Tarian press close against him, her heat and scent filling him, warming him, and he sighed as he closed his eyes. She took his hand in hers and laid her head upon his upper arm.

"Do you still feel this way?" she whispered.

"Yes." He leaned back, forcing her to lift her head to look at him. He did not know why he confided in her, but something about her fragile strength captivated him.

"Then we both feel the same way," she said. "I don't think I will ever truly feel safe again."

Suddenly, he realized he wanted Tarian to feel safe again and he wanted to be the one who did it. With a boldness he did not realize he had, he covered her hand with his free one.

"Eira says that you are leaving tomorrow. What if you stayed?" Her summer green eyes glimmered with unshed tears.

"I can't." He pulled his hands away from hers. Oh how he wanted to. The illusion of having a normal life with Tarian was intoxicating yet excruciating to know it could never be. Even had he not been Chosen, he was too different and that would always be a threat.

She stared at the ground in silence as he looked back at the festivities, watching a couple gently caress and kiss each other. Fearful that he was intruding on a private moment he brought his gaze back to his clasped hands and the ivory decorating his wrist. Silently, he slipped it off and placed it in Tarian's lap.

Picking up the majestic tusk, it gleamed in the firelight as she stared in awe. "What is this for?"

"I want you to have it," he replied, sitting up to look at her surprised expression.

"I can't take this." She pressed it back into his hand. "It's too rich a gift."

"It's worthless to me. Please take it." He held it out for her.

She took it from his bone white hand, eyes glued to it, as she slipped it over her hand to dangle from her wrist.

"Thank you," she muttered and went to brush a stray hair from her face. Her hand met his and she looked up into his beautiful crimson eyes.

He had not realized what he was about to do until her hand met his and she allowed him to brush back her hair. It was softer than he remembered, and as he paused at the pale smoothness of her neck he felt a sudden flush of heat. She leaned into the caress and he felt her strong pulse under his fingers pull at him. Her scent crowded out all thought except for her and her face and her full lips. Suddenly, he felt the need to kiss those lips, his fear mounting to new heights.

She leaned forward and he enclosed his lips around hers, her mouth opening to let him enter. He felt her hands reach up to brush back his hood, spilling long white hair around them as the kiss deepened to include an embrace.

Yessssss.

The intensity of the sensuous enjoyment he felt increased as the sound of her heartbeat pounded in his ears. The scent of her blood flooded his mind. He trailed kisses down the side of her neck.

Now!

The throbbing vessel teased and delighted him as he licked and sucked, making her moan under his gentle administrations. He so desperately wanted to break the skin with his teeth and drink in her essence.

Fulfill the covenant!

He was keenly aware of her hands caressing his chest, moving down. Her touch exploded his hunger, calling him to pierce her flesh with his teeth and drink her erotic blood.

Fulfill the covenant...NOW!

"No!" he shouted as he thrust himself away from doing their bidding.

Panting in terror of what he had almost done, he dropped his head into his shuddering hands. He did not want to see the disappointment on Tarian's face. He did not want her to see the terror the voices evoked in him.

"What's the matter?" she implored, pulling back the white curtain his hair made over the side of his face. She could see him trembling to regain control.

"Went too far too fast," he stammered, shaking his head. "This shouldn't have happened." He felt her warm hand caress his face, forcing him to swallow down the rising hunger that leapt at her soft touch, and pulled away.

"But it did," she said softly. "I don't regret it. Please look at me." He turned to gaze sadly upon her beauty. "You saved my life and that makes me yours. Our souls intertwined. I will never forget this, even unto my future lives, until we meet and I return your gift." She sighed and leaned back against the wall.

Baffled by her words, he stared at Tarian, drinking in the sight of her, knowing that what she hoped would never come to pass. Releasing the breath he unknowingly held, he sat back, their arms touching as they watched the festivities, each accepting the solitude together.

He had never heard music before. The drumming, flutes and stringed instruments wove an intricate pattern of sound that titillated him, drawing the faintest of smiles. Closing his eyes, he let the music carry and wash over him. He could almost allow the music to draw him into the circle around the fire, so hypnotic. Instead the sounds drew him out of himself and his worries until all that was left was the music.

The bass beating of the drums throbbed through him as though far and distant. They sang alone, flutes and strings forgotten as the others shouted in exultation. Gradually the drums began their slow crescendo that were met with much louder drumming, their beats at dissonance with each other. Opening his eyes, he noticed that no one was aware of the conflicting sounds. Everyone around the fire had taken to dancing and singing with the music. Closing his eyes, he turned his head, extending his Chosen sensitive hearing and realized the sound he heard was not drumming.

"What is it?" asked Tarian, concerned at his sudden change of behaviour.

He raised his hand, silencing her as he continued to search for the source of the ever increasing drumming. Opening his eyes, he looked out into the night but could see nothing and raised his hood in hopes that to cut out the light from the fire so he could see deeper into the darkness. The shifting of Tarian's body to a stand brought his attention to her wide eyed frozen form.

She whispered only one word. "Horses."

Name finally given to the sound he heard, he stood up and saw them approach. Their cloaks billowing behind them in demon wings, more than a dozen men on horseback rode hard from the north. The musicians, playing at the fire's edge, fell off their notes to allow for the roar of horses hooves. Faces full of happy tidings turned upside down, fear twisting features in stunned horror that raiders would attack at night, let alone during a festival. Women and children's screams and men's shouts crashed into the wave of horsemen leaping into the village.

Without warning a piebald horse bounded in front of him, forcing him back into Tarian who gasped in fright. The man on the horseback glittered in old mail and creaked with worn leathers while the horse's sides heaved and steamed in the cool night air. Brandishing a well-used and sharp sword, the raider brought it to bear at the tall young man's chest. "Move."

Closing the door behind Tarian and the young man, Eira shut her eyes for a moment to gather her strength for what was to come and turned to face her friend.

"Eira, what's wrong?" Notus quickly came to her side, noting her distress, and guided her back to the bench at the table.

Before she could allow him to make her sit, she pulled from his grasp. She had to do this. She had to know. "Where did you find him, Paul?" Her voice shook.

Confused at her sudden change and her question, Notus asked, "Is this the other part of the payment you wished?"

"It's gone beyond that." She shook her head sending long strands of black hair swinging. "Where did you find him?"

There was an urgency to her insistence so strong that it forced him to sit down. With careful editing he told Eira of the night in the forest where he came upon the lad, and finding him alone and living in the cave he decided to take the boy under his wing.

"So you never met him before this spring?" she urged.

"No," he replied, shaking his head, wondering what this was all about. This had nothing to do with her initial belief that he was a returned God of the Woods.

"Did he ever tell you anything about his past?" Her breath quickened and he could hear her heart beat match pace. There was something she wanted to hear that he was not telling her and he did not know what that was.

"Not much in the time we've been together," he cautiously replied.

"Did he ever give you his name?"

"No. Eira. What is this all about?"

Agitated, Eira paced, wringing her hands. She was always so calm and easy going. Seeing her like this worried Notus. He wanted to help her, but he did not know how.

"Did he ever talk about a man named Geraint or a woman named Llawela?" Her brown eyes bore into his searching for any answers he may have.

Taken aback by the first name, Notus could only nod mutely. He had heard the boy talk ever so briefly about a Geraint, but not any woman named Llawela, only the woman who raised him whom he called Auntie. In the expectant silence Notus told Eira this and watched her pale.

Alarmed, he grasped her, afraid she was going to faint, and made her sit. Crouching before her, he placed a hand on her forehead and then to the side of her throat. "Eira, please tell me what is going on."

Eyes threatening to spill over, Eira softly spoke. "Paul, please, whatever I tell you here, please never ever repeat it. Please never tell him for it would only hurt him. Will you swear to your Good God that you will?"

Whatever it was that Eira had to share, hiding it from his Chosen was something he did not think he could do. They would be together for a long time and even now the trust the boy felt for him was tenuous at best. "I can't, Eira."

Her grip on his hands was like steel and her eyes bored into his. "Please," she implored.

Notus could not see her in such pain and nodded, instantly regretting his choice, but was relieved to see her shoulders relax and a glimmer of a smile return to her face.

"Geraint was my father. Llawela was my great aunt. And the young man you brought into my life," she shuddered as she released a sigh, building her strength to finally speak the truth, "is my brother."

"*What?*" Notus rocked back onto his heels and stood up. He could not believe what he was hearing. The boy told him that he did not have parents, let alone a sister. He said that Auntie was a woman who took him in when he was left out as a changeling and raised him out of sight of others. Even Eira had said that she and three others had brutalized the boy when he was younger. What she was saying made no sense and said so.

"Please listen to me," begged Eira. "When I was little, my mother had another child, a boy, who she wouldn't care for because he was too different, too pale. She forced my father to expose him and that was the last I saw of my brother. My mother disappeared one night in the middle of winter shortly afterwards. Her body was never found.

"Several years later, my father was called away to my Auntie. She was old and needed help, he said, and went every fortnight to stay for a few days before returning to us. No one ever suspected anything. He was the Chief and one of the last remaining relatives Auntie had, so naturally he was thought of as exceptionally kind to go and help her.

"What no one else saw was that whenever he came home he was always bruised, and not the kind from doing chores, but rather from practicing the sword. He never said anything, keeping his secrets even from me, but he was happy for the first time in a long time.

"The day he left with my husband, Rhys, to fight with the King, he told me that should a young man of fair complexion come, I should help him.

"I never knew until he came this morning to leave the boar. I asked him who he was and he said, 'I am who Llawela raised. I am who Geraint trained. I am who Notus has made. I am crimbil made Chosen.'"

Notus gasped, his hazel eyes wide. He could not believe what he heard. Everything made sense and fit into the fragments the boy selected to share with him. What he could not fathom was why the boy revealed that he was Chosen. He had been told to keep that secret. Gut turning with a mixture of fear of being found out and anger at the boy, Notus knew he had to see how far the damage extended.

"Do you know what he meant by that," he cautiously inquired.

Eira shrugged her shoulders, releasing the knot between them and sighed. "I can only imagine that Auntie found him when my father exposed him. I don't know what could have convinced her to do that, knowing that children like that were best left to the Fay. She must have raised him in secret because everyone knew she lived alone.

"As to my father fitting into this, I'm not sure, but it somehow feels right. Does he know how to use a sword?" Her brown eyes penetrated.

"I believe so," commented Notus, "but I've never seen him actually properly use one. He made a wooden sword which shattered against a tree after only a move or two."

Her gaze fell back to her hands obviously disturbed by the lack of certainty Notus could give her. "I don't know what he meant by the rest except that maybe because you found him you chose to take care of him."

The tension flooded out of Notus as he breathed a sigh of relief. At least that secret was still a secret. Then he remembered the promise he made not to reveal to the boy his true parentage and family. "Oh, dear God, what have we done?" He sat heavily on the bench beside her.

"I don't know, Paul." Eira took his smaller hand in hers and looked into his eyes. "He can't know the truth, not if you are taking him away. And even if he were to stay, his differences already have others believing him to be the Horned Lord returned. I even thought that at first. Tarian believes him to be her Fairy lord saviour. Huw believes him to be a vengeful being out to destroy the village. My brother would never have a normal life." Sorrow filled her eyes as she broke contact. "Maybe that's why Auntie kept him hidden."

Silence filled the void. Notus had no answer to give. The boy was now in his care, and the secret pressed upon him ate at him until he realized that it was indeed better this way. Many other Chosen had families they left behind. It was that connection to seeing them be born and die and never being a part of it that drove some of them mad. Others saw it as an injustice and allowed hate to grow within them. Maybe it was just as well.

The quiet was broken by a commotion outside the roundhouse. They were not the ordinary sounds of a festival in full swing; to his Chosen ears Notus could hear the horses and shouts.

"What is it?" inquired Eira, noticing the return of tension in her friend, and then she heard it.

"Stay here."

Notus rose off the bench, causing it to creak and went to the door. Opening it ever so slightly, he witnessed the raiders invading the village. Some villagers fought and lost. Most allowed themselves to be rounded up around the fire. In the midst of it all he saw the cloaked boy and Tarian. Horror-stricken, Notus did not notice Eira standing behind him, viewing the spectacle herself.

"Bronwen," she cried, trying to push by her friend to get to her daughter who cowered behind Tarian.

Grabbing her arms, Notus pushed Eira back into the roundhouse. "You can't do anything for her right now." He found terror in her eyes and let go of her. "I'll go out and get her, but you have to stay here. Who else will take care of Llyr and Beti? Keep them quiet, if you can."

Eira mutely nodded, knowing that he was right and watched her friend enter a nightmare to save her daughter.

XV

said move it!" shouted the brigand atop his horse. His sword jabbed towards the bonfire. The man manoeuvred his steed to shove Tarian towards the fire and she let out a cry as she stumbled forward.

Still cloaked, the boy caught Tarian. His fear slowly turned to anger and he swung around to face the business end of the sword pointed at his shadowed face.

"Just try it," sneered the raider, obviously hoping that the young cowled man would rise to the bait.

He heard Tarian's sharp inhalation and noticed her eyes round in relived horror. Dearly wanting to protect her this time, he drew Tarian to his side, hoping that she would draw strength by his proximity. He did not want to go into the throng of people, but he had no choice. Fear did not dominate him as it once had. Instead anger boiled, threatening to break the surface. Regardless of what transpired, he silently swore that Tarian would not have to relive that night in the woods, and this time he would do anything to stop it.

Stepping back from the point of the blade, he felt Tarian's trembling hand on his arm.

"Come on," she urged, tugging him towards the fire.

Turning around, he walked slowly, feeling the hot breath of the horse through the thick fabric of his cloak. This was not the way he wished to be introduced to the villagers. The sight of all the frightened people before him tightened the clamp around his chest.

He felt Tarian stiffen and freeze as they entered the mass. Following her line of sight, he found the reason for her rising panic. Before them, issuing orders from horseback was the man who had nearly killed her daughter and brutally raped her, and beside him was a man in magnificent armour well worn and used. His black eyes showed no feeling. There was neither pleasure nor hatred at the people corralled where they had once danced. His long dark moustache moved every so often, giving directions to Cadwallader.

The raider who herded them drew his horse away to join in the offensive ring around the villagers.

More people were forced from hiding places and brought to the centre. With everyone's attention upon the marauders, the young man felt somewhat invisible under the cloak and was grateful to Eira for providing it. Glancing down at Tarian, he saw Bronwen clutching at her. Eira was nowhere to be seen; maybe they had not checked her roundhouse yet.

Gazing into the dark, he saw Notus silently emerge from the Eira's home. He did not know what his Chooser was going to do, but something had to be done. Bringing his attention back to the immediate threat, he saw the one who had raped Tarian scan the crowd only to land his eyes upon the girl. At first he seemed confused and then surprise followed by a dangerous smile forming on his lips.

A whimper escaped Tarian and she tried to burrow closer under the cloak to her once saviour. He allowed her, his arm coming around her in a protective embrace. His eyes locked on the one that got away.

The horseman's smile turned into a grin that did not match his eyes as he leaned over to the other man, whispering something. The once expressionless face moved, eyebrow rising as cold eyes locked onto Tarian. With a simple nod, Tarian's tormentor swung his horse around and cantered it to a stop before the young man and the two girls. One other horseman joined Cadwallader, making a formidable sight of potential violence.

Feeling the heaviness of fear and anger constrained around his chest, partly due to Tarian's grip, his jaw tightened.

"When I say so, take Bronwen and run." His whisper was

barely audible and he hoped Tarian heard him.

"I believe you have something of mine," stated Cadwallader, plainly, when he arrived.

Tarian whimpered.

Cadwallader's face clouded over menacingly when no answer was given. Before it could be stopped, the marauder sidled his horse closer and seized the girl away by her hair. Tarian screamed as she was ripped away and then tossed to the other man who leaned over his horse to hold his knife at her throat. Both men smiled savagely.

The motion of tearing the girl away from him caused the cloak to flap, unbalancing the hood to slip down his shoulders. Exposed in front of all the villagers and the raiders, he only focused on the men in front of him and how to free Tarian. The only pleasure he received was a flicker of fear on Cadwallader's face before it turned into hard hatred.

Any last remnants of fear he held were consumed in the anger he felt, his eyes locked onto Cadwallader's, but was fully aware of the other raider holding a knife to Tarian's throat. The promise of violence flashed in his crimson eyes. Nothing existed but the four of them. The world faded into the background, leaving the gasping of the Gods name on villagers' lips to slip into the night.

He could not bring himself to look at Tarian. Her fear and supplication on her face would unnerve him and bring forward his own fear. There was only what he needed to do to keep her safe and for that he needed a sword, and to procure one he had to take it.

Time stretched out and focused upon the moment. Peripherally, he could see the hilt of a sword sheathed at the opposite side of the man who held Tarian by knifepoint. Not wishing to place Tarian in more danger, he knew he had to use his Chosen gifts and move faster than they could expect.

Course of action chosen, he stated dangerously, for their ears only. "Let her go. You do not want to do this again."

"Do you think that you can stop us?" mocked Cadwallader. Boisterous laughter rang in the silence. "Here? Among all these sheep? I don't think so."

Tarian sobbed as the sharp knife pressed into her skin, allowing a trickle of blood down the pale smoothness of her neck. The smell of it rocked the young man, driving his need to shed blood. The men underestimating their foe were not prepared for the coil of violent fury unleashed.

Time halted. Even the buzzing of insects stopped in mid-flight. The sound of beating hearts slowed to near death as he stepped between the pulsations. Grasping the knife hand of Tarian's raider before the man could even comprehend the move, he pulled the knife hand roughly away before any more damage could be done to Tarian and hoped that she had the wherewithal to grab Bronwen and run like he had suggested. He did not dare look to see if that was the case. His only focus was on retrieving that sword.

Surprised, the raider cried out in pain as his shoulder audibly popped, causing him to drop the knife. Unbalanced by the tall pale spectre, he could do nothing as his sword was unsheathed and then sheathed in his chest. The last sights before death took him were red malevolent eyes.

The boy stepped into the next beat.

He tossed the newly made corpse down to the ground, the blood smell driving him to exact further justice from those who would harm the peaceful people of the village. Yanking the sword from the body, he switched hands to his dominant left.

Pandemonium reigned as others took up the fight against the marauders. There was nothing but a buzz of noise as he allowed Geraint's training to take over. Metal clanged and sparked against metal as his sword met Cadwallader's. Fear flickered momentarily in the raider's brown eyes as the force of the attack nearly unhorsed him. He did not see the flash of light the young man's blade made as it sliced through his belly. Entrails exploded onto his horses back before he too fell lifeless to the blood soaked earth.

The young man, entranced in the battle, allowed himself to let loose, to flow and move, easily cutting down raider after raider. Exhilarated, he allowed the smell of blood and fear to drive him. Never before had he felt so free, deflecting blows and landing his own deadly ones that it was a surprise to hear Tarian and Notus shout out to him together.

Out of his blind spot came the leader of the raiders on foot. The flash of steel hurtled towards him and was quickly blocked. What he did not expect was the horizontal strike the man made with the second sword. The blade bit deep into his upper arm, slicing muscle and threatened to break bone. Searing pain in his right arm nearly caused him to drop. He had never seen anyone, nor even conceived of anyone fighting with two swords. Blood flowed down his shield arm and he brought up his sword, barely deflecting both attacks.

The leader smiled coldly, eyes flickering to the wounded arm. The young man shifted his stance for another series of blows. They each took the measure of the other, waiting as the sounds of dying filled the air. Red eyes refused to move from black.

When the assault finally came, the young man was hard pressed to fight against such a foe, and with a well placed blow his sword flew out of his white hands as the other sword came to bare upon the nape of his neck.

"It is a shame I must kill such a fine creature such as yourself." The leader pressed the point to draw blood.

Disarmed and with a sword pointed at his neck bolstered his confidence that the man meant exactly as he promised. Somehow that thought did not frighten him. It enraged him. In the midst of all the blood, he felt the surge of hunger and watched the twin blades swing in slow motion to decapitate him. Time moved infinitesimally as he stepped closer and grabbed both sword arms. He twisted until he heard the satisfying pops of the shoulders dislocating. Both swords clanged to the ground as the man screamed in agony. He choked off the man's scream with the grip of his hand.

Under the firm grasp he felt the intoxicating rapid pulse. The need to replenish his own lost blood, the ever increasing pounding of the man's heart fuelled his hunger. He brought his face to the raiders, savouring the man's terror, focusing only on the pounding vessel. The smell of sweat, blood and excrement assaulted his senses, but it was the blood that drew him. Moving his pale hand around the neck, he uncovered the siren song of the large vessel. The unwashed neck and sweat did not hinder him as he pierced into flesh with his teeth.

The scintillating taste exploded in his mouth as hot blood flooded into him. He groaned in a pleasure he never had with the beasts he had fed off. Holding the man captive, he sucked on the life giving vessel, drawing more of the intoxicating blood into him. He did not care if it would kill the man. He would have died anyways, but this way was pure heaven.

He allowed the frightened heart to feed him as he suckled, each draught a delight. The man tried in vain to fight him as death clouded over him, and the young man held him tighter, exulting in the taste until the heart came to a flutter. Before the instant of death he tore himself away and looked at the man's dead face.

Hunger abated, the realization of his carnage hit him fully as he dropped the body.

The covenant is fulfilled!

Lightning pain flashed through him leaving him in agony and captured his breath. He did not feel the crashing of his knees into the bloodied mud nor Notus' strong hands holding him as he surrendered to the darkness.

So as not to attract any attention, Notus slipped out of Eira's home, carefully closing the ancient wooden door. He hoped that his friend would trust him to get Bronwen and stay hidden herself. Seeing the girl beside Tarian and his Chosen ringed by the marauders, Notus wondered how to get to them without drawing any attention to the roundhouse. Keeping his back to the stone wall, he shuffled sideways until the home no longer provided any coverage.

A sharp cry snapped his attention back to the bonfire. Fear forced his heart into his throat. Thankfully, it had not been Bronwen; unfortunately it was Tarian. She was now in the clutches of the raiders. Bronwen hid behind the lad, eyes wide in terror.

Standing in the open, he did what he reluctantly needed to do and with the speed of the Chosen he slipped past the horse backed men and entered into the throng of villagers. He easily went unnoticed; everyone's eyes were on the tall pale lad exposed to the villagers. It did not escape Notus' attention when several witnesses whispered the sound of Gwyn ap Nudd's name in awe.

There was no doubt in his mind that the situation was extremely volatile and prayed that the girls would come out untouched and the boy would back off before getting everybody killed. Moving forward, he tried to get to Bronwen and the boy. If he could get there in time he could use his other gifts to defuse the situation, and free Tarian, if that were possible. In any case, he had to try.

Stepping around a frightened young couple that clung to each other in shuddering terror, Notus did not see the lad freeing Tarian from the ruffian. All he heard was the song of steel as sword was released from sheath and then the wet gasp as it was impaled through the man.

Notus looked up in time to see the boy eviscerate the other man. The smell of blood assaulted his senses and he forcefully suppressed the hunger that surged to meet the odour, and in good time too as chaos exploded around him as others took whatever they had on hand to beat back the raiders. Many of the older men were well seasoned having fought in battles and survived, most of the young men were trained, even if green.

In the thick of it, Tarian and Bronwen slammed into him, sobbing for protection. He gave it willingly as he stared in horrific fascination as his Chosen slaughtered the raiders. He could hardly comprehend the boy who had seemed more likely to run away from violence was now a white phantom gracefully raining death to all that stood to oppose him.

Each move might have been part of a dance so well choreographed that it had been played out dozens of times before. In all his centuries Notus had never seen such a terrifying sight and a prayer to the Good God came unbidden to his lips. Raider after raider fell to the lad's blade. Most died completely unaware that they had been mowed down. When the man wielding two swords came into the fray Notus realized that he was not the only one in rapt attention upon the boy. Both he and Tarian shouted out a warning to the young man, the cry coming too late as he saw steel bite into flesh.

Notus knew not to be worried. It would heal in a matter of moments, but Tarian did not know that and both she and Bronwen had seen the slice. Then the unthinkable occurred and there was nothing Notus could do to stop it. If those watching were sceptical about the lad's otherworldly nature, they were now convinced as Notus watched in horror as the boy fed off of a mortal for the first time.

The leader was the last to fall, but not to the blade. Notus moved to get closer to the boy, to try and prevent any possibility of the boy going onto the next person. It was not unprecedented and Notus wanted to stop it from even potentially happening. It was even more shocking to hear the boy's cry of agony and see him crash to his knees.

Notus quickly made it to the lad's side, the mud squelching beneath his knees and firmly grasped the young man before he could topple forward onto the bloodied ground. Fear coursed through the monk. He had never seen such a reaction in a Chosen.

It was then that he noticed the deep cut in the boy's upper

arm. It should have healed. Instead, it gaped open under the ruined shirt. Shaking his head in confusion and a desire to discount
the reality of what he was seeing, Notus did the only thing his
fogging mind could think of.

"Get Eira," he shouted at Tarian who stood beside him.
"Now!"

Tarian stared at her unconscious saviour being held by the monk.
She knew Father Notus had said something but it did not register.
She was too scared at what she witnessed. It was only when Notus shouted at her again did Tarian break out of her reverie. Grabbing Bronwen's trembling hand, she ran to the roundhouse, her
urge to flee finally loosened.

It took a couple of tries to open the wooden door. Rewarded
at last with the creaking of hinges Tarian allowed herself some
sense of accomplishment. The night had not turned out in the way
anyone could expect and she absently touched the top of her neck
where the blade had cut her. It stung, but did not bleed.

Bronwen, seeing her mother within, cried out and ran inside
to be picked up in the fiercest of bear hugs.

"Oh thank the Goddess you're safe," cried Eira, brushing dark
locks from her daughter's tear streaked face and gave her a kiss
on the forehead. Turning to Tarian she said, "I'm so glad that
Paul was able to get you to safety."

"It wasn't Paul, Eira." Tarian shivered, the effects of the
assault and witnessing the violence finally taking its toll.

Worry washed over Eira's face as she clung to her daughter.
She could see something was terribly wrong on the young woman's face. "What happened?"

"It was the fairy lord, mama," answered Bronwen. Eira turned
to face her daughter, confused about the details. "He killed the
bad men. Mama, he saved us." Little sun golden arms wrapped
around Eira's neck, giving her mother a huge kiss.

Dark imploring eyes penetrated green before Tarian could
look away. "What happened?"

"He's hurt. Father Notus sent me to get you." Sadness and
concern filled Tarian as she went over to pick up her own
daughter, desperately needing to know that she was safe.

Eira blanched and placed her daughter back on the ground.
With a strict order for Bronwen to stay in the roundhouse with

Tarian she headed outdoors and stepped from a world of peaceful sleeping infants to a world of death and massacre.

"By the Goddess," she exclaimed, hands clutching at her heart in an attempt to gain control of its fearful racing.

It was a scene out of a nightmare, ones in which she had seen her father and husband cut down over and over without her being able to save them. The dimming light of the bonfire unattended cast a reddish glow upon everyone and everything as if they were all covered in blood. How many lay on the ground unmoving she could not count, but she could tell that not many were her own people.

Almost in the centre of the carnage Notus knelt, his brown robes a ghastly reddish colour, holding onto her brother splattered in red. Before she could get to them, she had to do something about the chaos that rained down upon her village. It had to be done no matter how desperately she wanted to be by their side. Knowing that Bronwen and Tarian were safe was small consolation in the tragedy of the festival.

Swallowing down her fear, Eira took another deep breath and took control of the situation. Head held high, eyes firm, she caught the first person she could grab and began issuing orders for the disposal of the marauders corpses. They had to be gotten rid of and preferably buried deep within the forest where no one would find them. If they had any allies, she did not want her village to be targeted for revenge.

With the next person she arranged for the wounded of the village to be brought to the central lodge where she would apply her healing arts as soon as able. She could see some of the men who had fought and won. Some with deep cuts still freshly bleeding, others with bruises still too new to be painful, to those who lost loved one's she left their families to take them home and prepare them for their final crossings.

With one last task left to delegate so that it would free her up to do what she desperately wanted to do, Eira quickly found her neighbour and asked her to go and take Tarian and the children in for the night. Her friend nodded knowingly. She had often done this in the past until Tarian came, when Eira was needed elsewhere for long periods of time. With a gentle hug the two women parted to their respective tasks.

Eira's gaze fell back upon Paul and her brother, fresh worry filling her heart. Skirt hiked up and bare feet squishing in mud not made with water, she rushed over. The fear and worry in Paul's eyes told her what she needed to know and did not want to recognize. Fighting back rising emotions to match the monk's, Eira donned the professional distance that a village healer must have in order to do what was necessary. Before she could do any healing they first had to get unconscious young man into her home, now.

"We have to get him inside, quickly," she ordered Notus who mutely nodded.

On the count of three, with Eira on one side and Notus on the other, they lifted the boy to his feet, half dragging, half carrying him to the roundhouse. She could see Paul trying to be as careful with her brother's right arm as possible. It was difficult going with the lad being so much taller than they, and made more so in trying to get the three of them through the door without dropping him.

"Onto the bed," stated Eira, pointing with a lifted chin to the bed Tarian had used, her voice focused on the task before her. Notus followed her direction without question.

Gently, they sat the unconscious young man down on the edge of the bed, allowing Eira to unclasp the cloak to lift it away. Unceremoniously, she rolled up the heavy fabric and plopped it against the wall behind her, laying the clasp on top.

Notus could not express how relieved he felt that Eira took charge in caring for the boy. He brushed the long white hair dappled in red out of the boy's face. He could see pain tensing the pale features, white brows pulled close. The boy should be fine, the gash gone. That was the way of the Chosen. Something was terribly wrong. It took him a moment to register that Eira had called his name.

"We need to get him out of those clothes," she stated matter-of-factly. Notus could see the lines of worry darkening her face and remembered the secret she had imparted to him. He knew that she was as concerned, maybe more so, than he.

As if she needed to say something, to keep going she stated, "Tarian and the children will spend the night at Arwen's."

Notus nodded as he stood, absently smoothing his robes in an attempt to find something he could control. Together they removed the once beautiful shirt, cutting it away in places once they saw the hand length slice in the lad's upper right arm. Notus was almost positive that had the boy not been Chosen, the arm would have been cleaved in two.

The remnants of the blood soaked shirt assailed his senses, quickening his hunger as Eira handed him the shirt to be placed next to the cloak behind them. Disgusted at the thoughts slamming through his mind, he quickly deposited the shirt on the floor to be discarded later.

With the shirt off and the wound finally exposed, Eira carefully laid her brother down on the bed on his left side, so as to keep the wounded arm off the bed and at a height she could easily work at. The small burn above the sternum was inconsequential to the one on the arm.

Turning around to join Eira beside the boy, he found her kneeling, examining the wounded arm.

"What is it? What's wrong?" demanded Notus as he moved to stand beside her. The red and black edged wound was sliced deep enough to see the white of bone. Blood oozed out the gaping gash that started just below the shoulder joint and ended just above the inside of the elbow. It was not even attempting to heal.

Eira took a shaky breath. "This is not good, not at all." She looked up at her worried friend; her own fears plain on her face. "There's a pail of water by the fire that I had boiled after you left, please get it."

He did as she bid, using a cloth to grasp the handle. Crystal clear liquid sloshed and threatened to mingle on the dirt floor as he carefully walked it over and placed it on the floor beside the unconscious boy.

Taking the rag from the handle, she dipped it into the boiled water and rung out the excess.

"Clean the wound first," stated Eira, passing the water soaked cloth to her friend. "Once the wound is tended to we'll clean the rest of him." Fatigue roughened her voice and Notus knew that her night was just beginning. There were so many more in need of her healing talents.

Standing, Eira went to the mantle to pick up a copper coloured wooden box that had been her grandmother's and her grandmother before her. Now it was hers and by morning it will have made her ancestors proud, she hoped. She took the gallon jug sitting on the shelving housing the foodstuffs next to the hearth. With the box in one hand and the jug in the other, Eira turned around to do what needed to be done and halted.

With her brother lying on his side, his long white hair no

longer covering his back, she could see wide silvered ragged tracks on his back. Rushing over, Eira placed the jug and box on the floor beside the bed and went around the other side where, with skirt held up over her knees, she scooted to examine him.

Notus glanced over his left shoulder and halted his washing of the wound. "What's wrong? What did you find?" asked Notus, panicked that there were other wounds the boy had taken that he had not noticed.

Eira placed her hands on the old scars, tracing them and stopped when her brother flinched and moaned at the touch. "Paul, what happened to him?"

Leaning over to see what she was talking about, Notus had his first truly clear look at the boy's back. Five nearly identical thickly silvered parallel scars tracked horizontally across both sides of the ribcage just below the shoulder blades.

Notus shook his head. "I don't know. He had them when I found him."

"They look as if they were from a bear." Eira shook her head disbelieving.

"There is a large bear fur he uses for his pallet."

Their eyes connected in realization. Eira huffed out a held breath, head shaking sadly. Climbing off the bed, she came around and she switched places with Notus to begin her work on healing the current wound.

Picking up her grandmother's box, Eira lifted the finely engraved lid and placed it on the bed beside her. Inside, sewing needles made of bone were lined up side by side next to small spools of very fine gut string. Next she picked up the jug and used her teeth to open it with a pop. The strong smell of grain alcohol filled the room as she stared intently on the cut, once again the healer of the village.

"Hold him," she ordered, preparing needle and thread with alcohol, the extra quickly absorbing into the dirt floor.

Kneeling by the boy's head, Notus grasped white strong shoulders. Warily, he asked, "Eira, what are you going to do?"

"I have to cleanse the wound before I can stitch it," she sated matter-of-factly, checking to see how she should start. Right now, all that existed was the wound, to think of anything more would cloud her judgment.

"Stitch it?" Notus had seen the procedure performed in the past, usually when warriors came back wounded, sometimes due to unfortunate accidents, but the necessity of it on a Chosen, when it should never have been necessary, only deepened his worry.

"It will not heal if left open like this and I don't know whether or not it will heal after I sew it up." Her voice matched Notus' unspoken concern, obviously for different reasons.

"What do you mean?" His voice rose in panic. He had come to care very deeply for the youth and appreciated his companionship. The accidental creation of his Chosen, as horrible as it was, meant that for the first time in a long time, he too was not alone, and the realization that he cared so much for the boy scared him.

Eira lifted her gaze. "The wound has been cauterized." She traced around the blackened edges with a bone needle as if to outline the real problem.

Releasing the boy's shoulders, Notus shifted over to really look at the gash, the sudden wrongness painfully clear. He had seen the sword hit. It had not glowed with forge fire heat. It did not make any sense that it could have caused such damage, and he told Eira so.

"I don't understand it myself," she said softly, almost disbelieving what she was about to say. "The only possible explanation I can think of is that what the villagers are saying is true."

"That the boy is some ancient forest god come back to life?" Notus could not believe what he was hearing. It was too ridiculous to even consider.

"I know. I know." Eira shook her head to dismiss her own theory. "But my mother believed him to be Fay. Even Bronwen and Tarian believe he's a fairy lord."

"That does not make any sense." His voice rose in frustration born of worry.

Softly, Eira replied, fearing to speak the truth. "It does since it was iron that burned him." Grabbing the opened jug, she poured the cleansing alcohol over the wound before Notus could support the boy from the biting pain that was just the precursor to her finally settling down to the arduous task of stitching the wound.

XVI

*e tumbled in a void of darkness.*
Out of control, scorching heat consumed him.
Curling into a foetal position, pain lashed through him.

There was no light.
    There was no Garden.
    There was no wailing.
    He whirled around in absolute blackness.
    Devoid of every sense except pain.
    Pain: the only constant.
    Fear ever present.

Slowly, imperceptibly, his uncontrolled descent reached its terminus.
    Conscious thought took hold through the pain.
    Uncurling, no sense of direction could be perceived.
    No up.
    No down.
    Nothingness.

*   *   *

Panic through the pain made its dominion.

Memories flooded in.

Fearing a renewed encounter he tried in vain to search the darkness.

Nothing.

Terror fuelled his furiously pumping heart.

A touch.

A single feathery touch as cold as death shocked up his arm.

Crying out, he pulled away, cradling his wounded arm.

Harsh and cold as the dead of winter, piercing the blackness.

He spun around.

"The covenant issssss fulfilled," the voice came from all around, filling the void.

Cold terror filled him. Shaking his head in denial he tried to back away and found he could not move. Frozen, stuck in a blackness gone solid.

A scratching rustling filled his ears, threatening to explode inside his head.

"Stop!" he cried out, imploringly.

As suddenly as it began, the sound vanished.

"Open your eyessssssss."

He did not want to.

He did not realize that he had closed them.

An icy cold touch under his chin forced his head up and he snapped his eyes open at the shock of pain through his head.

Red bloody eyes glared at him from a white rotting face. Its white half formed body floated in the unseen eddies and currents of the void. Its smile revealing a row of sharpened teeth.

He could not move. Frigid tendrils held him in place, lashing his body in fiery pain. He cried out.

"You are mine," it hissed. Its breath rotten with decay. "Finally."

He whimpered, wishing that it would release him. Let him go.

It cocked its head to the side sending other parts of it into the unseen breeze. "Now, why would I dooooo that?"

The tendrils gripped harder. Agony burst through him. Surrendering to the support of the tendrils he could only hang in the void.

"How did it feelllll?" Its fetid breath washed over him, nausea overriding the pain. The tendrils loosened just enough.

"Wh- wh- what?" he stammered, teeth chattering. He did not want to answer. He did not know the question.

Frigid fire laced through him as tendrils squeezed even tighter forcing a scream to ruin his throat.

"How did it feellll," it hissed. Its face closer to his. "How did it feelllll to feeeed offfff your fffffirst human?"

He tried to shrink away from the memory. Blood so full of life cascading down his throat filling him with energy no other creature had given him. The man's heart pounded in fear, finally succumbing to the inevitable. The essence of the man pouring in and filling him until there was nothing left. It was agonizingly intoxicating.

"Good. Good." It loosened its grasp. Its eyes closed, drinking in the memory.

It opened its eyes once the memory was completed. A malicious smile formed on his grey white lips. "Nowwww I will telllll you a sssssssecret. I know your sssssoul. I have owned it since the night of your conception. You are mine!"

He could not believe what he was hearing. It could not be possible. "N-n- no," he stammered. "You lie." His courage slowly returned as he shook his head in mute defiance. He could never believe this creature.

Suddenly, he was released. The force sent him reeling as laughter shattered the silence. The sound was thousands of insects buzzing angrily as it disintegrated into the darkness.

A blow across his face sent him flying.

"Believe what you wishhhhh." The voice came from everywhere and nowhere. "Believe that ridiculous monk. Believe that I cannot harm you. But know, beyond any doubt. That you are mine."

Pain ripped through his being as if thousands of hungry mouths bit into his flesh.

xⱱii

Strong hands gently laid him back onto the soft support of the bed under him. Shivering to regain control of his breathing, the echoes of his scream, real or imagined, still rang through his head. Even the side of his face throbbed and he attempted to bring his hand to the phantom wound before lightning pain stole his breath. He could not seem to stop shaking.

Eyes adjusting to the gloaming darkness, he could make out the rafters and the thatch above. Disoriented, he turned to look around, and to the right found Notus kneeling beside him, his face filled with relief. Swallowing down his dry mouth, he hoarsely whispered, "Where am I?"

He felt awful, worse than when the bear had attacked him and could not understand the smile filling his Choosers face.

"Thank the Good God," whispered Notus, enthusiastically, his hand coming to cup the side of the young man's face. "We're in Eira's home. You've been unconscious for three days. Everyone's worried about you."

Three days? But that was not possible, was it? He could not hide his astonishment from Notus. Three days without feeding. Three days of being in the clutches of the white faced demons. The thought made him shiver and he tried to sit but the movement brought renewed pain up and down his arm and he gasped.

Recognizing the boy's need to sit up, Notus slipped an arm

under the boy's upper back to provide support while his other hand grasped under the left arm and pulled.

Released from the warm blankets, his bare back met the cool stone of the wall that served as a headboard. It was then he noticed the linen bandages wrapped from shoulder to elbow, a red-brown stain seeping through the white. At first he could not recall how it could be there and then the memory of that night flooded back, especially the feeding off of the leader of the raiders. Hunger lurched through him and he grimaced. Three days without feeding. He had never gone this long.

"Here, drink this." Notus lifted up a wineskin to the boy's lips.

Using his good left arm, and with Notus' help, he drank the contents of the skin. The blood was still warm, but not hot, and it did not have the vitality of his last feeding. The blood satisfied the need, but the hunger still burned underneath.

"What is it?" he asked, taking the spout away from his reddened lips.

"Cow," replied Notus, taking a swig himself before placing the cap back on and lowering it onto the ground. "How are you feeling?"

He licked his lips, giving himself a moment. How did he feel? "Like someone sliced me open with a sword." His vain attempt at humour fell flat at the despair on Notus' face and realized what was wrong. "It should have healed, shouldn't it?" Anxiety clutched at him.

Mutely, Notus nodded. "Eira theorizes that it's because you were cut with iron."

"That doesn't make any sense." His voice rose in panic until Notus shushed him down and pointed to the other side of the roundhouse. In the other bed, Eira and her daughter slept beside the cradle that held two infants. It was where he found Tarian sleeping that made his eyes go round.

There in the bed with him Tarian slept peacefully, her chestnut hair dark in the subdued lighting caused by the banked hearth fire. Around her neck a white linen bandage was wrapped and he remembered the knife that had cut her as it was held at her throat.

"There are only two beds," explained the monk, seeing the boy's surprise. "Where else could Tarian sleep?"

It seemed reasonable and he was relieved to see that she was safe. She mumbled in her sleep and turned over to face away from him, pulling the covers with her. With his good hand he managed to save some of them for himself, wrapped up to his waist.

"My boy," whispered Notus, "we're going to wake everyone if we keep this up. I don't like to take advantage of your weakened situation, but we need to communicate better than this."

White brows furrowed in confusion. He found he was tired and wanted to sleep, but was afraid. He did not want to fall into the clutches of the demon again.

"I want you to close your eyes and relax," said Notus, his voice calm and soothing. "We should have been able to do this from the onset."

Pressure centred on his forehead and he felt fingers smoothing out the furrows.

Just listen. The words filled his mind and his eyes popped open to gawk at the monk. He could not believe what he heard, or more to the point how he heard it. *I did not want to introduce you to feeding on people this way. But it happened. Feeding off of people can be dangerous and can expose us to the human world if we're not careful. Fortunately, those that witnessed your feeding only saw it as proof to their delusions. There are other things I must teach you, but you must be open to it. Are you willing?*

He nodded, not knowing how to respond to this form of communication.

Don't worry about that. We'll work on it together. For now just think the words and I'll hear them.

Hesitantly, he tried. Instead of voicing his concern about his wound, he thought them.

Notus sighed and stared at the edge of the bed. *Eira believes it was the iron of the sword. When it cut you, it burned you. She had to stitch it and is afraid it might never heal right.*

He refused believe what he was revealed. *But that's not possible.* The words came unbidden to his mind. He had never before reacted this way. He could not count how many times he accidentally nicked or cut himself with his knife or even the arrow tips. Never before had they burned him. The stories Auntie told him always said that the Fay were afraid of iron. Auntie always thought him Fay.

That's not all, continued Notus. *You came down with a fever from the wound.*

The truth sent him reeling; his good left hand ran through his tangled hair and then settled over his mouth before dropping into his lap. Before he was Chosen he was different and had to be hidden away because Auntie believed him Fay.

Once he became Chosen he believed at last he was no longer completely unique, a curiosity, and was finally not different to those who were the same. And now…now, even among the Chosen, he was different.

Closing his eyes, he his head spun and he felt nauseous. "I need to lie down."

With Notus' help his head met the pillow and the covers were drawn up to his chest. He did notice that his feet stuck out the bottom of the bed.

The bed is made for shorter people, sent Notus with an apologetic smile.

"How long before dawn?" he whispered. He wanted to hear his own voice. It made everything more real.

"Not long," replied the monk, quietly. "Eira wants you to stay for a while until she's convinced neither you nor I would place you in a situation that would ruin her good work. We'll work it out. In the meantime, get your rest and heal. We'll be leaving for Ynis Witrin as soon as Eira says you can."

"I thought you were taking me to Londonium?" He could not keep his eyes open any longer. Sleep pulled at him.

"Not until you are completely healed. Ynis Witrin will give you the place and time to do so." Notus' voice drifted off into the distance.

A new realization forced his eyes open and caught his breath. "I killed them all, didn't I?"

Notus' resolute nod sent him trembling. Part of him was glad he had done what he could to save Tarian, but the boy Auntie raised was horrified that he could easily have dispatched those vile men. He closed his eyes at the memory of their faces fraught with pain and dying anger as blood exploded out of wounds he rent into them. He never believed he could be the source of such violence and it rocked him to the core.

A cool hand touched his forehead. *Try and sleep, my son. I wish I could tell you that taking a life becomes easier, but it does not, no matter the circumstances. If it did, I would truly worry for your soul.*

He opened his eyes and stared into Notus' sad face. *I don't want to kill again.*

I'm glad to hear that, my son, smiled Notus, sadly. *But sometimes in life we have no choice when it comes to defending those we care about and ourselves. Try and sleep, tomorrow night will be better.*

This time, when the darkness embraced him, it was a normal sleep, filled with normal nightmares.

He did not know how long he slept. He did not know if it was day or night, or for that matter, which day or night since his strange conversation with Notus. All he knew was that through his exhausted slumber raised voices pulled at him, eroding a peaceful sleep gratefully without dreams.

He could not make out what was being said. He could not figure out who was talking. Everything was still a fog until his eyes fluttered open. Lying on his uninjured side, he found he was alone in the bed. Even the other bed was empty. The only explanation was that it was daytime and he should still be asleep. He still wanted to be, but the voices kept him from doing so.

"He's staying, Huw. He's injured, he's in my home and he's staying."

His eyes widened to hear the venom in Eira's voice and fear fluttered his heart to know that Huw was there in the house with him incapacitated.

"Do you think I'll allow such a creature to stay in our village?" ranted Huw, his voice carrying violence restrained. "It's the one that has brought nothing but evil to our family."

Silence filled the space for only a moment before Eira responded her voice low and filled with hatred. "The only one who has brought evil to my family is you."

"How dare you!" roared Huw, his voice filling the roundhouse, his feet stomping.

"Back off, Huw." The young man was surprised to hear the monk's weary tone.

Eira pressed her advantage. "If you hadn't fled during the battle, my father and Rhys would still be alive. If you hadn't stirred up the villagers, attacked, and killed my Aunt in an attempt to regain your failed honour, I would still have family alive. You are coward and a recreant man. I have never wanted anything to do with you and I will never want anything to do with you. Get out of my home *now*."

The sound of flesh smacking flesh and Eira's cry rang through the room.

"Huw!" yelled Notus. The sound of a chair sliding preceded shuffled steps.

"You're not the Chief here, no matter what you wish." Eira's voice was slightly muffled but still full of force. "This is my home and what I say goes. He will stay. Now don't make me repeat myself. Get out!"

"This is not over, Eira," hissed Huw. "I have friends on the Council." The overt threat pressed the tension in the house.

"Eira asked you to leave," said Notus, firmly. Then the air in the room seemed to shift and the monk's cadence changed as he began to talk slowly and calmly. "Huw, it would be wise of you to leave. Go. Visit your family—your brothers and sisters—and leave Eira and her family alone."

The next sound was the hinges of the door creaking as the door opened, letting in a wash of sunlight, and then banged closed, returning the home to darkness.

"I don't know what you did to Huw, Paul, but thank you," stated Eira, relieved and tired from the conflict.

"He won't bother you any longer," said Notus, his voice reflecting Eira's. "And we won't be a target for any more problems for you and your family."

"What do you mean?"

"Tonight, the boy and I will be leaving."

He gasped at the revelation and realized that he did not want to go. For the first time since Auntie's death he felt at home and he did not want to give that up.

"He hasn't even woken up, Paul," concern filled her voice.

"He did last night and we talked," said Notus, tiredly as he stifled a yawn. "It would be best for everyone concerned."

Silence filled the room to give Eira time to accept her friend's decision. It did not give the young man the same benefit.

"But his arm—"

"—is not his leg. He can still walk, Eira. I know you would like him to stay longer, but we can't. I thank you for your generosity, but it's clear we have outlived our welcome in your village. Huw is not the only one who feels this way, I'm sure, and I can't send everyone away."

Eira sighed in defeat.

"Now, if you don't mind, my dear, I really do need to get some sleep. I've been up far too long as it is."

"Y-yes, of course," said Eira, distractedly. "Please, take my bed. My home is yours for as long as you need."

"Thank you, my daughter."

The boy watched Notus push the curtain aside and walk to the other bed.

Go back to sleep, sent the monk, slipping beneath the covers.

The flutter of fingers gently sweeping his hair from the side of his face lifted him from a dreamless sleep. Confused by the touch, he opened his eyes, blinking in surprise. Tarian sat beside him, her side warm against his naked back and a slight smile on her lips. Unable to roll over to see her without straining his neck, he moved and then eased over carefully trying not to strain his wounded arm.

"Tarian," he spoke her name softly. He did not know why she was here. Looking around the room, she was the only one in the roundhouse except for Notus' sleeping supine form in the other bed.

"Shhh." She placed a finger across his lips and then replaced them with her own.

The unexpected kiss was exhilarating but did not answer his question. Gently, with his good arm, he pushed her away. "What are you doing here?"

"I wanted to see you before you left tonight," she whispered, her smile gone from her lowered green eyes. "Eira told me. She thought I would like to know."

He did not know what to say and found that he was glad that Eira had told Tarian. Glancing from her face to her neck, he saw the bandage was gone, only a single thin scab no longer than a finger was evidence to the attack. Reaching up, he cupped the side of her neck, feeling the captivating pulse and lightly ran his thumb under the wound. Surprised at his own boldness, he dropped his arm back to his abdomen. Realizing his uncovered state, he reached to pull up the blankets.

"I'm sorry I couldn't stop them from hurting you again." He could not bring his eyes to meet hers.

He felt her warm touch on his face and looked up. "But you did," she said earnestly, her dazzling eyes picking up the fire of her chestnut hair. "If it weren't for you I might be dead. Everyone in the village might be dead if not for you."

He had not thought of it that way and then another thought came unbidden to his mind. "Is everyone else alright? Beti? Bronwen?"

"Yes, everyone is fine." She rewarded him with a smile. "Only Garth was killed in the skirmish. There were a few injuries, but nothing Eira could not handle. She's an amazing healer and she's offered to teach me."

A slight smile lifted his lips at her enthusiasm and with the knowledge that the people he had surprisingly come to care about were all right. "Then why are you here?" Curiosity stole the smile away.

"Because I needed to thank you," she stated in all seriousness. "Because no one ever has given me so much when I thought everything was gone, and because I wanted to be with you without fear of anyone ruining it. You saved me not once, but twice, not because of any responsibility to me, but because you are a good person who chose to do the right thing. But most of all, because you never asked for anything in return."

He could not believe what he heard, and then he could not believe what was happening. Tarian leaned over and kissed him again, her mouth pressing onto his. Opening his mouth, he drank her in. When she finally pulled away, her pupils were dilated and he could hear the speeding of her heart. All this drew him, driving a need he never he knew before.

"Why are you doing this?" he asked shakily once his breath returned. He did not know where this was leading and was afraid that his hunger would rise up and then he would be the one causing her harm. That was something he desperately did not want to do.

"Never before has anyone given so selflessly to me," she smiled sadly. "You are so sad and afraid that it makes my heart ache, but then there is a fierceness within you that is good and true. I see so much loneliness in you and the only thing I want to do is take that away, if only for a moment."

She leaned forward to kiss him again and was stopped by his firm pale hand on her arm, confused disappointment washed over her fine features.

He could not believe what she offered. A part of him cried out in sorrow that despite everything come this evening he would most likely never see Tarian again. But to be touched, to be wanted in a way that he was told would always be denied to him offered a glimmering of hope. "I–I—" he stammered.

Understanding filled her eyes. "I trust you."

This time when she leaned forward, he welcomed her kiss. No one had ever said those words to him before. No one trusted him so openly, and believing her he opened himself to his growing desire for her that was unlike any hunger he had felt before.

Tongues touched and caressed each other and then pulled away as lips trailed kisses along his jaw and then down his throat. Sensation exploded through him causing him to writhe and gasp as she teased his great vessel. The touch sparked his sleeping hunger, but it was still not supreme in his desires.

Suddenly, her lips were gone from his neck and he looked down at her. She smiled back, her hair cascading around her face as she slowly administered gentle kisses down his chest, gently teasing one nipple erect with a soft moist tongue and then the other. Lightning shot through him and he groaned wanting more, trusting her as she trusted him and closed his eyes at her ministrations.

Gently, methodically she kissed his chest, then down to his abdomen, leaving a cool trail in the dissipation of heat. He did not open his eyes when he felt her move the blanket off of him, revealing him completely to her. He did not have time. White fire encapsulated him and he stiffened as she took him into her mouth.

He shuddered at the touch, wanting more. He never knew it could be like this, especially since he grew up with the expectation he would never have it as no one would want to be with him in this way. Gripping the bedding beneath him, he arched his back, trying in vain to catch his breath. Every time he thought he managed, Tarian did something new to send shocks of pleasure racing up and down his body.

He wanted more. He wanted to consume her, to make her his, and a small part of his mind knew that it was not just the hunger making itself more known. He wanted Tarian, as she seemed to want him. No one had ever wanted him with such desperate need and he allowed himself to fall into it, to ride it, to allow his own need to rise.

Unexpectedly, all sensation disappeared and he opened his eyes to find Tarian removing her dress in one fluid motion over her head, tossing the green fabric to the floor. Sitting beside him, her breasts large and round, she leaned over and this time he brought her to his lips, greedily entering her mouth. He was rewarded with a soft sigh.

Tarian shifted, almost disconnecting from the kiss, until she straddled him. The sound of her racing heartbeat and her heat sent his head swimming. Her body pressed his. Sweeping her hair away from her face, she found what she was looking for and then she moved down and sat up, impaling herself on him.

Crimson eyes snapped open as her pulse raced through his body and her soft wet heat threatened to consume him. When he thought he could not experience any more pleasure, she moved.

Hunger for her body and hunger for her blood rode the waves as she rode him, her breath coming in short gasps. They moved together, eyes locked on each other. His pale hand reached for her breast, feeling the full firmness and he wanted to do to her what she had for him. Carefully, so not to aggravate his injured arm, he sat up, his good arm around her back and was rewarded with a gasp as he reached as deep as he could go.

This time his lips found hers and she opened them willingly, welcoming him in. He wanted to drink, but he did not want to hurt her. Following down the front of her neck, to avoid the pulsating vessels in her neck, he leaned Tarian back, supporting her with his embrace until he found what he wanted. Her areola was large and dark. He could hear the pounding of her heart. Hungrily, he encapsulated the sensitive tissue and licked, teasing the hardening nipple and was rewarded by Tarian's cry, her nails digging into his shoulders. Sweetness exploded into his mouth and he drank. It was not what he desired. He needed more.

They moved together, faster to the rhythm of their heartbeats. The tense need to fulfill his desires grew, meeting Tarian's. Finding each other's mouths for a brief moment, he could no longer resist the call of the pounding vessel at her neck.

"Yes, now," she cried out, seeming to know his needs, and he bit.

Soft white flesh separated as he pierced with his sharpened teeth. This time he was rewarded with his desire. Liquid fire poured into him with each convulsion that shuddered through the two of them, feeling his own throbbing release in time with hers. Her cry rang through him as she clutched at him. He so desperately wanted to suckle the vessel but he knew that would kill her.

The rapture of their release came to an end and he reluctantly released her neck, lifting his face away from the quickly healing wound. Worried, he looked into her glazed smiling face.

Soft hands caressed both sides of his face and then she lightly kissed him, tasting her blood on his lips. On unruly legs, Tarian lifted herself off of him and sat heavily down on the side of the bed, hand to her head.

"Are you alright?" he asked, worried that he had taken too much of her blood.

She turned, her smile radiant. "I'm more than alright."

He met her smile with his own as she leaned over to recover her clothing. He enjoyed watching the way the fabric floated down over her breasts, her slightly rounded stomach, and her full hips, to cover her completely. Tarian ran her fingers through her long wavy hair and sat back down beside him.

"You'd better lie down and get some sleep," she suggested, gently pushing him down to the bed and covering him with the blankets. "You start a long journey tonight and I think we've done enough to test the bounds of your healing." Her sad smile said what did not need to be said and with a shared kiss Tarian rose to leave. Turning to look at him once at the drapery, tears glistened on her cheeks. Mouthing a thank you, she dipped around the tapestry and was gone.

With a shuddering sigh, he turned onto his left side. Thoughts of what transpired between the two of them filled his mind. Closing his eyes and fighting back his own tears, he was surprised that he did not want to leave. He wanted to stay with Tarian.

Sleep was long time coming and when it did he was unaware of Notus lying awake in the bed next to him.

He barely had time to register Eira crying out "Bronwen, no!" before the impact drove the breath from his lungs and stole the sleep from his mind. Landing on his back, he snapped his eyes open to find that the world contained the brilliant smile of Eira's daughter, her dark brown eyes hardly a hand span away from his own.

"Yea! You're awake!" she cried, pushing off of his chest to lounge on him, pinning his only good arm.

Stunned at the awakening, he tried to sit up using his wounded arm as leverage. The pain brought him back down onto the soft bed. Bronwen took no notice of his grimace.

"Bronwen, get off of him, now," ordered Eira, as she picked through a swatch of white cloth.

"Mama says that you're leaving tonight," the girl chattered, taking no notice of his discomfort or of her mother's directive. "I don't want you to go. Everyone in the village is here. Lots of folk think that you're one of the Ancient Ones. Some say that you're the Horned Lord, Gwyn ap—"

"I told you to get off of him," said Eira, eyes glaring at her daughter in a way only mothers could do. With a swatch of cloth in one hand and a jug in the other, she walked over to the bed.

Bronwen, recognizing the look in her mother's eyes, scurried off. "Sorry, mama."

"Don't tell me you're sorry, tell him. He's the one you jumped on." Eira walked around to the other side of the bed where a stool had been placed.

Abashed, Bronwen flickered brown eyes that still held the hint of mischievousness at their guest. "I'm sorry," she drawled.

For some strange reason that he could not understand, he did not believe her and thought that if a second chance arose she would take it and jump on him again. Some part of him did not mind that.

Eira harrumphed, obviously not taken by her daughter's performance. "Take Llyr and go outside. We'll be out shortly."

"Okay, mama." Disappointed, Bronwen melodramatically stomped across the roundhouse creating little clouds around her bare ankles. Shoulders sagging, every line of her body made it clear for all to see that she did not want to do what she was told. Before Llyr could crawl to one of the hot stones that lined the front of the hearth Bronwen swept up her baby brother and deposited him on her hip. His gurgling laughter filled the room.

"C'mon, Llyr," moaned the girl, as she headed to the door. "Mama doesn't want us in here right now."

The closed door cut off any further complaints, leaving the two of them alone in Eira's home.

"I'm sorry about that. Bronwen is more like her Aunt—may she rest with the Goddess—than she'll ever know." Eira smiled and sat down on the stool. Placing the cloth on the side of the bed, she uncorked the jug before depositing it on the earthen floor.

"Despite Bronwen's usual way to wake a person from a deep slumber, I'm glad to see that you are finally awake." She smiled and reached to pull down his covers and met resistance. "You can let go of the blankets. I have to take a look at your arm."

Not realizing his grip on the fabric, he relinquished his hold, allowing Eira to lower the blanket enough so that she could gently lift his injured arm from under the covers and lay it back down, exposed for her examination. The movement caused shooting pains down into his fingers and up to the side of his head causing him to suck in a breath and close his eyes.

"It still hurts, doesn't it?" she asked, lifting her hands away.

Nodding, he opened his eyes and saw the concern in hers.

"I need to change the dressing and see how the wound is healing," she explained, folding a piece of cloth. "And to do that, it would be easier if you would sit up. You can lean against the wall if you need. Do you think you can do that?"

Again, he nodded, and with Eira's help sat up, the covers falling to his waist. Suddenly embarrassed, he grabbed the blankets with his good arm, holding them secure. He did not know why he felt this way. Maybe it was because of what happened with Tarian. Not to mention, he did not arrive in this bed this way. Notus must have had some help. The thought sent a flood of heat to his face and he dropped his gaze to his lap.

His shyness did not go unnoticed. Eira smiled knowingly and slapped his outstretched leg. Without another hint, he crossed his legs, making room for Eira to sit before him, but also disrupting the covers so that he had to snatch them back into place.

Scooping her long straight black hair behind one ear, she leaned forward, examining his arm with cautious probing. A hiss escaped his lips and his eyes briefly caught hers as she glanced up at him. "I'm going to remove the dressing now. It may hurt when it comes off. I'm going to be as gentle as I can. If you need me to stop for a moment, just let me know."

He took a deep breath to brace himself and nodded. She unwound the bandage, forcing his arm agonizingly up and down. When it came time to lift off the portion directly over the wound she found it stuck. That was not uncommon and she was prepared. Picking up the jug, she wet the portion of bandaging with the grain alcohol and pulled it back.

Unfortunately, he was not equally prepared, and he gritted his teeth in an attempt not to cry out. As quickly as the pain came, it went with the removal of the bandage and he sighed his relief. Glancing around the roundhouse, he noticed Notus was gone. A flutter of panic filled him. "Where's Notus?"

"He's outside with the others, waiting for you," she answered, distractedly.

He turned back to find Eira worrying her bottom lip and saw the reason why. A thick dark line, black against his pale white skin, held with blood stained sutures, ran from his shoulder to the inside of his elbow. Around the wound a ring of red inflammation smouldered. He audibly swallowed, his mouth gone dry. He had not wanted to believe Notus but even though the truth was stitched in his arm he asked, "Why? Why is it like that?"

Eira met his terror filled eyes. She wanted to reassure him, but found that there was nothing truly she could say except, "You are Fay and the iron in the sword not only cut you, it burned you." She cupped his face in her hand and let it fall along his milk white hair before taking her hand back. "I only pray that you will heal fully in time as I have done what I could."

He could not believe the words and he looked away. Notus said he was Chosen. Auntie believed him Fay. He did not know what or who he was.

Cold stinging brought his attention back to Eira as she began to carefully clean the wound, respecting his desire for silence. Once done, she stood up and went over to what served as her pantry and brought over a little jar.

Opening it up, the sweet scent of honey wafted and he watched her place a dollop onto the linen to serve as his bandage. He knew from Auntie how honey helped with infections because the bees brought the blessing of the Goddess. He doubted that the Goddess would help him.

As carefully as she could, she redressed the wound until he was wrapped snugly in the white clean linen. Task complete, she stood, wiping her hands on her blue apron.

"How does it feel?"

He tried to bend his arm and was rewarded with another shock of pain, but not as bad as the first time. He told her so.

"Good," she smiled, her eyes lighting up. "Now let's get some food into you. You must be famished."

Before he could refuse, Eira turned back to the hearth where a pot hung from an iron hook. The mention of food roused his hunger, but not for what she brought to him in the brown wooden bowl. Before Notus had come, the smell of beef broth would have set his stomach gurgling in anticipation. Now it smelled wrong.

"Here, drink this," offered Eira, sitting down beside him on the stool. "It will help you to regain your strength."

Taking the sloshing bowl of brown liquid shimmering with melted fat on the surface, he grimaced and passed it back.

Surprised at his reaction to her broth, Eira reluctantly accepted the bowl. "Oh come now. It's only beef broth." She tried to hand it back only to see him retreat from it as if it would sting him. Exasperated, she stated, "Do I have to force feed you?"

Believing she would do exactly what she promised, he accepted defeat and took the bowl back, staring at the brown liquid. Quickly glancing at Eira's stern face, he realized there was no way out and brought the bowl to his lips. The pungent taste, so unlike blood, exploded across his pallet and he spat the mouthful back into the bowl.

"Sorry," he stammered, giving back the bowl.

"That's alright," she sighed, giving him a rag to wipe his face. "You'll eat when you're ready."

Handing back the cloth, he turned to snuggle back under the covers.

"Uh, uh, uh. It's time to rise. Paul is waiting for you. You know he wants to leave tonight."

He frowned. He did not want to leave. Not after what he had shared with Tarian. He did not want to be taken away from people that seemed to truly care and accept him. He also did not want to leave sleeping in a real bed for the first time in his life. He knew Notus' desire to go to a place called Ynis Witrin and then to Londoninum, wherever they were, but he wondered if the monk knew his wishes. He doubted it.

Sitting back up, he swung his legs over the bed, keeping the blanket securely around his lap and noticed that he had no clothes. As if reading his mind, Eira smiled and went to her bed.

"I knew you would need something to wear," she called, "and managed to grab these before Paul had your trunk packed in the cart." From under the bed, she re-emerged holding his boots, his trousers cleaned from the blood splatter and a simple forest green long sleeved tunic. Her smile expanded at the astonished look on the young man's face. In her other hand, she held a length of un-dyed cloth and laid both piles down beside him.

Discomposed at the thought of her presence while he dressed, he shyly asked her to leave.

Eira raised a perfect dark eyebrow. "Well, if you wish." She walked to the hanging that helped separate living quarters from sleep quarters and gave it a tug. "But you may find it difficult to dress using one arm."

He watched her disappear behind the fall of multicolour fabric, relieved to be alone. He did not know why he felt so awkward in her presence. She was always kind and attentive to him, but the thought of dressing in front of her was, well, like dressing in front of Auntie once he started to become a man.

Picking up the trousers, he flipped them out and found that getting a pant leg over one leg was tricky enough, let alone two, but he could not even attempt to pull them past his thighs. Flustered he sat there and looked up to find Eira peeking around the drapery, a smile on her face.

"I–I think I am going to need your help," he finally admitted. A rush of heat flooded his face and he looked away.

"I thought you might," she laughed and moved to help.

It felt strange having someone help him dress. He had stopped needing Auntie's help by the time he was four and now he found Eira's willingness oddly comforting. With her help, they managed to fit the trousers with minimal embarrassment to both.

"There. Now for your tunic," said Eira, smiling.

Lifting the soft green cloth, she instructed him to sit back down and carefully pulled the tunic over his head, helping him thread his bandaged arm into the sleeve and then into the sling she made with the extra length of cloth she had brought. Her touch was stunningly hot as he intently watched her every move. It took both of them to get his boots on.

Finally dressed, Eira went to her bedside table and picked up a silver backed brush made with stiff hair and brought it over. He had never seen such a thing before and he twisted in his seat to see her come behind him.

Noticing the inquisitive look on his face, she turned his face away from him and lifted his hair out of the tunic. "I'm not about to let you leave looking like you've been abed," she answered and began to brush out the tangles in his thick hair. A smile played upon her face and she began to hum as she worked the brush through.

No one had ever done this for him. At first it felt strange, and then he began to relax, especially once she began to hum. Untangling his hair was always relatively easy, but he never had a brush or a comb. Fingers, either his own or Aunties, did the job adequately, and sometimes in the fall the thistle flower would work well, but this was bliss.

Finally, she halted. "All done." Eira smiled, rising to stand as he stood, admiring the transformed young man. She could not believe he was the same person who had alighted her threshold with nothing more than the ratty stained clothes on his back. Now he was going to leave her, probably forever, looking like the fairy lord her daughter believed him to be.

"I know that Notus is waiting to leave," explained Eira, "but before you go, there is something else you should take with you."

Curious, he watched as she went and reached under her bed once again, this time drawing out a swatch of black cloth obviously hiding something in its folds. Once she stood before him, Eira opened the wrapping to reveal a long-sword with a black grip. The guard was also steel, but shaped in the style of two dragonheads and the pommel was plain. His eyes widened in shock. He had seen this sword before. He had trained against this sword and the man who once carried it.

"I cannot take this," he said. He shook his head and pushed the sword towards Eira, his mind swimming at what he should not be seeing.

Eira held it out again, her sad eyes imploring him. "My father—" Her voice caught and she coughed to clear it from the emotions threatening to halt her from what she knew she needed to do. "My father was a good man—the Chief of this village after my grandfather. After I married Rhys, my father started to spend time with my Aunt who lived alone on the other side of the woods. He said it was because she needed help and we all believed him because he was a good person. Before he left with my husband to fight with the king, he told me that should a young man the colour of my name come, I was to help him. I didn't know what he meant until that morning I found you with Bronwen in the milking shack. When my father was killed, along with Rhys, I kept his sword. I believe he would have wanted you to have it."

Stunned at the revelation of her story and its implications, he reverently grasped the sword and released it from its simple dark brown leather scabbard, setting the blade ringing. Firelight caught the blade with the single deep blood groove and lit up the delicate etching of two dragons intertwined on each side of the blade.

It was Geraint's sword.

"He never told me your name," she quietly stated, watching the young man's face fill with sorrow.

"I never told him because I never knew it," he quietly admitted.

Eira laid her hand over his on the hilt, holding the sword with him and smiled into his watery blood coloured eyes. "It's Gwyn."

He closed his eyes, stopping any tears from flowing, and nodded.

Together they sheathed the sword, and with Eira's help, fit the sword on his right hip with a strong, wide leather belt. He would not be able to wear the baldric until his arm healed.

Hand in hand they walked to the door, and before she opened it, she turned to face him once more, tears glittering in her eyes. "I don't want you to ever forget that you will always have a home with us."

"I will not," he promised in a husky voice. More than ever he did not want to leave. He wanted to stay and talk with Eira about Geraint and about Auntie who was her Aunt. He wanted to be part of her family and knew that could never be.

"I'm glad." She reached up and cupped his face with her hand, caressing his soft cheek with her thumb. "My mother had a son that died before the madness took her. I wish he could have been you." Stretching up on her toes, she lightly kissed his cool cheek.

Stunned by the confession and head spinning at all that had happened, he stood dumbfounded as she opened the door.

It seemed that most of the villagers were there to see them off. Many of them were milling about in twos and threes talking quietly with one another. The chatter instantly ceased as they finally took notice of him. The only sound was the wicker of a horse. Taking a fortifying breath, he stepped clear of Eira's home and into the inquisitive sight of so many people.

He could see Notus talking avidly with an average looking man who radiated an aura of authority and strength. His sensitive Chosen hearing brought that the man was the Chief and Notus was thanking him for the horse harnessed to his cart and the one next to it, saddled and ready. The Chief seemed quite happy to give them the horses and the tack since they originally belonged to the raiders, and now that they were dead, the village acquired a new herd of fine warhorses.

A man standing next to the Chief whispered into his ear and without any further ado, wished Notus well, and walked back to his hall with several others in tow. With no one to talk to and noticing the strange quiet, the monk turned and noticed him.

"My dear boy," exclaimed Notus, briskly walking to meet him. "I am so pleased to see you up and looking well." He turned his attention the Eira who was only a few steps behind, "How is he?"

"Well." She stopped next to the young man.

"Good. Good. Wonderful," interrupted Notus, oblivious to her agitation. Then he is—"

"But he will need to have the bandage changed regularly," interjected Eira, "and he will need help with some tasks. Other than that he is fit to travel."

Notus nodded satisfactorily. "Then we shall be on our way."

"Not yet," announced Eira. She grabbed his long brown sleeve and pulled him aside until she was sure they were far enough away to have a private conversation.

Distinctly aware of all eyes upon him, he walked over to the saddled black destrier. Lifting his hand for the horse to get his scent like Geraint had taught him, he was rewarded with lips nibbling at his hand in acceptance. The horse pressed its head against his chest forcing him to take a step back and he began to scratch its ears and nose, enjoying the soft velvety feel.

He did not mean to hear, but Eira's fervent whispers drew him.

"You cannot tell him," she whispered. "Never."

"My dear, I gave you my promise as one who serves the Good God. Do not fear. Your secret is safe, though it is a tragedy that you cannot tell him the truth."

He frowned, wondering what was being hidden from him. Notus wanted him to trust him, but now he was keeping secrets from him. He shook his head, white hair falling against the black of the horses face. Realizing that someone had come up beside him, he could not focus upon the continued conversation between his Chooser and Eira.

Tarian stood with Beti gurgling in delight in one arm and a draping of cloth in the other. Beside her Bronwen struggled with Llyr on her hip.

"I'm sorry I jumped on you." Bronwen gazed up at him and

he knew this time the apology was sincere. A smile lighted on his lips. "I just wish you didn't have to go." Without warning she grabbed his legs in an awkward hug and let go before she almost dropped her brother. Bronwen hastened to her mother without looking back, ashamed of her tears.

Standing alone with Tarian, he could see her beautiful liquid eyes. "I thought you might forget this," she uttered and held out his cloak.

He took the cloak from her, and in the palm of her hand was Geraint's broach. With her one handed help they managed to get the cloak over his shoulders, the heavy fabric pressing his wound uncomfortably, and closed the cloak pin in place. She sadly smiled as he freed his hair.

He wanted to say so much to her and found not a word. What could he say? Instead he timidly took her hand in his. "Tarian?" he ventured and found that his voice caught.

She gazed up at him, eyes brimming with tears. "That's going to be the last time you say my name," she whispered. "Please say it again."

He did and she folded herself around him, weeping as he repeated her name over and over, stroking her soft curling locks, tears streaming down his face.

The touch of Notus' hand on his side brought his attention away from Tarian. "It's time to go."

Sympathetically, Notus stepped over to the cart, allowing them a final moment alone.

Releasing Tarian, he wiped his tears away and then hers, her face so soft he lingered for a moment.

"I have to go," he mumbled.

She nodded sadly. "I won't ever forget you. My life is yours, twice over now."

"I will never forget you." He turned on his heel to walk to the cart and stopped at Tarian's grip on his hand.

"I never heard your name," she said as he turned back to face her.

He stared into her eyes not knowing what to say, and then it came to him. "It's Gwyn."

Her eyes widened in awe and he walked to the horses and Notus, holding her hand until the last possible moment before the distance was too great.

Notus smiled proudly and passed the horse's keys to him as

he held onto his own horse's reigns. They led their horses and their belongings out of the village. The only sound was the horses' hooves trampling hard packed earth, creaking leather, and the jingling of metal, followed by the turning of the carts wheels.

Just as they were about to follow the track into the woods they heard farewells called out by the villagers, Eira's and Tarian's the loudest. Without turning, eyes focused only on the road ahead, Notus quietly said, "Do not look back, my boy, salt stings."

The Chosen Chronicles continues with

Angel of Death

about the author

Karen Dales is the Award Winning Author of the widely acclaimed *The Chosen Chronicles,* having won Siren Books' Award for Best Horror and Best Overall 2010. *The Chosen Chronicles* include *Changeling, Angel of Death, The Guest (a Short Story of the Angel of Death), Shadow of Death,* and *Thanatos.*

She is currently at work on the next book in *The Chosen Chronicles - Resurrection* as well as a historical fiction novel.

Born in Toronto, Ontario, Canada, she shares her life with her two cats, one son and husband.

www.ingramcontent.com/pod-product-compliance
Lightning Source LLC
Chambersburg PA
CBHW070055260626
47160CB00004B/1215

Also by Karen Dales

THE CHOSEN CHRONICLES

Changeling
Angel of Death
Shadow of Death
Thanatos
(Resurrection)